JK

The new Zebra Regency Romance logo that you see on the cover is a photograph of an actual regency "tuzzy-muzzy." The fashionable regency lady often wore a tuzzy-muzzy tied with a satin or velvet rib-and around her wrist to carry a fragrant nosegay. Usually made of gold or silver, tuzzy-muzzies varied in design from the elegantly simple to the exquisitely ornate. The Zebra Regency Romance tuzzy-muzzy is made of alabaster with a silver filigree edging.

A MOST PROVOCATIVE CHALLENGE

"Come, Miss Wilde. I cannot believe that you have forgotten our first encounter," Simon mocked.

When she refused to answer, he raised her chin with one hand and looked deeply into the puzzled blue eyes which met his.

"No, I have not forgotten. You treated me as if I were a lightskirt. Should I apologize for disappointing you?"

"You did not disappoint me, hardly that. In fact I found you quite intriguing."

"I don't like your tone, sir, and I think you presume far too much considering our short acquaintance," Katherine replied, her anger rising at his impertinence.

"Ah, but I hope that acquaintance will deepen. Is there any reason why it should not? Do you take me in abhorrence on such a pretext? That would be a great shame," he teased.

"Hardly a pretext! You kissed me, without my permission," she retorted, her judgment yielding to her mortification. She had not meant to mention that kiss.

"Yes, and you tempt me to do it again. You are a most provocative challenge, Miss Wilde."

THE BEST OF REGENCY ROMANCES

AN IMPROPER COMPANION   (2691, $3.95)
by Karla Hocker
At the closing of Miss Venable's Seminary for Young
Ladies school, mistress Kate Elliott welcomed the invitation to be Liza Ashcroft's chaperone for the Season at
Bath. Little did she know that Miss Ashcroft's father, the
handsome widower Damien Ashcroft would also enter her
life. And not as a passive bystander or dutiful dad.

WAGER ON LOVE   (2693, $2.95)
by Prudence Martin
Only a rogue like Nicholas Ruxart would choose a bride on
the basis of a careless wager. And only a rakehell like Nicholas would then fall in love with his betrothed's grey-eyed
sister! The cynical viscount had always thought one blush-
ing miss would suit as well as another, but the unattainable
Jane Sommers soon proved him wrong.

LOVE AND FOLLY   (2715, $3.95)
by Sheila Simonson
To the dismay of her more sensible twin Margaret, Lady
Jean proceeded to fall hopelessly in love with the silver-
tongued, seditious poet, Owen Davies—and catapult her
entire family into social ruin . . . Margaret was used to
gentlemen falling in love with vivacious Jean rather than
with her—even the handsome Johnny Dyott whom she secretly adored. And when Jean's foolishness led her into the
arms of the notorious Owen Davies, Margaret knew she
could count on Dyott to avert scandal. What she didn't
know, however was that her sweet sensibility was exerting a
charm all its own.

*Available wherever paperbacks are sold, or order direct from the
Publisher. Send cover price plus 50¢ per copy for mailing and
handling to Zebra Books, Dept. 3222, 475 Park Avenue South,
New York, N.Y. 10016. Residents of New York, New Jersey and
Pennsylvania must include sales tax. DO NOT SEND CASH.*

A Traitorous Heart
Violet Hamilton

ZEBRA BOOKS
KENSINGTON PUBLISHING CORP.

ZEBRA BOOKS

are published by

Kensington Publishing Corp.
475 Park Avenue South
New York, NY 10016

Copyright © 1990 by Violet Hamilton

First printing: November, 1990

Printed in the United States of America

Chapter One

The idea of attending the masquerade at the Pantheon had immediately struck Katherine as a splendid way of irritating her father. His Gothic notions of propriety and his plans for her future had aroused her anger and defiance. It was after he had informed her, in quelling tones which brooked no argument, that he had hired a lady of impeccable breeding, if straitened means, to introduce her into society that she had become intent on rebellion. It was not the idea of making her bow, but his suggestion that the object of this introduction was a marriage to further his own ambitions that she resented. Katherine, shocked and outraged at being used in such a fashion, had decided to attack him where he was most vulnerable, his self esteem. It would wound him to have his daughter the target of scandal-mongers. Her anger, however, at being used as a pawn in his schemes had faded somewhat in the face of the reality. She felt not only disgruntled but disappointed. The masquerade was turning out to be both a tawdry and unexciting affair.

She had persuaded her escort, Ronald Pemberton, Viscount Chomeley, much against his judgment, to escort her to the masquerade, and since the young peer was most anxious not to offend her, he had consented. Katherine was beginning to wonder about Ronald. On first meeting him she had been flattered and charmed by his attentions, although she now suspected his motives in dancing attendance upon her might not be entirely unconnected with her father's wealth. She had escaped his rather fulsome compliments after their last dance by pleading a need for fresh air, and promised to wait quietly in the garden while he procured her a glass of ratafia, if he could find such a tame beverage. Most of the guests at this rather bizarre entertainment appeared to prefer much stronger drink. Katherine sighed. Her instincts were to obey her father's requests, but his manner in informing her that she had been educated and protected in order to fulfill some antiquated dynastic hopes of his own, with no concern for her own happiness, had infuriated her. Her temper often led her into disgraceful scrapes, but this particular one was proving to be not so much shocking as sordid.

Beyond the gardens she could catch a glimpse of the large ballroom, surrounded by boxes and alcoves, cunningly designed for trysts. Crystal chandeliers glittered on the masked throng cavorting beneath the tapers. At one time these rooms had been patronized by the haut monde, but the first structure had been burnt to the ground and the new palace of dance was considered too vulgarly ostentatious. The evening was growing late and the revelers were fast abandoning any pretensions to decorum. Katherine drew her purple silk domino more closely about her, despite that heat of the night. She did not want any of the guests to discover her identity or seek her out as one willing to join the boisterous behaviour now rising to a dangerous pitch. If any august member of the ton should by some mischance recognize her, they would not be surprised, she thought a bit cynically. What else could be expected from a cit's daughter? Katherine's few weeks of experience in London society had led to the realization that her father's wealth and his intimacy through his business affairs with many of the leading members of society did not mean that his daughter would be welcomed among them. Peter Wilde was acceptable as a money lender but not as a social equal.

Although his merchant bank dealt with the highest in the land from Prinny to a whole stable of dukes and earls, his presence at the more exclusive gatherings of the season was not guaranteed. Of course, he could not be completely ignored. His wealth made him a man to be reckoned with, but that necessity did not always apply to his daughter. Katherine scorned her father's ambitions, but she was also hurt by the snubs and unkindnesses she had received. Some of the girls who had been her intimate friends at her Bath Seminary treated her with less than charity.

It did not occur to her that she represented a real threat to their hopes of making a desirable match. She was not unaware that she had some claim to beauty, with her midnight black curls, cut fashionably in the latest crop, and her brilliant, luminous blue eyes which several besotted officers at the Bath Pump Room had found enticing pools of temptation. Still, her attraction was of an uncommon type, not at all in the mode of the serene blond beauties who reigned as the season's incomparables. Her personality was too vivacious, her conversation too frank, her manner too candid to meet the approval of the more starched doyennes of London salons. She did not realize that her very attraction lay in those distinct qualities which singled her out from the usual debutante. And, of course, there was all that Wilde money. As much as London's matrons might sneer at her background, too many of them envied the handsome settlements that Peter Wilde would no doubt eagerly bestow on his only child if she was able to capture a suitable title.

Katherine stirred restlessly. This evening's rather pathetic attempt to challenge her father was not turning out quite the way she had planned. And as soon as the laggard Lord Chomeley returned with the ratafia, she would suggest they leave. Whatever could be keeping him? But her musings were interrupted by the looming figure in a black domino, who suddenly grasped her by the shoulders and pulled her up from her seat.

"Ah, there you are, my fair Titania. You have led me a merry chase. There must be a score of purple dominos at this dratted masquerade, and none of them the right one. But, at last, I have found you. Now, come, what can you deliver?" he asked in a deep voice with undertones Katherine neither understood nor quite liked. There was a menacing aspect to this man who had appeared out of the night and obviously mistook her for some light skirt.

"I beg your pardon, sir. I think you have made a mistake," she said in her most repressive tone, drawing back into the shadows, and pulling the domino more closely about her. It would never do for this stranger to discover she was not his chosen Cyprian but a naive girl who had foolishly thrust herself into this disreputable situation.

"Have I? Perhaps I have made a more exciting discovery than the one I planned. Are you awaiting some gallant, who has callously abandoned you? If so, will I not make a suitable substitute? Let us see what you are hiding, my pretty," he taunted. Before Katherine could guess his intention and move to thwart it, he had swept aside her mask and gazed from hooded dark eyes into her face.

She struggled to escape the tight grip and avert her face from his searching gaze, but he would have none of it.

"Not at all what I expected. What are you doing here, my dear? Hoping to attract some exceptional protector? You should have no difficulty. You have a certain enchanting air

8

of innocence—assumed no doubt, but alluring for all that. How mean spirited of me to interrupt," the stranger continued, in that mocking tone which raised Katherine's hackles. How dare he make such assumptions.

"You have made a mistake, sir. I am not what you think, and I find your insinuations vastly insulting," Katherine replied bravely, not sure how to handle this engimatic gentleman, for that was what he was. He had none of the appearance or the tone of an encroaching cit or a boisterous parvenue. Not that she could tell much about his appearance, for while he had removed her mask he had kept his own, and all she was aware of was a pair of dark eyes and unusual height. The advantages were all his.

"Do not protest so much. I am not such a flat as to be taken in by whatever Banbury tale you will try upon me. Whatever your reasons for lurking here in the gardens, they are not innocent ones I am sure. I rather regret that you are not the party I sought, but I must leave you to whatever mischief you are planning, and can only repine that I am not the fortunate fellow who will win your favors," he insisted, still in that taunting voice which signified his contempt.

"Begone, sir. I want nothing to do with you, and if you persist in annoying me, I will scream. I am not without protection," she cried, not realizing the ambiguity of her words.

"Just as I thought. Well, screams will cause no comment in this tawdry palace, and your protector is strangely elusive. Before he returns to find me poaching on his preserves, I will take my regretful adieu, but not without a forfeit."

Tilting her chin, he looked for a moment into her bemused eyes, and the hardness of his own expression seemed to dissolve for a moment. Then—to Katherine's amazement—he dropped the most gossamer of kisses on her unresisting lips. Before she could take him to task for his liberty, he had slipped away into the darkness, leaving her astounded by his effrontery. She had come to the Pantheon masquerade looking for an adventure, and she had certainly found one. The man had taken her for a light skirt, and not without cause, because there were dozens of that fellowship cavorting boldly in the ballroom. But there had been more than a suggestion of mystery beneath his offensive remarks. Obviously he had intended to meet some unknown woman wearing a purple domino in the Pantheon Gardens, and knew her only as Titania. Katherine remembered vaguely from Miss Molesworth's literature readings that there was a character by that name in Shakespeare's "Midsummer's Night Dream." Titania, Queen of the Fairies. Did this have some ulteriour meaning? Before she could ponder the enigma any further, Ronald Pemberton appeared, clutching a glass of ratafia, as if it were a precious chalice.

"Here you are, Katherine, and I must say I had the deuce of a time getting it," he remarked a bit peevishly. "Matters are heating up in there and I am not sure that we should remain much longer. You might see some shocking sights, and I am sure I should not have left you here in the garden unescorted. Who knows what you might have encountered?"

Katherine, who had no intention of mentioning the incident with the mysterious gentleman, dismissed his words. "Don't be silly, Ronald. What could happen to me here? We are not in the stews, you know. This is a very respectable part of the city and I am quite able to cope with any unwarranted approach," she answered a bit sharply, annoyed by his proprietery tone and not about to endure this lecturing.

Sensing that he had annoyed Katherine, Ronald Pemberton hastened to temper his manner. He was a well set up young man, of some twenty five years, with blond hair con-

10

trived into the latest windswept style, a thin-boned face and a sculptured mouth which now tightened with annoyance. He much valued his own consequence, and believed Miss Wilde should show a proper deference for his position and title. That he was as near to dun street as nodding did not particularly worry him, as he was convinced he would easily come about with an advantageous marriage whenever he chose to throw the handkerchief. Unfortunately. Miss Wilde did not seem as appreciative of his assets as he considered she should in view of her own undistinguished lineage. But he would win her round yet. If he had to marry a City's daughter, there could not be a more attractive choice than Katherine.

He forced a smile at her reproof, restraining his inclination to tell her he was a better arbiter of manners than a banker's chit such as she. Until he had safely wed her, he would step circumspectly.

"Perhaps I am overly anxious, afraid that some rubbishy fellow should see you and be struck by your beauty," he said in what Katherine thought an affected manner, but she could not help but warm to his attentions. A girl who craved affection and received little of it from her austere father, she was vulnerable to the lures of a handsome, well-born, attentive young man.

She smiled in a forgiving fashion at her escort. "I am mean to rip up at you, Ronald, when I know you brought me here against your wishes. But I must say I have not found this masquerade as shocking as expected. It is quite flat, don't you think?" she asked, casting a teasing look at his disapproving face.

"If your father knew that I had been a party to this madcap scheme he would deny me the house, and rightly so. I can't think how you cozened me into such a plan!"

"My father deny Viscount Chomeley his house? Never!

11

He is too aware of your consequence.'' Cynicism darkened her words. She had no illusions about her father's desire to gain Ronald as a son-in-law.

Ronald frowned, annoyed at her percipience. "Now, Katherine. Your father is an estimable man.''

"And a very rich one," Katherine smiled in what Ronald considered a very undutiful way. "But enough of this tedious prosing. Let us join the dancers. I am dying to experience the thrills of the masquerade. Who knows? I might yet see what all the shocked disapproval is about.'' She ignored her escort's critical expression for she was determined to stay. A small warning nagged her. Ronald would no doubt make a very censorious husband, apt to throw her background in her face whenever she behaved in a fashion less than proper. Well, they were not married yet, so he had no choice but to assent to her coaxing.

As they moved carefully through the throng of revelers, many beginning to behave in a fashion which bordered on the licentious, Katherine found herself examing the passing couples for the stranger who had accosted her in the garden. But the dominos and masks of the masqueraders, designed to protect their identities, made this a formidable task. Finally, she abandoned her scrutiny, but she did not completely forget the encounter in fending off Ronald's ardent expressions of regard as the evening progressed. It was well past midnight when he delivered her to her Wigmore Street home and took his leave with many warnings not to divulge the shocking nature of the evening's entertainment.

She prepared for bed, having avoided any meeting with her father. She suspected he had retired early, forbearing to wait up for her, since he believed she had spent a most proper evening at the theater chaperoned by Ronald's married cousins, a device she had arranged providentially. Not that she was afraid to face her father with the news of her escapade,

12

but she preferred to do it when the exploit could serve to her advantage. In the few weeks since she had come to London Katherine had learned more about her father, his ambitions and his character than she had known in the previous eighteen years. And she did not enjoy what she had been forced to conclude. His regard for her was tempered by her usefulness to him. But she would let herself be used by no man, not even her father. She had set the stage for her rebellion and he would soon realize he had foe worthy of his most tortuous stratagems.

Chapter Two

Katherine tripped light-heartedly into the dining room in a bouyant mood the morning following the masquerade. A warm-hearted girl whose character did not incline her to hold a grudge, she had decided after a good night's sleep that she would forgive her father for his intentions, and talk him into a more reasonable frame of mind. He must have some affection for her and if he realized that she took his scheme to marry her off to some decadent aristocrat in order to secure his own place in society as a despicable one, surely he would desist. And she wanted no part of the chaperone he insisted upon—no doubt a dessicated dowager who would prose and condescend.

She looked beguiling enough to soften the hardest heart, in a jonquil silk morning dress cut decorously across the bosom, but cleverly designed to show off her slender figure to best advantage.

"Good morning, Father. Isn't it a beautiful day?" she trilled, settling herself opposite her parent who was buried beneath the newspaper. He looked up and frowned, barely acknowledging her cheerful greeting.

"I understand most ladies of fashion prefer to remain in

bed until the late hours of the morning," he said, implying there was a lack of decorum in her joining him for breakfast.

Katherine, shook out her napkin, and nodded her thanks to the butler, Saunders, who offered her some shirred eggs and deviled kidneys, before replying saucily, "But I am not quite a lady of fashion, Father, despite your efforts to make me one."

Peter Wilde's rather severe countenance did not lighten at this attempted jest. He was a handsome man, who looked more aristocratic than many of his clients, with a carefully combed shock of white hair, a trim stature, and well defined features. Only his cold gray eyes, under quite forbidding dark eyebrows hinted at the ruthless intelligence that had propelled him to the top of his profession. He had begun life as the son of a country solicitor, but had early decided not to follow in his sire's footsteps. He was clever with figures and had an unerring eye for the fluctuations of the exchange. Before he was thirty he had made a fortune through judicious investments in the East India Company.

It was then that he had made what was perhaps the only imprudent action of his life. He had married the penniless, vivacious Amelia Langely, after her first season. Amelia, well connected, if not aristocratic, had burst upon the London scene, a refreshing tonic beside the dull simpering debutantes of her year. She had been presented by her mother's cousin, Lady Beauville, whose entrees into the most distinguished drawing rooms could not be denied.

Despite Amelia's lack of fortune she took immediately and received several exceptional offers, which made it all the more surprising when she finally accepted Peter Wilde, whose mercurial rise in the City could not disguise his lack of background, no matter how determinedly he studied to ape his betters. London's ton did not welcome parvenues, and even his alliance with Amelia Langely, respectably born, did not insure him the acceptance he craved. His disappointment was acute and did not lessen when his wife presented him with a daughter rather than the son he desired. Living with a disappointed man had evidently dimmed Amelia's own enjoyment and vivacity, for she did not long survive the birth of her daughter. She died when Katherine was barely out of leading strings.

Katherine had a dim memory of a laughing face, sheltering arms, and a delicious scent, but her father never talked about her mother, and her own efforts to learn more had been rebuffed brusquely. There was no portrait of the late Mrs. Wilde. Katherine's only relic of her mother was a charming miniature painted on the occasion of Amelia's come-out. Katherine often wondered if her father's austere character could be laid at the door of her mother's death. Perhaps his heart was buried in her grave, she mused soulfully, but then scorned those romantic notions as being too like a Mrs. Radcliffe novel and not at all appropriate to the somber merchant banker.

She looked at him a bit wistfully, hoping for a sign that he regarded her presence in his home with some pleasure. Surely after all these years burrowing away in the financial intracies of the exchange, he must long for some other reward than a monetary one. She yearned for some acknowledgement that he welcomed her for herself, not just as a valuable pawn in his desire for social prestige.

"I rather thought you might enjoy having company over your meal, Father. It must be dreary eating alone these many years," she said, hoping to wring some response.

Indeed, Peter Wilde was not so hard-hearted that he could not appreciate the charming picture his daughter made over the breakfast table, and he rewarded her with a wintery smile. But as if annoyed at this small departure from his normal disciplined reaction to any frivolity, he spoke in the repressive tones which Katherine had come to expect from him.

"I have never found my own company dreary, Katherine, and you must not allow any sense of filial duty to interfere with your preference." He smiled tightly as if to rob his words of any sting, But Katherine could only feel rebuffed.

She persevered in her campaign to establish some rapport with this solemn parent. Katherine was not a girl who could live happily in such an arctic atmosphere. "Oh, but it is my preference to breakfast with you, Father," she replied brightly, wishing not for the first time that she could abandon that chilly appelation, for the more intimate "Papa."

But Peter Wilde was not a man who would easily relax standards, and he did not see himself as "Papa".

"As you wish, my dear," he responded as if humoring an eccentric whim. "When you have finished that rather lavish breakfast, Katherine," he added, looking at the amount of eggs, kidney and toast his daughter was managing to eat with some amazement, "I would like to see you in the library. I find the dining table is not the best scene for serious discussion, and there are a few matters I would like to clear up with you before I leave for Lombard Street."

He then bundled up his post and newspapers and stalked from the room without waiting for an answer.

Katherine, tempted to put out a saucy tongue after her obdurate parent, was restrained from such an unladylike action by the arrival of the maids asking if they might clear the covers.

She had no recourse but to follow her father into his sanctum, feeling very much as she had on those many occasions when Miss Molesworth had bade her attend a disciplinary session in her head-mistress' quarters. Katherine mused as she walked slowly across the impressive marbled hall toward the library that her former instructress and her parent had a great deal in common. They both seemed determined to take her in hand, both disapproved of her high spirits. Well, it was too nice a June day to mope over her situation and she would not let her father depress her tendencies toward adventure and gaiety. If he hoped to badger her into behaving like some prim, prissy maiden who never raised her voice or her eyes to her lord and master, he was due for a surprise. Katherine decided rebelliously. She was a girl who had always been led by her affections but balked at any attempt at coercion.

"Please be seated, Katherine," Peter Wilde commanded at her entrance into his library, a rather awesome room of noble proportions relying heavily on panelled bookcases and rich leather chairs for its effect. Not even today's bright sunshine penetrated the gloom of the high-ceilinged room, and Katherine suspected her father preferred this grim environment, so like his banking offices, to any more cheerful furnishing. Feeling rather like a client whose overdraft was being called into question, she settled herself in the chair he indicated.

"You have now been in London two weeks, Katherine, and I fear, that if steps are not taken to restrain your obvious penchant for troublesome escapades, you will never find a husband. Well brought up girls do not cavort in the streets of London without chaperones. It has come to my notice that you were seen in the Park a few days ago strolling alone and eyeing the motley like some housemaid from the country." He spoke in a censorious tone which immediately sent Katherine, whose temper was easily roused by injustice, up into the boughs.

"Hardly a housemaid, Father. You have seen to it that I am too well dressed for that mistake! And surely a small saunter in the Park cannot lead me into the path of sin," she teased, hoping to lighten the atmosphere. Really, her father had some old fashioned ideas.

"Respectable girls do not roam about carelessly without a maid or some other suitable escort. I hope you will not force me to speak to you again about this, Katherine," he said severely. Then, perhaps seeing the defiant expression on his daughter's face he softened his tone with an effort. "But enough of that. I mentioned yesterday that I have secured the good offices of an exceptional lady who will initiate you into London society and guard you from the pitfalls which lie in wait for a naive girl making her Come-Out. Mrs. Basingbroke has entree into all the best drawing rooms. She might even secure you vouchers for Almacks, for I understand she is a close friend of Lady Sefton's. You will do well to be guided by her experience and I am sure you will find her an amiable lady."

"I understand, Father, that I must be introduced by some suitable chaperone, but I think you mistake the situation if you believe I will be received in London's most august salons," she said sadly, remembering past snubs. "I would much rather be left to my own devices, you know, for I fear that my background is not to everyone's taste."

But if she was expecting some sympathy from her father, she had mistaken her man. He had planned her debut much as a general planned a campaign and he would brook no interference from an ungrateful chit of a girl. In well-regulated families daughters did not defy their parents, and he did not feel he was behaving harshly.

"Katherine, you have been afforded an excellent education, and every luxury that a girl could desire. It is not unreasonable for me to expect that you honor your obligations by making a desirable match."

"I do not want to be married right from the schoolroom. I would like to enjoy a season, see something of the world, before I am married off to some suitor who meets your exacting standards of birth and position," she blurted out unwisely, but faced her father's growing anger bravely. She must make him see the justice of her position.

"Since Napoleon has put the Continent out of bounds, I fear you must wait until after you have achieved the status of a matron before a jaunt of that sort," he replied a bit sarcastically. Peter Wilde was famed for his ability to reach a lucrative compromise in business matters. But he was not dealing with a balance sheet or an exchange bill now, and it was only with great difficulty that he held on to his temper.

"Katherine, be reasonable. As your father, responsible for your future welfare, it behooves me to guide you into making a judicious union. I am not asking you to wed an ogre or a gouty old man, but simply an eligible young man who will offer you an enjoyable life, a London town house, a place in the country, children, acceptance into the best drawing rooms," he argued. "A young man like Ronald Pemberton, for example. You do not find him obnoxious, I notice." Wilde thought he had made his point, and he had introduced the Viscount with just such an outcome in mind. In the normal course of affairs he would not have run across such an exceptional party, but Ronald had served as his father's agent on a matter of business in which Wilde had been able to oblige the hard-pressed peer on very favorable terms.

"Ronald is all right, but I have not fallen in love with him. And I rather doubt the sincerity of his own attentions. I understand you would be willing to pay handsomely for a title," she challenged outrageously.

"Don't be impertinent, Katherine. And I will not entertain your foolish romantic vapourings. Marriages in the best families are made for reasons of property and inheritance, not because two young people feel some wild emotion which soon dissipates under the exigencies of daily living. You would soon lose your illusions married to some half pay officer and struggling to survive in a dreary country barracks town, I assure you.''

"Was mother a passing infatuation for you?" Katherine asked boldly, unwilling to surrender, but dismayed by her father's cold reaction. She wondered why he was so anxious to get her off his hands. A different stamp of man would have welcomed the company of a loving daughter to brighten his loneliness.

"We are not discussing my marriage, Katherine, but yours. I do not think that what I am asking is an occasion to enact a Cheltenham tragedy. Just be thankful you are not auctioned off to a senile old fool who is lured by your youth. That is the fate of many a girl, sold to rescue her family from penury. Be grateful your lot will be a happier one. And do not turn your nose up at young Pemberton. You could do a great deal worse.''

"And you could not do better," was Katherine's inclination to argue, but she bit her tongue. No point would be served by brangling with her father over Ronald or any other hypothetical suitor.

Thoroughly out of patience, Wilde hurried to bring the distasteful interview to a close. Why couldn't the girl be biddable, show some gratitude? "That is all, Katherine," he said dismissing her. "I must be away to Lombard Street, but I will remind you that Mrs. Basingbroke will be joining us within the week, and I expect you to receive her politely, and not plague her with your unnatural notions.''

Katherine was not prepared to leave affairs in such a state, but she shrewdly realized that she must save her attack for another day, after she had decided on the proper tactics. She would not be paraded before the ton, auctioned off to the best title, to satisfy her father's ambitions. And he had not been honest about those. She would respect him a great deal more if he had not wrapped up his eagerness to gain an aristocratic connection in such fustian. There were several questions about her father's attitude she found puzzling, but for the moment she felt it prudent to retire to protest another day, to brood over his motives and his reasoning. She sensed there was a great deal more here than a father's desire to improve his social status by arranging a brilliant marriage for his daughter.

Chapter Three

If such a guarded and aloof man as Peter Wilde could evidence smug satisfaction, that was the expression he sported on this occasion. His host, experienced at concealing his own emotions, was not deceived. Rarely were bankers, even men of such influence and wealth as Wilde, admitted into the portals of White's, the club which listed the most aristocratic names in England on its roster. Since Simon Stafford, Marquis of Staines, had the bad taste to invite what "King" Allen called "his tradesmen" to luncheon, the only recourse his fellow members had was to ignore both Staines and his guest. If the Marquis was aware of his solecism, he was indifferent to it, having enough consequence to carry off almost any offense against the unwritten code with aplomb. He had invited Wilde to the club because he wished to gain his confidence, and this flattering acknowledgement of the man's importance was sure to put him at a disadvantage. Staines, himself, cared little for such snobbish notions, but he recognized that he was committing a definite breach of manners in hobnobbing with a "Cit" within the sacred portals.

White's had begun as a chocolate house in the early eighteenth century, serving as a gathering place for Tory gentlemen who wanted to discuss politics, but more than twenty years ago the club had been organized along more formal lines with a subscription fee and a rule that no one should be elected if one member blackballed him. The exclusive nature of the club had deepened over the years so that Wilde was under no illusions that he could ever gain admittance unless he managed a more intimate connection with one of the members, through marriage perhaps. Which reminded him to ask his host a question of great import to his plans.

"Could you tell me, my lord, is Ronald Pemberton, Viscount Chomeley, a member here?" he asked with some diffidence.

If the Marquis of Staines found the question ill-advised, even surprising, he was too skilled a strategist to show it. He raised an ironic eyebrow and answered in his lazy drawl, "I believe so. I know his father, The Earl of Wexford is a member, but the Viscount's circle is a trifle jejune for me."

Wilde, astute enough to realize that he had presumed, did not pursue the matter, but settled down to the business at hand. Wilde knew the Marquis had not invited him to White's for the pleasure of his company. The fellow wanted a favor and this was his method of beguiling the banker into a receptive frame of mind. Wilde wondered if it would be a request for a loan, and if so what guarantees the Marquis would give. He was willing to pay dearly for entree into the circles he desired to join, but not at the expense of business. He had made a few inquiries about Staines and had not discovered any rumors that the Marquis was in queer street, about to be rolled up. The peer had one of the country's most impressive fortunes, and he was not a gamester, so Wilde doubted that he needed any personal financial assistance. He was not a customer who Wilde, despite his vast experience, could easily read. Apparently affable, with a neg-

24

ligent, careless ease of manner, the Marquis would not be easily impressed or influenced. Fortune had not only blessed him with wealth and position but also dark, good looks. His tanned face showed generations of breeding with high cheekbones, a disciplined mouth and distinguished brow, topped by dark brown hair combed a la Titus. But his most striking feature were his slate gray eyes, cold and assessing one moment, warm and inquisitive another. Wilde felt confident that the Marquis was fully in control of his life, unlikely to entertain fools or charlatans and possessed of a formidable intelligence. He would walk warily with Staines, a judgment shared by most of the men who had dealt with Simon Stafford in his thirty years.

The two men had dined well off on a baron of beef, some crisp whiting and had now reached the cheese and bisquits finale of the meal before Staines gave any hint of the subject which had impelled this strange invitation. Wilde realized the Marquis considered it bad ton to discuss business over a meal.

"Perhaps we can adjourn to the library, which is rarely occupied at this hour, and can discuss the small matter of business which I hope can be completed to our mutual advantage," Staines said affably. Wilde agreed and the two men walked from the dining room, his host ignoring the stares and whispers of his fellow members lingering over their port and madeira.

Wilde envied his host's sang froid in the face of such conjecture, but could not emulate it. Although he knew his own wealth exceeded that of many of these starched-up critics, he could not throw off the inferiority he felt, even if he was successful at hiding it. He knew they regarded him as a good enough fellow to borrow money from, but not well born enough to join their club or be entertained in their houses. If Peter Wilde were vulnerable in any area of his

25

well-arranged life it concerned his fervant desire to be accepted in the highest circles of London society, an ambition his daughter had begun to realize as a consuming force in his life. The Marquis of Staines had also taken pains to discover this weakness in the banker's armor, and intended to capitalize on it for his own reasons.

The library, as he had promised, was deserted, the members for the most part not men of scholary tastes, who might spend their hours delving into the musty books lining two sides of the dark panelled room. The Marquis, now that courtesy had been satisfied, quickly settled down to the subject of the moment.

"I will put it to you frankly, Wilde, "the Marquis began." Several of us, I am not at liberty now to name the principals, have decided to form a syndicate to take advantage of the profits in eastern trade. We are thinking of an initial investment of fifty thousand pounds, and you appear the best man to handle such a project. Naturally, we would want this business to be kept secret. You understand, it is not quite the thing for us to be delving in these matters, for personal gain."

Wilde looked over the aristocratic face with mixed feelings, and restrained his cynicism and scorn. These fellows, as greedy as the most common merchant, were not above turning a profit as long as the sordid changing of money did not endanger their social standing. At least Staines was honest enough to admit he wanted to increase his fortune, if not honest enough to be seen doing it. This so-called syndicate needed him and he intended to see that these disdainful peers paid dearly for the privilege, if not in the coin of the realm, in another way far more to Wilde's taste. It would never occur to Peter Wilde to deal dishonestly in business affairs, and the notion that he would exert social blackmail did not compromise his business ethics, but he had been the victim of too many snubs not to indulge in a human desire to further his own aims at the expense of the syndicate's fortunes.

"I understand, my lord. Naturally, you would not want to dirty your hands with an obvious incursion into the market place," Wilde replied, unable to resist a slight note of sarcasm.

Staines smiled lazily in response to the barbed words.

"Quite so, Wilde. I see we shall deal well together. Now what is the first step in the proceedings? You will want our draft for the money, of course, and we will want some undertaking as to the investment." The Marquis showed a surprising grasp of the financial intracies involved.

"Yes, well, I will look about for the best venture. The East India Company would once have been my choice but lately I have not found the company well managed, and several ships have foundered with valuable cargos. This needs some consideration, my lord, but I am honored that you would consult me."

"Capital, capital! I knew I could rely on you. My friends will be pleased we can settle this to our mutual advantage, for of course, your commission will be a generous one," Staines concluded, reminding Wilde that business was their only point of contact.

But the banker had more in mind. "I wonder, my lord, since we are going to be partners, so to speak, in this exciting venture, if I might prevail upon you to join me for dinner later this week, where we can discuss it in more detail. I would naturally wish to return your hospitality."

For a moment Wilde thought he saw an expression of distaste darken the Marquis' face, but it quickly passed, and Staines agreed easily to the invitation. Before parting, the two set the day.

Staines escorted his guest to the entrance of the club and bade him farewell with impeccable politeness, watching the banker walk off confidently in search of a hackney. He was about to take his own leave when he was approached by a tall saturnine gentleman, of equally aristocratic mien.

"Well, how did it go, Staines? You certainly caused some chin-wagging in the sanctum. Not exactly the done thing, old chap," Lord de Lisle mocked as he joined Staines in retrieving their hats and sticks.

"I am just off now to see Valentine now and report," Staines responded as the two men hesitated on the steps of White's. "Are you coming along to add your bit to the council of war?"

"No, I will have to catch up on all the doings later. Melissa is expecting me to fetch her from Sally Jersey's and she will ring a peal over me if I am late," de Lisle excused himself, giving the impression of a much-tried benedict which Simon Stafford knew to be false.

Theron de Lisle had recently married a very young charmer who was not above joining him in some of his dangerous escapades. Indeed, that was how Theron de Lisle had met his Melissa and fallen completely under the spell of this gamin girl, so different from the legion of women he had pursued in the past. Caught by a mere school girl, he had endured the teasing of his friends with good natured composure and showed no signs of tiring of his folly in taking a wife of such youth.

"Till later, then. And my best to your Marchioness. I think you are a fortunate fellow, Theron," Staines concluded before swinging off with a brisk stride on his errand to the War Office.

General Lucien Valentine, (only in his late thirties), was young to have achieved such exalted rank. He had won his promotion after years fighting the King's enemies on many battlefields and crowning his efforts with a brilliant coup against local traitors in the war against Napoleon. Although

28

the French and British were now ostensibly enjoying a truce in the hostilities, neither side had relaxed its intelligence efforts nor its vigilance. Valentine and his superiors believed that the wily Corsican had sued for peace in order to build his armaments and strengthen his finances. He was not above conniving with his enemies for money and that was the conspiracy Valentine, with the help of Staines and de Lisle, both veterans in his intelligence network, intended to thwart.

Valentine greeted his lieutenant eagerly when Staines entered his office.

"Well, did the fellow bite, Simon?" he asked after indicating that the Marquis be seated.

Simon nodded and then smiled roguishly. "And I am not at all sure that I shall not be shunned by Alvaney, Allen, Sefton and the rest for inviting a Cit into the White's exclusive halls," he said in dismay mock.

"Nonsense. You have enough consequence to carry off the most outrageous insults to the ton without any retribution. But what is your opinion of the man?" Valentine asked. Experience had led him to believe that traitors could flourish in the most unlikely places. "I know he would not be trafficking with the enemy for the money. So what would his motive be?"

"Ambition. He badly wants entrée into the best circles, and even a knighthood is not beyond his dreams, I suspect. Granted, betraying his King and country is a strange way to achieve those aims, but no doubt he believes himself invulnerable. After all, what evidence do we have, beyond some very garbled information that he tendered the Italians a hefty loan. And that was before the fellows surrendered, bought off by their republican hopes."

"The Italians and then the Austrians. Very damning, and even more damning are the rumors of Wilde's dealings with the Papacy," Valentine insisted.

"He would claim it was all a matter of business, and that at the time the debtors were our allies," Staines pointed out. "And now, if Wilde is in deep waters because he has not collected on those loans—highly likely with Europe in its current state—then he might be tempted to recoup through treasonable dealing with Napoleon, who always needs money."

"Yes, I agree. Wilde is extremely clever, as well as ambitious and will be sure to cover his tracks smoothly. Did you get any hint of associates of his who might play some part in these dealings?" Valentine asked, idly jotting on the pad in front of him, but with little hope of learning any pertinent information at this early date.

"Only one. He asked me if I knew Viscount Chomeley—Wexford's sprig. Since Wexford is almost under the hatches, Chomeley has to marry money. Perhaps that will prove to be a useful bit of information," Simon mused. He had been puzzled by the irrelevant introduction of the Viscount's name into their business discussion.

Valentine nodded. He was not surprised, for his vast network turned up some unsavory facts about England's most aristocratic families. "Wilde has a daughter, just returned from her seminary, whom he hopes to marry off to satisfy his ambitions, I warrant. I doubt that Wexford's son is anything more than a possible suitor. Much as he tries to hide it, there is no denying that Wilde's vulnerability lies in his social ambitions. He has an unholy interest in gaining acceptance into the highest circles." Valentine's lip curled with distaste.

"Well, I will no doubt meet the daughter. I am dining with Wilde next week. Much as I dislike accepting his hospitality, I thought it best to accept. What I do for my country!" Simon smiled derisively. He did not like pursuing traitors in London drawing rooms. His preference and his experience had led him to fight the fellows in much less comfortable if more dangerous environs.

"See that you are not led astray by Miss Wilde's charms! I understand that she is an uncommonly attractive girl," Valentine jibed, his dark eyes crinkling with amusement. Every eligible woman in London had tried to lure Simon to the altar, but the Marquis had remained impervious. Nor did he cultivate light skirts, and Valentine had never known of his keeping a mistress. He was singularly devoted to the army and his acres, but as the General knew from his own history, the right woman could undoubtedly change Simon's mind and heart.

"Do you suspect the girl of being in on Wilde's dubious dealings? I doubt he would confide in a schoolgirl," Simon replied lightly, rising to his feet. "But you need not worry, Lucien. I am forwarned."

Valentine bid him a warm farewell after making arrangements for a further meeting which would include De Lisle. But after Staines had departed he smiled reminiscently to himself. The man was entirely too serious-minded, too sure that he would never fall victim to some charmer. Valentine thought it would be quite a turn-up if the charming Miss Wilde should prove to be the instrument of Staines' romantic downfall. Then he shrugged and returned to his memos. He would leave such romantic twaddle to his beloved wife. Discovering what Peter Wilde was plotting was the chief item on his crowded agenda right now.

Chapter Four

Whatever Katherine had expected of the dreaded chaperone, Mrs. Basingbroke, she was pleasantly surprised. A woman of some forty-odd years, widow of an improvident younger son of a baronet, an Honorable herself, she had neither the haughty air of the aristocrat toward the less nobly born nor the sycophantic manner of the impoverished genteel. Plum, cheerful, with merry brown eyes and a wealth of chestnut hair arranged stylishly, she dressed simply but elegantly. Most importantly, she treated Katherine as a contemporary, not trying to admonish or cajole, but explaining the situation in which they found themselves with practical good sense.

"You see, my dear," she said confidingly over their tea cups, "I have a commodity to sell, and your father the money to buy. It's as simple as that." She settled her skirts with a brisk twitch and sipped her tea daintily.

"I'm not sure I want to buy, but father does. This whole business of securing me a desirable match is his idea, you know," Katherine replied with some asperity, but unable to hold any animosity toward this engaging matron.

"Well, naturally your Papa wants to see you suitably settled. Unfortunately men really have no idea of how to go about such affairs. They have such antiquated notions of propriety, and no fancy for romance, poor dears!''

"I don't think I am very romantic myself," Katherine answered briskly, wishing to settle any mistaken notions Mrs. Basingbroke might entertain of her own expectations.

"How sensible. Alas, I was swept away by dreams of romantic bliss, not realizing until it was too late that marriage demands certain realities. I loved my husband, but he really was a most improvident man. Perhaps it is just as well we weren't blessed with children, for without a feather to fly with we could not have given them a secure life. And since I married over the anvil my parents were not very sympathetic when we ended up in the hands of the ten percenters.

Gerald died in a hunting accident, before the baliffs were actually in the house, but if he had gone on much longer it would have meant the Fleet. And then my father and mother died, leaving the estate to a cousin, and I was hard pressed to manage. But now I have come about, and have had some success in getting off lovely young girls, all I may add, into very desirable situations, as unlike mine as possible. So that is my story, Katherine, and enough prosing from me," Mrs. Basingbroke concluded. "But don't be concerned that I will forever be warning you of the pitfalls of romance. We must just see to it that the young man fortunate enough to win you is one for whom you can entertain both romantic and practical feelings."

Katherine, touched despite herself by Mrs. Basingbroke's recital of her past misfortunes, and the matter-of-fact acceptance of her unenviable lot, thought the two of them would deal very well together and accepted her chaperone with more enthusiasm than she at first had deemed possible.

Mrs. Basingbroke preferred not to live with the Wildes

33

during Katherine's season, but lodged instead with one of her numerous cousins. But she would spend most of her days and evenings at the Wigmore Street house and chaperoning Katherine to the various entertainments to which she would secure entry. A doughty campaigner, she intended to launch her charge with an introduction to Lady Cowper, at one of the patroness of Almack's Wednesday "at homes."

The afternoon, which Katherine had viewed with some misgivings, proved not to be so alarming, due largely to Mrs. Basingbroke's skilled and easy touch. Lady Cowper, a small slender woman with merry brown eyes, welcomed Katherine with the charm that had made her one of London's most popular hostesses. As a patroness of Almack's her endorsement was essential if a debutante was to be acceptable in the best circles. Despite her imposing reputation she was not untouched by scandal. For it was well known that she had enjoyed a liaison of many years with Lord Palmerston. Still, this marital infidelity in no way detracted from her impregnable social position, and the affair was conducted with the utmost descretion on both sides.

Her manner toward Katherine was both kindly and interested. She willingly overlooked the fact that she was entertaining the daughter of a Cit. Her guests, for the most part, followed her lead, with the exception of Sally Villiers, Lady Jersey, whose own background was tainted with trade and who was most sensitive to any encroaching by parvenues. She looked Katherine over with a critical eye and said in a rather sneering tone to Cecilia Basingbroke, "Well, Ceci, you should have no trouble with this one. She's a beauty, and her settlement will soften any taint of the market place."

Mrs. Basingbroke, reproved gently, "Well, you should know, Sally. Like the Childs, Katherine's father has loaned money to the highest in the land, and she is too clever to marry over the anvil!"

Lady Jersey, her bright eyes sparkling with malice, seemed about to reply sharply, but then thought better of it. It was all too true that Sally Fane had married Lord Jersey at Gretna Green, and her considerable fortune was inherited from the redoubtable Joshua Childs of the merchant baking family whose ancestors had been goldsmiths. Tainted with trade indeed!

Katherine, pleased at her mild-appearing chaperone's quick riposte, decided that it would be wiser for her to ignore snubs and leave her defense in Mrs. Basingbroke's capable hands.

Afterwards, as they rode toward Wigmore Street, Katherine was not tardy in her gratitude.

"You make a formidable guardian, Mrs. Basingbroke! I was quite amazed at you facing up to Lady Jersey. I understand she has routed some very impressive challengers. And you did it so quietly."

"Poor Sally," Mrs. Basingbroke responded." She is so conscious of her own background and fights like a tiger if anyone casts doubts on her pedigree. But she is not averse to spending the Childs fortune, which won her a top-of-the-trees husband, even if they are not too happy together. So much spite can often be laid at the door of unhappiness, you know. But it is not wise to make an enemy of her, and you were clever to bite your tongue no matter the temptation."

"What a wise and compassionate woman, you are," Katherine replied, much impressed with her chaperone's understanding and tolerance. Even if she decried the necessity of these maneuvers, Katherine was intelligent enough to understand that it served her better to accept Mrs. Basingbroke's counsel and keep any rebellious thoughts and plans to herself. If she objected to Mrs. B., her father would only supply another woman whom Katherine might find much less to her taste.

What really bothered Katherine was not Mrs. Basing-broke, but the whole idea of being paraded through the London season for the approval of any young man with aristocratic credentials, no matter what his character.

With great bitterness Katherine had accepted the fact that her welfare was less important to her father than his own schemes for advancement. She wondered if the fault was hers, that he could not love her or accept the love she was prepared to offer him. He must have cared for her mother, even though he was a man of reserved and aloof temperament. Why did he treat his daughter with such insensibility, using her as a pawn in his designs with no consideration for her own feelings? Having spent so much time at school Katherine, with a child's acceptance of her situation, had not realized how indifferent her father was to her. She knew that many parents ignored their children, leaving them in the hands of others, but perhaps because she had lost her mother so young, she craved some sign of affection from the only relation she had.

Even Mrs. Basingbroke's kindly attentions were bought. Money seemed to be the only commodity her father respected.

Katherine had to admit he had spared no expense in providing her with every luxury a girl could want. Since her arrival in London she had become aware that the majority of the populace did not live in such comfort and ease. But she felt she would have sacrificed her pretty gowns and pleasures for a little honest affection. However, Katherine conceded, no one had all of life's gifts and she was a ninny to repine over her father's attitude. She would just have to hope that a prolonged and more intimate exposure to her delightful self would change his mind, she ruefully concluded. It never did to take oneself too seriously.

The next morning, Katherine received her father's orders for that evening's entertainment with determined cheerfulness. He called her into his library, the place for all their consultations—that was what Katherine considered them—feeling rather like a dubious borrower, requesting a loan from a grudging lender. She doubted that even the Prince Regent and other august members of society faced such a stern banker when they made their submissions.

"Well, Katherine, you seem to have settled down well with Mrs. Basingbroke. She tells me you were well received at Lady Cowper's at home."

Peter Wilde viewed his daughter with a certain amount of complacency. She did appear in the best of looks, wearing a sapphire blue French dimity dress edged in scallops, the color accenting her eyes, her complexion glowing. She might not be in the popular mode of pale blond beauties but she had an attraction all her own, her father was forced to admit. He did not wait for her opinion of Mrs. Basingbroke, but continued issuing his orders.

"Tonight we are having a small dinner party which will help you get into the way of managing these things. Mrs. Basingbroke will act as hostess and you must take your lead from her. She knows how to go on in these matters. Several important guests will be attending, including the Marquis of Staines, and I expect you to exert yourself to be hospitable, but not forward. Mrs. Basingbroke has been given the list and I have spoken to Alphonse about the menu." His managing tone set Katherine's back up, but she knew this was not the occasion to challenge her father.

"May I ask if Ronald Pemberton is included in the list?" she asked, trying to restrain her annoyance.

"Yes, and his father, the Earl of Wexford, has also accepted. We will be twelve at table. But you need not concern yourself with that. I assume you have a proper gown for the evening, considering the extent of your dressmaker's bills." Though he wanted to launch his daughter on the ton in a fitting manner, Peter Wilde couldn't help wincing at the expense.

"If you expect me to shine in the beau monde, father, I must be gowned accordingly. This marital parade is not my choice you know," she said gently ironic.

Peter frowned. Whenever he talked to Katherine about her responsibilities and future he felt at a disadvantage, suspecting she laughed at him.

"If that is all, I will leave you to your ledgers, then," Katherine announced, trying to keep any sign of her frustration from her voice. She intended to choose her own husband, but no good would come of tilting at her father in advance of the expected rebellion. It would serve him right if she ran off with a half-pay officer and brought all his plans to naught.

As Katherine left the library she smiled at her own foolishness. She would be cutting off her nose to spite her face, for she would not relish life in some barracks town, no matter if she loved her husband to distraction. She had enough of her father's practicality in her nature to know that she enjoyed the luxuries he provided. What an ungrateful girl she was, she decided, and determined to put all thoughts of marriage from her mind and enjoy the moment, even if her freedom proved temporary.

That evening, Katherine dressed with care for the important dinner. She chose a white silk gown of youthful simplicity, designed to show off her creamy shoulders, but it was cut lower than her usual style, the hem and bodice intricately woven with a shell seed pearl design. She made a moue at herself in the mirror, observing that she looked a bit like a virgin lamb ready for slaughter. She turned her maid's fulsome compliments aside with a short demur. How ridiculous society was, judging a girl by her gown and looks and caring little for the character beneath the handsome facade.

Only her father and Mrs. Basingbroke were present in the drawing room when she descended. The chaperone looked quite distinguished in a dress of plain gray taffeta and some rather nice amethysts. Katherine herself wore only her mother's pearls, but an impressive string, whose cost her father must have begrudged.

"You are looking very well, Katherine," her father commented as she crossed the room to join the pair who were seated on the Sheraton sofa. Obviously they had been discussing her, for her father looked a bit chagrined. Katherine wondered what Mrs. Basingbroke had said to him. Before Katherine could more than greet her chaperone and compliment her on her looks, the butler announced the first of the guests, the Earl of Wexford and Ronald.

The Earl, looked a great deal older than his fifty years for he was a stooped crabbed-looking gentleman with sparse white hair and a lined face. Whether this was the legacy of either dissipation or care, Katherine could not decide. He had cold blue eyes and narrow features and in no way resembled his son. Katherine did not care for the assessing look he gave her when they were introduced, and she turned with relief to Ronald, greeting him with more enthusiasm than she had intended, finding him a welcome ally in what she felt might be a difficult evening.

The Wexfords were followed quickly by the other guests, and Katherine was surprised to see the Jerseys among them. How had her father achieved such a coup? Or was Mrs. Basingbroke the persuader? If so her influence was indeed considerable. This evening the capricious Sally Jersey was on her best behaviour, and greeted Katherine with a suspicious amiability. The other guests included two dowagers of impeccable lineage, and a young couple whose only claim to inclusion was their affability, for the Otterlys accepted any invitation offered, so unwilling were they to spend an evening alone. The last guest entered with polite apologies for his tardiness to Peter Wilde. Mrs. Basingbroke brought him over to Katherine.

"May I present the Marquis of Staines, my dear. Simon, this is Mr. Wilde's daughter, Katherine," she said in her soft voice.

For a moment Katherine thought she saw a flash of recognition in the dark eyes which gleamed in appreciation as they assessed her, but if so, it passed into a casual courtesy as he acknowledged the introduction.

"Delighted, Miss Wilde. I do hope I have not delayed dinner by my unforgiveable lateness. If your chef is typical he will be having hysterics over the souffle," he said in a teasing, strangely familiar voice.

"Alphonse is the most placid of men, most unlike a Frenchman," she replied, impressed with this dark saturnine man of impeccable appearance. He looked completely at ease in a drawing room which she felt was not his natural arena. He belonged in a wilderness or in some other dangerous environ, for he had an aura of mastery and indifference to the usages of polite society, for all his fashionable manners and dress. In a moment they were joined by Sally Jersey, who trilled intimately at the Marquis.

"Why, Simon, I am surprised to see you. I thought you were still off in some mysterious errand or sequestered at those vast estates of yours in Somerset. If I had known you were in town I would have pressed you to visit us. This is the *last* place I would have imagined to meet you." She said with a significant glance at her host.

Despite a warning look from Mrs. Basingbroke, Katherine could not restrain a sharp reply. "Is there some reason the

Marquis should not be my father's guest, Lady Jersey?'' she asked, anger over-riding good sense.

"I'm sure Sally did not mean to sound so cavalier. After all, she is a guest here herself. Do behave, Sally, and remember your manners,'' the Marquis reproved, but with a smile the Countess could not resist, drawing her fire away from Katherine. Not that Katherine welcomed his support. She could defend herself and would not be patronized by Sally Jersey even if she were one of the most important doyennes of the society her father craved to enter. However, before she could utter any ill-timed reply to the Countess dinner was announced. The Marquis indicated that he was to take her in, which Katherine found somewhat unusual, and Sally Jersey watched with raised eyebrows.

Katherine peeped from under her demurely lowered eyes at the Marquis of Staines after he had seated her politely at the table, fittingly arrayed for this dinner party with Peter Wilde's best silver plate and Sévres china. In matters of furnishing Katherine conceded her father had elegant if austere taste. He would spend money where it mattered, she believed, but he expected value for his money. She hoped he did not consider her future a funded investment. And how had he lured the noble Marquis to his table? She doubted that she was the attraction. Ambitious as Peter Wilde was he could never dream of snaring such an eligible party for his daughter. Her curiosity aroused, Katherine hurried to satisfy it, although with a proper hint of modesty.

"I was not aware that you were numbered among my father's acquaintances, my lord.''

"And are you aware of all your father's acquaintances, Miss Wilde?'' he countered smoothly, with an edge to his tone she found rather insulting.

"Not the men he meets in the marketplace, my lord, 'tis true, but then he rarely brings those men to his table,'' she replied tartly, hoping to score a hit. She would not be patronized by this noble lord, whatever her father wanted to gain from this invitation. He was exactly the type of man to set her back up, puffed up with his own consequence and probably aware of his condescension in honoring the "Cits" by gracing their dinner table. She stared boldly at him, wondering how she could make polite conversation with such an arrogant man.

Simon smiled into her eyes, ignoring her sarcasm. She would have to learn to mask her emotions if she wanted to succeed in capturing a husband, he thought. Such frankness was not the style, but he found it rather refreshing. Surely the delectable Miss Wilde was not as innocent as she appeared, or what had she been doing in the garden of The Pantheon masquerade? As yet she had not recognized him as the mysterious intruder on her tryst. Looking at her with appreciation he wondered what she would do if he revealed their prior connection. Deny it, of course. Well, that was an advantage he would hold in reserve. However, if he were to learn what he needed to know, he would have to first win her confidence and dispell the bad opinion she seemed to have formed.

As the turbot replaced the soup, be bent his considerable efforts onto erasing the first unfavorable impression.

"For some reason, Miss Wilde, you seem to have taken me in dislike. I find that most dispiriting, and wish I could know what I can do to redeem my reputation in your eyes," he said in a tone of light cajoling.

"Why, nothing, my lord. I suppose I am simply overwhelmed by your company." she answered with a gamin grin, but wondering a bit at her audacity in teasing this daunting character. Mrs. Basingbroke would certainly chide her for such forward behaviour.

"I shall have to improve your erroneous impression of me,

for I would not like to be in your black books, and I quite look forward to furthering our relationship," he said with telling significance, although Katherine was not quite sure what he meant. Was he just a practiced flatterer, unable to accept the notion that any woman would not be overcome by his attention? Well, she might be a green schoolgirl but she was not such a flat as that. He had some motive which would bear careful scrutiny. For the moment she would depress his pretensions.

"Much as I would like to pursue this fascinating discussion, my lord, courtesy insists I now engage my other dinner partner in conversation," she said with a small smile. She then turned her back upon him resolutely, to talk to Lord Jersey as the saddle of mutton was passed.

What an impertinent minx, Simon decided, but intriguing for all she was barely out of the nursery. Such assurance could only come from experience, and what that experience entailed he was determined to explore further.

Chapter Five

If Simon Stafford found the evening at Wilde's frustrating he gave no sign of it, exerting his considerable tact upon the disparate company and ignoring Katherine for the rest of the evening. She found his attitude maddening. He had insinuated that he found her alluring, and then abandoned her to chat with Lady Jersey and Mrs. Basingbroke, much to those matrons' delight. What Katherine could not know, as she flirted with Ronald Pemberton, was that Simon was skillfully extracting from those two ladies some very illuminating information about the Wildes.

With Lady Jersey, Simon took a confiding approach, knowing that she responded to flattery and the sophisticated fliration she expected from any attractive young man.

"Sally, you are looking especially fetching this evening. I have been intending to call long before this but affairs of moment have kept me in the country," he confessed with a winning smile which begged her indulgence.

"I don't know if I will forgive you, Simon, for you have neglected me shamefully," Lady Jersey replied coquettishly. "And I suspect you want something from me, hence this sudden attention," she said with mock coolness.

"You wound me, dear lady. I have only the most pure intentions," he smoothly replied.

"Simon, you are the most complete hand. And I must say, the Wildes' drawing room is the last place I would expect to find you. Not our sort at all." She raised her eyebrows to punctuate this pronouncement.

Simon pretended doubt. "Oh, I don't know. The daughter is quite stunning, and Wilde seems an innocuous sort, terribly plump in the pocket, too. He certainly made his pile while still young enough to enjoy it."

Lady Jersey glanced at him sharply. "I don't believe you have any need of his money, and I haven't heard you are in the market for a bride. Can it be that the girl has some special appeal?"

"I am merely curious, Sally. Our host is quite a figure of mystery, you know."

"Not at all. Just a county solicitor's son with a talent for money grubbing. Of course he cheerfully lent money to Prinny which gives him a certain entree, I suppose," she admitted reluctantly.

"Well, you would know about that," Simon remarked coolly, alluding to the foundation of Sally's own family fortune, achieved in just the manner she criticized in Peter Wilde.

Mindful that the Marquis of Staines was not a man to snub, she let the stinging barb pass and merely rapped him playfully with her fan and proceeded to tell him of the latest scandal engaging the gossips.

With Katherine's chaperone, on the other hand, he assumed an artless air. Charmed by the Marquis' attention, Mrs. Basingbroke was quite open, confiding in the Marquis about her arrangement with Peter Wilde to launch Katherine upon the ton. The Marquis did not appear to find their bargain in any way shocking.

"Well, dear lady, I suspect your task will be an easy one. Your charge should easily snare an eligible suitor. She is exceptionally attractive, if not in the usual style."

"Yes, indeed. She is a darling, although a bit hot in hand. But then not every gentleman prefers a demure simpering ninny for a wife," Mrs. Basingbroke said rather more frankly than was her want, for there was something about the Marquis that seemed to invite indiscretion.

"And naturally her settlement would be a most handsome one" he suggested.

Mrs. Basingbroke would have none of that. "Of course her father will be generous, but any man would be fortunate to win Katherine!"

"I beg your pardon. I did not mean to imply that her fortune was her chief attraction," he apologized. "Young Pemberton appears enthralled," he noted looking across the drawing room at the tête à tête.

Mrs. Basingbroke hastened to clarify the situation. "I am not convinced that the Viscount has won Katherine's approval, although he is a pleasant young man." If there was any chance that he himself might be interested in Katherine, she must do her best not to discourage him, although admittedly the likelihood of the elusive Marquis being smitten by her charge seemed small.

"Wexford could use an infusion of money. His estates are sadly encumbered," was the Marquis's cynical observation.

"I understand Mr. Wilde has assisted several financially embarrassed peers, and not been the loser for it," Mrs. Basingbroke replied, surprising the Marquis with her perception. So she was not the empty-headed society matron she appeared.

"Indeed. He is a very clever man, and completely trustworthy into the bargain."

Mrs. Basingbroke glanced sharply at her partner but encountered only a steady gaze. "Of course, or he would not have achieved such a reputation," she said. "The Prince Regent himself has found him most obliging."

For the moment the Marquis decided it would be imprudent to quiz the obliging woman further. He must persevere in his efforts to win Katherine's confidence. If her father thought the Marquis was interested in his daughter, so much the better, he thought cynically. And if she misread his attentions she deserved as much. The Marquis of Staines, who had been pursued by the most determined of parents with marriageable daughters, was well up to eluding the most blatant lures, although always with the chilling courtesy which distinguished him. He was too downy a bird to be taken in by a Cit's daughter, no matter how attractive her charms.

He had to admit, later, as he took his leave of Wilde and Katherine, that those charms had a piquant appeal rarely found among debutantes. But the Marquis' preoccupation with spies and conspirators overrode his interest in dalliance. If Katherine Wilde was committing treason or taking part in her father's suspect schemes, she would not escape retribution, no matter how fascinating her wiles.

Unaware that the Marquis of Staines suspected her of such doubtful activity, and not recognizing him as the mysterious stranger who had kissed her in the garden of the Pantheon, Katherine wondered at his interest. She was both intrigued and flattered, and despite her determination not to be taken in by a practised flatterer, she could not help wondering if he would attempt to deepen their acquaintance. Certainly he was far more interesting than Ronald, attentive and eager as that young man appeared to be.

Actually, as she thought about the evening later, she concluded that the whole business of being launched upon an unreceptive society was not to her taste at all. Why could she not just enjoy the routs, balls and theater parties of the season without all this blatant husband hunting? But she knew that a young woman had few choices. Only after marriage could she indulge her own whims, and then only with the utmost circumspection. Katherine was sensible enough to laugh at fancies which belonged in the pages of gothic novels. She might entertain fantasies of attracting the Marquis of Staines but she knew that should any such circumstance come true she'd be a fool to go through with it. He did not seem the sort of man who would allow his wife to pursue her own desires unless they agreed with his own.

The next morning as she was crossing the hall in her riding dress, intent only on a brisk canter in the Park to clear her thoughts, she met her father talking with a strange young man. He could not fail to introduce her.

"Katherine, I do not believe you have met my associate, George Lang, a clever young man who has been of inestimable help to me in my affairs," he said with unusual affability. Obviously he approved of Lang.

Of average height, with a pair of keen brown eyes and sandy hair cut en brosse, Mr. Lang lacked any pretension to fashion. He was dressed soberly in a brown superfine coat and a cravat tied without intricacy. His rather somber features lightened at the picture she made in her emerald green habit, with a dashing hussars coat and cockaded hat, and he greeted her with an open smile.

"Charmed, Miss Wilde," he acknowledged.

Katherine, warming to his frank admiration, responded with her usual candor. "How nice to meet you, Mr. Lang. I know so little of my father's business, I welcome the opportunity to hear of his associates. We must have a chat and you can introduce me to some of the mysteries of high finance," she invited, though she wondered why she had never heard of this acquaintance before.

"I will look forward to that, Miss Wilde," George Lang responded, seeming only too happy to oblige his employer's daughter.

"Young Lang here is a comer. Knows all about the 'change,' " her father said with some enthusiasm, a surprising endorsement Katherine thought. "But we must not keep you from your ride, Katherine. Perhaps you will be home for luncheon and can quiz George here to your heart's content."

Katherine promised to be home in plenty of time for luncheon and continued on her way.

"A lovely girl. You must be very proud of her," George Lang commented to his employer.

"I have great hopes that Katherine will make a splendid marriage. In fact I intend to see that she does," Wilde responded. George Lang could not aspire to such an alliance, and would be warned off shortly if he chanced his luck. Peter Wilde was quite prepared to encourage Lang, who was a bright student of financial intracies. But that encouragement did not include entertaining a match between him and his daughter.

"Let us repair to the library and go over this loan for the Italians again," Wilde suggested, his mind once more focused on the matter in hand. "They are already in arrears on the interest, and may hope to avoid payment now that Napoleon has rolled them up so smartly. We must guard against any possibility of them reneging on the obligation."

"Of course, sir." Whatever Lang's thoughts on the information Wilde had tendered about his daughter's matrimonial prospects, he appeared to have taken the warning.

Cantering briskly through the Park with an obliging groom following her at a decorous distance, Katherine forgot

Lang, her father and the memories of the dinner party. The morning was fine, with just enough breeze to dispel the heat, and the trees glimmered with morning dew. It was still too early for the more fashionable throngs to take the air, and the Park was comfortably empty. There were so few opportunities for her to enjoy this kind of freedom she reveled in every moment. If only she had more chances to escape from the rigid dictates of society!

She pulled up her grey mare, Sophia, and looked down the long avenue with pleasure. She would have preferred to ride in the country where she was not confined to well-raked gravel paths, but in lieu of that these morning rides were the best substitute. She hoped whoever she married would have a country house. But there, she had promised herself not to worry about her future!

Tightening her hands on the reins, she turned Sophia and prepared for another gallop to blow away the vague uneasiness which assailed her. Before she could put her intentions into effect, a large black stallion appeared out of the trees to her right and trotted up to her. The rider was the Marquis of Staines.

"What a fortuitous meeting, Miss Wilde," Simon greeted her, his all-encompassing glance taking in the delightful picture she made. "Shall we ride together for a pace? I want to thank you for the charming evening. I intended to call later today, but this is much more pleasant and private," he said, lingering on the last word.

"Of course, my lord," she replied politely, inwardly taken aback by this unexpected encounter.

They rode side by side in silence for some moments, until Simon espied a convenient bench and suggested they dismount and continue their conversation in a more relaxed setting. She had no reason to refuse, but was a little discomfited by his warm and admiring glances.

Just what did this distinguished peer want of her, she wondered? He was quick to answer her unspoken question, after he had helped her down from her horse and tossed the reins to the waiting groom.

"I have been wondering what a girl of your respectable background was doing in the gardens of the Pantheon the other evening."

Katherine, a sudden suspicion darkening her mind, did not respond immediately.

"Come, Miss Wilde. I cannot believe that you have forgotten our first encounter?" Since she was refused to answer, he raised her chin with on hand and looked deeply into the puzzled blue eyes which met his.

Katherine shook off her dismay and answered forthrightly.

"No, I have not forgotten, but I am surprised that you wish me to remember. Your conduct was not that of a gentleman."

"Gentlemen do not always act as they should, and I mistook you for another woman, if you remember."

"Yes, I recall. You treated me as if I were a light-skirt! Should I apologize for disappointing you?"

"You did not disappoint me, hardly that. In fact I found you quite intriguing. What is a debutante doing evading her chaperone and dallying at a masquerade, if not for some nefarious purpose?" he asked sharply, putting his suspicion to the test. If she had arranged a rendezvous at the Pantheon she would not confess it, but he felt a skilled enough interrogator to read her evasions.

"I don't like your tone, sir, and I think you presume far too much considering our short acquaintance," Katherine replied, her anger rising at his impertinence.

"Ah, but I hope that acquaintance will deepen. Is there any reason why it should not? Do you take me in abhorrence on such a pretext? That would be a great shame," he teased.

"Hardly a pretext! You kissed me, without my permission," she retorted, her judgment yielding to her mortification. She had not meant to mention that kiss.

"Yes, and you tempt me to do it again. You are a most provocative challenge, Miss Wilde."

Katherine rose, annoyed at his casual assumption that she was ripe for a flirtation. If his were an example of ton manners, she did not think much of them.

"I think this conversation has gone on long enough, my lord. I do not enjoy being made mock of," she said severely, ignoring his ironic smile. Obviously the Marquis of Staines rarely encountered a woman who dared to reject him. Well, she was not available for his experiments in dalliance, Katherine decided, but could not help a passing regret that their association, such as it was, had to be conducted on such vapid lines.

"If you think I am mocking you, Miss Wilde, I am deeply sorry. Be assured I feel only the deepest admiration for you," Simon protested, all sincerity, but Katherine suspected that beneath his facade of concern he was yet laughing at her.

She made no answer, determined not to surrender to his cajolery. With nothing more than a toss of her head she stalked toward her horse, eager to put an end to this disturbing encounter.

But he refused to be dismissed and insisted on helping her mount her horse. She did not look at him. Raising her head haughtily she gazed intently at the leafy trees in the distance. He laid a restraining hand on the reins as she prepared to spur her mare forward.

"You are most cruel, Miss Wilde, but I do not promise to leave you alone. I have hopes that I may change your unfortunate impression of me. I am not your enemy, you know, and I greatly desire to be more than a friend," he assured her, with all the irony gone from his tone.

Katherine was not to be cajoled, for she did not trust him; his words seemed to hold a threat. Before she could weaken in her resolve, she jerked the reins from his hand and spurred Sophie into a canter, riding rapidly down the bridle path.

Simon watched her disappear into the distance, feeling a trifle ashamed of himself. He had deliberately tried to charm her in order to discover her game. He could not believe that she was as innocent as she claimed, but all the same, he was not proud of his own conduct. Luring schoolgirls into confidences in order to unmask his country's traitors was not a ploy he enjoyed. Damn the chit, she had rebuffed him with all the skill of an experienced courtesan, while not in any way diminishing his interest. If he was not careful she would ensnare him in her toils, and that he would not endure, not even in the service of his country. She might be involved in her father's suspect dealing, or she might be completely innocent. But, whatever the outcome of his investigations, he would not be seduced by a pair of speaking blue eyes and an intriguing air, into making a fool of himself.

Simon very much feared that Katherine Wilde would cause him a deal of trouble before their duel of wits was at an end.

Chapter Six

Riding as if all the furies were at her back, Katherine rushed from the Park heedless of her direction. Unused to such harsh treatment, her mare, reared, and almost ran down a gentleman strolling across Park Lane in the direction of Grosvenor Square. Katherine, appalled at her carelessness, reined the nervous horse to a halt and jumped unaided from Sophie's back.

"Oh, sir, I am most undone. I did not see you in my haste. I do hope you have suffered no harm," she pleaded, looking into the stranger's face. He was a man of middle years, of erect carriage, dressed conservatively but elegantly in black pantaloons and a wine-colored coat of impeccable cut. He did not appear to have suffered from his encounter with Sophie, and smiled reassuringly at his anxious questioner with eyes as blue as her own.

"No harm done. My own fault, for I was wool-gathering and should know better than to walk so idly near the Park without keeping an eye out for impetuous riders," he said, kindly taking the blame for the mishap.

"That is kind of you, sir. But I am afraid my impulsive behaviour was the culprit. I was in a temper and not paying

54

attention," Katherine explained, grateful that he should behave so gallantly when she knew herself to be at fault.

"Well, if I have to be run down, I prefer it to be by such an attractive young woman. Allow me to introduce myself. Sir Richard Overton, at your service. I suppose we must observe some of the proprieties." His smile invited her to join him in affability.

"I am Katherine Wilde, Sir Richard, and entirely at fault. Although it is most generous of you to say differently." Katherine was pleased with his elegant manners, and she thought that he had the kindest eyes she had ever seen.

"Well, Miss Wilde, no harm done, and I must not keep you. Perhaps we will meet again, in more conventional circumstances. I hope so."

He tipped his hat politely and continued on his way, while Katherine watched him with a bemused expression.

What a nice gentleman, she thought. Another man might have behaved in an entirely different manner, rating her with the scold she deserved. And it was all that irritating Lord Stafford's fault for arousing her temper! She must learn some control or they would be at dagger's drawn every time they met. She shook herself with some anger. Really, it was not as if there were to be countless meetings!

Following her admonition to behave with more propriety, Katherine appeared at the luncheon table after her tumultuous ride prepared to be decorous and cooperative, no matter how intransigent her father appeared. It was rare that he stayed in for the mid-day meal—he generally ate near his place of business—so there was all the more reason for Katherine to mark this occasion by a particular display of pretty manners.

Of course, George Lang's presence made it easier to converse with some degree of enthusiasm. Mr. Lang seemed to inspire Peter Wilde to forsake his usual severity. There must be some excitement in the intracacies of high finance which eluded her, Katherine decided whimsically. Her father appeared most animated when he discussed money, a topic considered not acceptable by more fashionable members of the society to which he aspired.

"Well, my dear. You look glowing. Your ride chased away the shadows of last night's dissipation," Peter Wilde approved, turning with an explanation to George Lang. "We had a small dinner party here last evening, to launch Katherine on her Season. Some quite unexceptional guests, the Jerseys and Earl of Wexford and the Marquis of Stainess," he almost crowed in his delight at attracting such aristocratic non pareils to his table. Katherine found his pride more pathetic than embarrassing.

"I am sure Miss Wilde proved equal to the occasion," George Lang replied smoothly, leading Katherine to wonder if he was secretly amused at her father's pretensions. If so, she would not allow him such license.

"My father is well accustomed to meeting such notables, Mr. Lang," she reproved, tossing her head.

He hastened to retrieve his mistake. "Of course, Miss Wilde, and I doubt not that you are traveling in the best of circles under Mrs. Basingbroke's guidance," he said, rather mysteriously, Katherine thought.

Whatever his feelings, Katherine thought he was all too adept at hiding them, and her first felicitous impression of her father's associate dimmed somewhat. No doubt he was clever and ambitious, but was he loyal and appreciative? Katherine set herself to discover more about his background.

"You were going to tell me all about finance, Mr. Lang, and how you, at such a young age, have achieved such success in this world of guineas and pence," she said.

"George has risen high in his few years," her father said approvingly. "He is an orphan, and gained his way completely by his own efforts, without any support from relatives of means or influence." Peter Wilde considered hard work even more of a virtue than talent.

"I fear my background is rather dull, hardly of interest to a young lady such as yourself. I grew up with some cousins in Lancashire, and entered an actuary's office there as an apprentice before seeking my fortune in London," Lang said a bit reluctantly.

"Well, you should be proud of making your way so quickly and to such heights," Katherine replied charitably, although not sure that she had learned the entire story. There was more to George Lang than she had imagined. At first meeting he appeared intelligent, frank, and grateful for his employer's patronage, but Katherine wondered what he really felt about his subservient position. Did he envy Peter Wilde, have ambitions beyond his station, resent being treated like a clerk? In truth, he gave no evidence of this, as he explained patiently what he did to assist her father.

Katherine was recalled to her initial desire to learn more about Sir Richard Overton by a remark her father made in passing.

"We are due at the Foreign Office at three o'clock with the requested documents, Lang, and we must be sharp on the hour," Wilde said, waving away the sweet, a delicious conconction of strawberries and creme a l'anglais offered by a servant. "These government bureaucrats can be sticky about protocol, and I want no difficulty with them over this affair."

Katherine wondered if her kindly Sir Richard could be numbered among that company. He looked like a man who undertook important affairs, rather than a tulip of fashion or an idle man about town.

"Father," she asked as that gentleman was preparing to excuse himself from the table. "I meant to ask you about

57

someone I unfortunately almost ran down emerging from the Park this morning. Do you know a Sir Richard Overton?''

At her words Wilde sank down in his seat again, an ugly frown passing over his usually impassive face. But he quickly recovered.

''The name seems familiar, but I can't say I have met the gentleman. Really, Katherine, if you can't control your mount you have no business riding in the Park, running down innocent passers-by. Your manners are atrocious!''

Katherine had learned through long experience to accept her father's frequent criticism of her behaviour with equanimity. She sensed that the name Sir Richard Overton was responsible for his anger, not her own deeds.

Peter Wilde left the table abruptly signaling to Lang to follow him. Katherine gave the young man a sympathetic smile, knowing he might expect to reap the results of her ill-timed question.

Katherine wondered what Sir Richard could have done to incur her father's wrath. Somehow Katherine did not believe Sir Richard was the sort of man to acquire a mountain of debt and be forced to borrow from the ten per centers, or even from a respectable banker like her father. He appeared, at first sight, to be a man of utter probity. Well, if she wanted more information about Sir Richard, she would ask dear Mrs. B, as she now called Mrs. Basingbroke. Her chaperone knew a great many on dits about society and she would be able to tell Katherine if the man had a mystery in his past, whether he was of the first stare, and all the exciting bits if there were a scandal attached to his name. Really, Katherine chided herself, she was becoming as bad a rumor chaser as Sally Jersey!

When Mrs. Basingbroke arrived soon after luncheon to take Katherine to another ''at home'', this one at the imposing Mrs. Burrell's, she was able to satisfy Katherine's curiosity with a story which had every dramatic element any young girl could desire.

Katherine introduced the topic artlessly by describing her encounter with Sir Richard, deliberately concealing her prior interview with Simon Stafford, an incident she had also carefully hidden from her father. She did not want either to think that the Marquis of Staines had any romantic interest in her.

At the end of her account, she pleaded with Mrs. B. to tell her what she knew of Sir Richard.

At first her chaperone hesitated, though she did not deny that she knew of the gentleman. But her natural desire to be accommodating and a feminine penchant for gossip, though of a kindly nature, impelled her to tell Katherine what she knew.

"Sir Richard has always been somewhat a figure of mystery. His father wanted him to pursue a career in the Foreign Office, but the young man had hankered after an army life and defied his parents by purchasing a commission in a line regiment with money left to him by a maiden aunt. He fought in the colonies, where he was either captured or reported missing in action. For the longest time he was feared dead, but suddenly, after the shameful surrender at Yorktown, he turned up as bright as a new penny." Mrs. B. paused, as if further confidences were imminent, but then seemed to think better of it, and closed her lips firmly on any untoward revelations.

"How exciting! But then what happened to him? He seems to be most respectable and sober now although completely charming."

"Not a great deal. He re-entered the Foreign Office where he served with some distinction, spending many years on the Continent and at the Tsar's Court, before returning at the beginning of the recent truce. He is a most unexceptional man, and he does not now go much into society."

"What about his family? Surely such an attractive man must have married," Katherine queried, determined to wrest every bit of romance from the account.

"No, he has remained a bachelor, and a much pursued one, although he has successfully eluded the most determined attempts to lead him to the altar. He is quite a catch, with a considerable competence. I fancied him myself as a young girl," Mrs. Basingbroke confessed wistfully, "but he did not return my regard, though he always behaved with the utmost politeness toward me and any young woman he met."

"A man of mystery! I wonder if he was a spy?" Katherine's imagination was caught by this intriguing tale.

Mrs. Basingbroke suddenly recalled her duties as a chaperone. "Whatever his past, he is not a proper figure for your interest, Katherine," she warned.

"Oh, I would never entertain such ideas, dear Mrs. B," Katherine reassured her, amused at her suspicions. "I just found him excessively kind and forgiving, and with delightful manners."

"Yes, he has all of those estimable qualities. But I doubt you will meet him again. As I said, he does not go much into society." Mrs. Basingbroke rose with finality, obviously not wanting to discuss Sir Richard any further. Katherine wondered why but did not pursue her enqueries, though she was by no means satisfied.

She entered enthusiastically into Mrs. Basingbroke's plans for her introduction to Almack's, for her chaperone had been successful in securing the much-coveted vouchers for that most holy of holies, called irreverently by some wags "The Marriage Mart."

As the Wilde equipage approached the King Street entrance of Almack's that evening, Katherine viewed the coming ordeal with some trepidation. She wondered how Mrs. Basingbroke had persuaded the patronesses of Almack's to admit her into its hallowed portals, and she worried she would be shunned by the gallants and debutantes who were habitués of this famed sanctum. At school she had heard her classmates discuss Almack's as the ultimate destination of every marriageable girl of good family. Only the most distinguished and well born were admitted to its lists, and Katherine knew her breeding and background made her suspect in the eyes of many. Her father had been so pleased that she would at last enter the sacred doors, she had not the heart to confess she would as lief refuse the honor. She took comfort in the fact that Ronald Pemberton had requested the first dance, but she wondered if she would spend the rest of the evening propping up the wall.

Her first impression of the place was disappointing, a huge assembly room some ninety feet long, with little of interest in the decoration. That evening Lady Jersey, who welcomed her with hateur, Lady Cowper, who was all affability, and the grande dame Mrs. Drummond Burrell were present. With Lady Castlereagh, Lady Sefton, Princess Esterhazy and Countess Leiven they formed the body of patronesses whose rule of society was stringent and over-riding. However, Mrs. Basingbroke's standing covered Katherine like a protective cloak, and she was received more pleasantly than she had expected. Ronald was on hand to lead her into the opening country dance and she greeted him with enthusiasm, glad to meet a friend in such a nest of critics.

She was unaware that the appearance of such a new beauty whose fortune was well known would cause such a stir. She certainly looked her best in a gown of white silk with an overdress of silver gauze, her dark ringlets cleverly dressed à la Sappho. Several of the jealous matrons whispered among themselves as they watched her daintly step through the intracies of the dance.

And in truth it did appear that Katherine's debut at Almack's would satisfy even the most demanding debutante. The moment the opening country dance drew to a close, she was surrounded by young men requesting an introduction from Mrs. Basingbroke, and demands for a dance. Katherine smiled very prettily on all comers, but she wondered if the rumors of her father's fortune were as responsible for the full dance card as her own attributes. Most of the young men appeared a trifle callow, and Ronald shone by comparison, being just that much older and more sophisticated.

Ronald was soon eclipsed however, by a strikingly tall dark gentleman of some thirty years who managed to disperse his rivals with the ease of long practice, and beg an introduction and a dance, which Katherine was not loathe to grant. Count Guido Alessandro Crespi possessed all the fabled address of an experienced man about town, allied to that romantic facility which Latin males seemed to exert in dealing with females of all ages. Katherine wisely did not believe his rather fulsome compliments but she could not but be flattered by his attentions as he led her through the minuet. The movements of the dance made conversation difficult, but the Count was more than able to compensate for the lack of opportunities by gazing soulfully at his partner and murmuring "bella, bellisima" every time he passed her in the figures.

As Katherine was later to learn, Count Crespi had his detractors, especially among the male members of the ton. The Marquis de Lisle, who had his own share of inherited Gallic charm, had been known to remark that the Count deserved to have his cork drawn for his oily, ingratiating manner, but the ton dowagers and debutantes alike found him fascinating. His English mother, daughter of a Duke, assured his entree into every important drawing room, and his own charm made him a favorite with hostesses. A refugee from the Napoleonic assault on his country, he enlisted sympathy for his plight, the occupation of his Piedmont estates, which denied him the position and fortune necessary for an aristocrat. Those who deplored England's open door for every impoverished emigré, wondered just how the Count managed to support himself in such style. He lived in fashionable rooms at the Albany, belonged to White's, and appeared very plump in the pocket for an exile. One could only conclude that his uncle, the crusty Duke of Ryland, kept him in funds.

Whatever the source of his income Guido Crespi spent lavishly, prompt with nosegays to favored ladies, and hosting comfortable dinners to his male cronies. He had even succeeded in wresting the latest Convent Garden beauty from her recent protector without the lavish gifts such an exalted Cyprian expected. Doubtless, he had heard of Katherine's fortune and hurried to pay his obeisance, the more uncharitable members of Almack's decided, as they watched him pay her court.

Katherine was chatting happily with the Count at the conclusion of their dance, and trying to repress his intentions of claiming several more dances when Simon Stafford made a rare appearance just before the doors closed at eleven o'clock. He had not intended to visit Almack's that evening, for he found the place flat and stultifying. But he had heard that Katherine would be making her bow and could not resist continuing his investigation—or at least that was how he put it to himself, unwilling to concede that any reason except duty drew him to the chit.

He greeted Sally Jersey and bowed to Mrs. Burrell, who honored him with one of her frosty smiles. Almost immediately he noticed Katherine and her companion, and his eyes narrowed. If he needed fuel for his suspicions, her obvious intimacy with Count Crespi would seem to supply it. Why else would the Count bother with a naive debutante?

As Simon approached the pair, he noticed Ronald Pemberton glowering in the background and had to suppress a smile. It seemed Miss Wilde was becoming an Incomparable, the rage of the season, with gentlemen of all persuasions fighting for her interest. Not one to be deterred by rivals, Simon entered the lists himself.

Chapter Seven

"Good evening, Miss Wilde. Your servant, Count," Simon greeted the couple, noticing with some pleasure that although he was too polite to make it obvious, the Italian did not welcome the interruption.

"I do hope you have saved a dance for me, Miss Wilde, as you promised," Simon said outrageously, for he had neither told Katherine he would attend Almack's that evening nor asked her for the favour of a dance.

"I do not recall any such a request, my lord, and as you see I am fully engaged for the evening." She extended her dance card which was covered with the scrawled initials of eager partners.

"Depressed again. You are hard-hearted, Miss Wilde. I will have to see whom I can bribe to relinquish his claim." Simon, aware that he was annoying both the Count and Katherine, found the sensation quite enjoyable. "Perhaps I can prevail upon you, Crespi, to surrender a dance to one who has been laboring all day in the service of his country."

"Laboring in your country's service, my lord? I had no idea you were so patriotic and industrious. Where do you ply your skills? Not in the army, I think," Katherine replied in what she considered a very insulting tone, but unable to help herself, for the Marquis of Staines had succeeded, as usual, in raising her hackles and making her forget the minimum courtesies.

If she had angered him he was too skilled a campaigner to show it. But before he could answer her barbed question the Count rushed to his assistance with that annoying affability which made Simon long to wipe the smile off his face.

"The Marquis of Staines has a very important post in the Foreign Office, Signorina, although the nature of it eludes me. Perhaps you will enlighten us, my lord," the Count suggested silkily.

"I am afraid it must continue to elude you, Count, while I see whom I can persuade to yield his prior claims to my pressing need to partner you, Miss Wilde. Until later." Simon made his bow and departed. His quick eyes had caught the initials of a young subultern in the Guards who happened to be a distant connection of his. He had no difficulty in persuading that awed youth to sacrifice his dance with Katherine. The young guardsman, having relinquished his dance, stared after Simon. It was quite unlike the aloof Marquis of Staines to pursue a debutante, no matter how great her fortune. A fortune which Simon scarcely needed his young relative conceded, sighing uselessly over his own financial dilemma.

Ronald Pemberton, who took Katherine down to the meager refreshments supplied by Almack's, made known his own jealousy at the attentions of two such intriguing gentlemen as Count Crespi and the Marquis of Staines. Setting his chin in determined lines, he challenged Katherine as to what she meant by flirting with them.

"Flirting, Ronald? What can you mean? I was merely observing the decencies. And I wonder what gives you the privilege of reproving me for my conduct," she protested, thoroughly annoyed by his possessive manner. Really, between the Marquis of Staines who suspected her of intrigue and conduct becoming to a lightskirt, the Count who expected to overawe her with the flattery of his regard, and Ronald, behaving as if he were an acknowledged suitor, she was completely disgusted with the male sex. Even her father treated her as if she were dim-witted, unable to make intelligent decisions about her life.

"I most humbly beg your pardon, Katherine, but you do make a fellow jealous. I had hoped that you had come to care for me just a bit, that perhaps . . . ," he stuttered to a stop at the warning in Katherine's eyes.

She put down the fork with which she had been toying with a piece of stale cake and faced Ronald with determination to make her point.

"I am fond of you, Ronald, but I do not think I have given you any reason to think that fondness has deepened into a more lasting affection as of yet. I enjoy your company, and I hope you look upon me as a friend, but that does not give you the license to criticize my conduct."

He flushed and his blue eyes dropped before hers.

"You know that I have your father's permission. . . . I mean I had intended to ask you a most important question . . . ," Ronald seemed overcome with embarrassment and emotion, and Katherine could only take pity upon him.

"This is hardly the place to make a declaration, Ronald," she said gently. "Mrs. Burrell is already looking askance at us, and I think you had best take me back to Mrs. Basingbroke before we are both ejected scandalously from these sacred precincts." Katherine did not quite know how she felt about the young Viscount but she was sure that she was not ready to rush into an engagement with him, nor entertain a proposal of marriage at Almacks.

Realizing his solecism, he escorted her back to her chaperone, eager to redeem his credit.

One of Ronald's most engaging characteristics was his inability to hold a grudge or fall into the sullens—a valuable asset in a husband, Katherine thought. And not one which he shared with many men, she surmised. She suspected she would be able to manage him adroitly but did she want such a malleable husband?

Before she could ask her chaperone if they could leave, prepared to plead a headache, she was approached by Simon Stafford for his dance. Much to her surprise he had not taken her rebuff with any seriousness and had prevailed upon his young Guardsman relative to surrender in his favor. He explained this to Mrs. Basingbroke, while Katherine stood by, both furious and flattered.

As they approached the floor Simon looked at his partner with some amusement, aware that she was puzzled and annoyed by his interest in her. Unlike many gazetted beauties she did not immediately assume that every man who paid her the most cursory of attention was besotted with her. She had a certain refreshing modesty considering her piquant beauty and vivacious personality, not to mention her wealth. He set himself to calming her suspicions, at the same time wondering why he was taking such pains to cajole a young woman who could only cause him trouble in the end. He reminded himself that she might easily be a traitor to her country.

"As you see, I have been quite diligent in securing you as a partner despite your reluctance to admit me into the favored ranks," he teased, noticing the flush on her cheeks, wondering whether it was inspired by anger or pleasure at his persistence.

"I am sure you are rarely defeated in your purpose, however frivolous the goal, my lord," Katherine replied, accepting his hand as they stepped through the paces of the dance. She cast him a speaking look before tripping away to the end of the set.

When they came together again, he accepted her challenge. "This is a difficult maneuver for conversation. We must arrange a more suitable setting." He smiled at her with an expression which he knew would be noted by Sally Jersey and the other patronesses. It would stir up a hotbed of gossip, but then that was part of his plan.

Katherine looked at him crossly, wondering why he was taking such a tack, but before she could voice her objections he said with a teasing glance, "Come, you must not glower at me so. The dowagers will think I have made an improper suggestion."

"You are perfectly capable of it, and probably most adept at it, too," Katherine replied sharply, but aware of a small burst of excitement which she did her best to repress. Somehow arguing with Simon Stafford was far more intriguing than parrying the fulsome flattery of Count Crespi or the dogged devotion of Ronald Pemberton. She must be in danger of behaving like a fashionable flirt despite Mrs. Basingbroke's influence.

All too soon the dance came to a close and as he punctiliously escorted her back to her duenna, causing all kinds of conjecture in the chaperone's corner by whispering in her ear: "I refuse to take my congé, and will be around tomorrow afternoon to take you driving. See to it that you are ready, for if I have to rout you out I will exact a forfeit."

Leaving her with a bow, he quitted Almack's, causing some consternation that he danced with no other young ladies, and leading Sally Jersey to comment to Emily Cowper that Simon Stafford was behaving in a quite remarkable manner toward Katherine Wilde.

Both ladies and Katherine herself would have been

astounded to learn the real reason for Simon's pursuit of Katherine.

The next day at White's, Simon put his suspicions to Theron de Lisle when they had retired to a secluded corner.

"What do you know about Crespi, Theron?" Simon asked somewhat abruptly.

"Just the usual gossip. That he has been dispossessed by Napoleon, sought sanctuary here and receives an allowance from his uncle, the Duke of Ryland, who spends all his time in the country but ushered Crespi into London society." Theron de Lisle, who had no trouble in deciphering Simon's thoughts asked, "Do you suspect him of some traitorous activity? Or is it just that a ladybird you have your eye on prefers his continental charm?"

"You might say both," Simon laughed. "He seems uncommonly interested in Katherine Wilde, and I am not convinced that he is as grateful to his adopted country as he should be. Most emigrés would traffik with the devil himself, much less Napoleon, if it guaranteed their estates would be returned to them."

De Lisle, a skilled negotiator and spy chaser, was not completely in agreement with General Valentine and Stafford that Wilde was conniving with Napoleon to secure his Italian loan, but he could be convinced if evidence showed otherwise. At one time de Lisle's own loyalty had been suspect, so he tended to be more cautious in suspecting others in a like situation.

"Tell me, mon ami, why you are so satisfied as to Wilde's guilt?" de Lisle asked.

"Come, Theron, we are certain that money is being purveyed to Napoleon, and has been since the beginning of the Revolution. This niggling truce is a poor excuse for its legality now. Our contacts in Paris have established without doubt that English guineas are helping Napoleon to rearm and pay his troops, a shocking affair which must be stopped. Wilde loaned money to the Italians before Napoleon conquered the country. It was perfectly proper then, but if the loan is still outstanding and we are sure of that, he will take means, either legally or otherwise, to redeem his money."

"And you intend to cultivate his innocent daughter in order to discover his machinations? Hardly an admirable ploy, my gallant defender," de Lisle protested.

Simon smiled grimly. "You have become incurably sentimental since you married your delightful Melissa."

"I suppose so," Theron admitted, for contrary to all expectations he was a most devoted husband, despite his past reputation as a rake. "But I almost lost her through my cynical propensity to suspect the worst, and I would not want to see you follow that tortuous path. Be careful, Simon, that you are not caught in your victim's toils, or for her sake, do not engage her affections and then abandon her."

"That is highly unlikely, Theron. I am not such an easy mark and even if she is the most accomplished adventuress, which I doubt, I am well armored against her schemes."

De Lisle shook his head. "You are entering dangerous waters, mon ami, but I can see my warnings fall on deaf ears. I can only wish you *bon chance* and be ready to assist with any demands you may make of me." He had met Katherine Wilde at a recent levee and found her most engaging. It seemed to him that not even his cynical friend could be completely impervious to her charms.

"Thank you, Theron. I only hope the matter can be solved swiftly. It is not a comfortable position," Simon admitted. If Wilde should prove to be a traitor then the baiting of his daughter would be well worth whatever shabby treatment he meted out to her.

Still, as he left his friend for a meeting with General Valentine he was not settled in his mind, for Theron had only voiced his own disquiet.

Katherine had almost decided not to be at home when Simon appeared for the promised drive in the Park, but an uncomfortable interview with her father changed her mind.

Peter Wilde called her into his library to acquaint her with the news that Ronald Pemberton had indeed made an offer for her, and he expected her to be over the moon with delight. He was irritated and confounded by her hesitation.

"What is your objection to the young man, Katherine? He is exactly the husband I would choose for you, and you have shown no signs of taking him in distaste, even allowing him to escort you unchaperoned, to a shabby masquerade, where your presence was noted and could easily have ruined your chances."

Katherine wondered how her father had discovered her little rebellion. One of the reasons she had prevailed upon Ronald to take her to the masquerade was a gesture of defiance against her father's intentions of bartering her hand in marriage to further his position in society.

"Perhaps I am light-minded, father. But I wonder you are not more concerned with my future happiness!" she said with spirit. "Would it be all the same to you if Ronald were an ugly, lecherous aged peer? Do you care so little for me you would sell me off to the first bidder?"

"Don't be missish and ridiculous, Katherine. I am not asking you to wed such a man. Pemberton is a fine young man, and unless I am much mistaken you hold him in some regard. He is also quite fond of you."

"Fond of me, yes, I suppose he is. But he is also fond of the settlement you would be compelled to make. I am not denying that I must marry, but I would like some time to

72

look about me. I have barely begun my season," she argued. Suddenly she hit upon the perfect means of placating her father: "You know, father, Ronald is not the only gentleman who has paid me attention. Why, just this afternoon I have been invited to drive in the Park by Simon Stafford, who you must admit is quite a catch!"

"Don't be vulgar, Katherine," he replied automatically, but Katherine could see her words had given him pause. Should Staines be seriously interested in his daughter, he would have second thoughts about young Pemberton, whose father, the Earl of Wexford, would demand a huge fortune for his assent to the match. Staines had no such need of money. And his patronage would be far more effective in satisfying Wilde's ambitions.

Wisely deciding not to labor the point, Katherine changed the subject tactfully.

"How did your meeting go at the Foreign Office yesterday, Father? You seemed quite worried about it."

But for once business seemed less important than personal matters to Peter Wilde. "Troublesome, these government lackeys, but let's not talk of that. Women should never meddle in business. Now I want to hear more about Stafford. Has he given you any inkling of his intentions toward you?"

"He has merely solicited a ride in the Park, Father, not my hand in marriage. What I was trying to make you see is that if I accept the first offer made to me before meeting other gentlemen during the season, I may not be making the best choice." Katherine rose and shook out her skirts. "Well, if I am to be ready when the Marquis calls I had best change my dress. I will see you at dinner, Father, with Mrs. Basingbroke. We are going to the Esterhazy ball this evening. She seems to know everyone of note in London and has more than fulfilled your requests to introduce me to the ton!"

"Yes, yes. She is well worth her fee. And as for Stafford,

Katherine, remember that you can't play ducks and drakes with that one, so tread carefully,'' he warned with a puzzling air of hidden information.

Mounting the staircase to her room, Katherine wondered what he knew about Simon Stafford. Well, she had no intention of leading on that enigmatic lord. If her father was waiting for a proposal he could save his breath to cool his porridge, Katherine decided impishly, smiling at the vulgar adage which would have shocked society matrons had she dared to utter it in public. Someday her sense of the ridiculous would overcome all her Bath Seminary training and the careful guidance of Mrs. Basingbroke with shocking results. Perhaps she should try such tactics on Simon Stafford. He appeared to expect the most outrageous action from her anyway, and she decided not to disappoint him.

Chapter Eight

Katherine promptly forgot her plans to shock the Marquis of Staines, in the pleasure of his company, for he set out to beguile her as only he could.

At first it appeared the outing would be a disaster. As the pair was leaving the Wigmore Street house, they encountered none other than Count Crespi, who expressed his desolation at discovering Katherine had a prior engagement.

His Latin gallantry and expert social sense carried off the meeting with no untoward unpleasantness, but Katherine sensed Simon Stafford's irritation at the Count's interest, which goaded her into welcoming the Italian with more warmth than she intended. As they dallied on the doorstep, Simon impatiently twitching his riding crop against his boot, Count Crespi chanced his luck by asking Katherine if she were planning to attend the Esterhazy ball that evening.

"Can I hope that you will give me the supper dance this evening, Signorina? I must make my bid early, as you will be beseiged by beaux and I will be cast into the outer darkness," he complained with a melting glance from his expressive dark eyes.

Before she could either refuse or accept, Simon leapt into

the breach. "I am afraid you are too late, Count. Miss Wilde has already promised the supper dance to me, and now we really must be on our way. I don't like keeping my horses standing." Simon gestured toward his groom holding the fidgeting pair of matched chestnuts in the roadway. His manners could not have been easier. Still, Katherine would not allow him to think he could override her preference and impose his will.

As they cantered deftly to the end of Wigmore Street, turning left toward the Park, Katherine voiced her objections. "I was not aware, sir, that I had engaged myself to you for the supper dance, this evening," she said severely, though it was most difficult to retain her irritation at the Marquis' high-handness when he smiled at her in such a fashion.

"I know, it was quite diabolical of me, but really, Kate, you cannot want to waste your time with that Italian puppy. He is not a fit person for your acquaintance."

"Neither do I recall giving you permission to choose my friends, my lord, nor call me Kate," she protested.

"How presumptuous of me. But you may call me Simon, Kate, so let us cry pax," he urged, thinking what an attractive minx she was in her cherry-red spencer faced in cream silk, and a dashing Agrippa straw hat tied saucily with a matching red ribbon. If he were not careful he would forget just why he was paying her such unmistakable attentions and fall under the lure of those luminous blue eyes like any callow youth. For a moment de Lisle's warning flashed across his mind, causing him to frown.

Katherine did not fail to notice his abstraction and was piqued. What was he thinking beneath this facade of badinage? She wondered what his real intent was toward her. She could not really believe he had become enamoured of her, when so many others had failed to gain his regard.

"You know, my lord," she blurted out, "I am not certain you do not think of me a deep-dyed adventuress, mistaking me for your lady of the tryst at the Pantheon. Let me assure you that I am exactly what I seem, an innocent female, intent only on enjoying the delights of her first London season.

Amazed and rather disarmed by her frankness, Simon, dropped the reins and his horses shied nervously. Recalled to the moment, Simon pulled them to order. What could he say? Was this an honest explanation of the confusion at the Pantheon or just a clever ruse to dispell his suspicions?

"I must yield to your protestations, dear Kate. I stand revealed as the most villanous cad to suspect any girl with your candid eyes of any chicanery. It is due to my naturally suspicious nature, a legacy of my chequered past, I'm afraid."

She was not sure he believed her, but she was too intrigued by his reference to a chequered past, as he knew she would be, not to take him up on this dramatic hint to his true character.

"You fascinate me, Simon," she replied glancing at him with a wide eyed expression which begged for confidences. "What kind of a past have you? No doubt one with legions of heartbroken women cluttering the landscape," she teased.

"You wound me, Kate. I was not referring to women," he answered, aware that he had almost committed an indiscretion. Her manner was so disarming that it was difficult not to reveal more than was wise. Was this how she managed to wrest information from her victims?

"Returning to the matter of the loathesome Count Crespi, I wonder if you met him on a trip to Italy," he suggested carelessly, as if the acquaintance was a long-standing one.

Surprised, Katherine looked at him searchingly. He seemed obsessed with the Italian. "Of course not. I met him for the first time at Almack's last evening. I have only recently come

77

to London from my seminary in Bath, you know," she explained, twisting her reticule in some annoyance. Why did he constantly quiz her, as if trying to catch her out in a lie or a discrepancy?

"You seemed on such intimate terms. Of course, I cannot chose your friends for you, but Ronald Pemberton is much more your style," he offered helpfully as they cantered sedately down the graveled paths of Hyde Park.

"Really, do you think so?" Katherine replied, nettled that he should contemplate her suitors with such a brotherly indifference. But she had some quizzing of her own to do. "Tell me, Simon. You appear to be privy to so much information, what can you tell me about Sir Richard Overton?"

Simon, too experienced to reveal his amazement at the introduction of the middle-aged statesman, whose services to the government were known to but a few knowledgeable men, appeared to consider his answer. In reality her question confirmed his suspicion that Katherine Wilde was a clever and perhaps dangerous intrigante.

"Sir Richard is a quiet respectable man of the utmost probity, who has spent most of his time abroad. How ever did you meet him? You are a woman of catholic tastes, my dear Kate," he responded silkily.

Not liking his tone, Katherine refused to explain further. "Oh, I just ran across him," she said carelessly smiling to herself at her choice of words.

Katherine had a feeling that they were talking at cross purposes, and she turned the conversation to inconsequential matters.

Simon, following her lead, was now convinced that the enigmatic Miss Wilde deserved the closest scrutiny, and he was aware of deep disappointment. He would prefer her to be innocent, but his reasons were personal, and must not be allowed to hamper his investigation. If she had indeed spent the past year at a seminary in Bath, it was easily proved but that did not absolve her from intrigue in London these past weeks. Could her father have enlisted her as an ally in whatever deep game he was playing? Simon disliked the idea but could not put it out of his mind.

For the rest of the drive they bantered easily but with an underlying restraint, which caused Katherine some disquiet. She did not understand Simon's interest in her and felt that he had other motives in pursuing her than the obvious ones. Well, she would not be gulled by his attentions into foolishly offering her heart to a man who neither respected nor believed her protestations of innocence in whatever dark doings he thought her privy to.

Simon drove her back to Wigmore Street, bidding her a polite farewell but reminding her she was promised to him for the supper dance at the Esterhazys that evening. He had not finished with her yet.

Peter Wilde had turned away Katherine's inquiries about his meeting at the Foreign Office with a brusque comment that the matter did not concern her, but in that he was wrong. He had endured a searching examination of his negotiations with the Italian government in the past months, and he had not entirely satisfied his interlocuters. He disliked explaining his methods to outsiders and his manner consequently appeared evasive and suspect. Not so George Lang, who flew to his employer's defence.

"If you will excuse me, sir, perhaps, I can enlighten Sir Edward and the other gentlemen," Lang offered obsequiously. Although Sir Edward Ponsonby was directing the investigation, it was Lord Castlereagh whom he correctly assumed was the man he must satisfy.

Wilde, who disliked being interrupted, opened his mouth

to protest, but then thought better of it. "Go ahead, George, and see if you can persuade them that we have been doing nothing treasonable or dishonest."

"Mr. Wilde" Lang explained, "loaned the Italian government a considerable sum at a good rate of interest, assuming it would use the money to pursue the fight against Napoleon. Whether they did so, we have no way of knowing. The Italians paid the first interest installment, but are now in arrears. Naturally, as a good businessman, Mr. Wilde is intent on collecting what is due him. As you can see from these notes," George shuffled papers toward his questioners, "the loan was instigated before Napoleon's victory over the Austrians at Marengo, enabling northwest Italy to come under French control. Since Italy now claims to be a republic it will not honor the former royalist debts. Mr. Wilde does not look favorably upon such a decision and has been endeavoring, without much success, to collect what is owed him—quite a large sum."

"How much?" asked Lord Castlereagh succinctly.

Lang looked at his employer, but could gather little from that impassive face. He considered only briefly whether he should answer and then decided, "In the neighborhood of one million pounds," he said flatly, eliciting several gasps from around the table.

"Surely, Mr. Wilde, you cannot afford to lose such a sum?" Castlereagh asked.

"No businessman can afford to let a debt of that amount go uncollected, but the matter will not drive me into bankruptcy," my Lord," Wilde replied with some assurance. He had been within an ace of losing his temper, but George's interruption had restored his usual aplomb.

"What methods are you using to collect the money?" Sir Edward asked. As permanent secretary of the Foreign Office he was accustomed to dealing with facts and figures, and distrusted ideology. Unlike Castlereagh he had no passionate convictions or moral imperatives. He was chiefly concerned with legality, and here he had some reason to suspect Wilde.

"Perfectly legal ones, Sir Edward. I have contacted the new republican government and requested payment, but have received no reply."

"Are you prepared to go further, sir?"

"Short of sending in an army I cannot see what more I can do."

"I believe you must leave that decision up to His Majesty's government, Mr. Wilde," Castlereagh intervened with asperity.

"Of course, my Lord. I do not expect Napoleon to honor the debt, so I will just have to be patient. I hope you are now satisfied with my bona fides."

"I must warn you, Mr. Wilde, that His Majesty's government would not look favorably upon any dealings you might instigate with the Corsican," Sir Edward intoned.

"I quite understand, Sir Edward," Wilde replied drily. "Now, if you gentlemen are satisfied, I have a pressing appointment." He was tired of toadying to bureaucrats who had no notion of the power of money, except to spend someone else's.

For a moment it appeared that Lord Castlereagh was not satisfied, but finally he nodded, and Wilde and Lang were dismissed with a polite word of thanks.

After the door closed on the pair, there was silence for a moment as the committee, four men in all, digested the interview. Sir Edward finally said, "Well, Wilde seems clear of all treasonable activity. I doubt that he will treat with the enemy. He values his business too much."

"I am not so sanguine about his intentions," Castlereagh said. "Wilde is primarily a businessman, and cannot afford to allow patriotism to intervene. Of course, technically we are now at peace with the Corsican and whatever dealings he has with him cannot be considered treasonable. But the man bears watching. I do not trust him or his rather unctuous assistant. Wilde himself may be cleared of any wrongdoing, but that very ambitious young man with an eye to the main chance could have other ideas.''

"Of course, we will keep them under surveillance, for any dealings with the Italians or their emissaries. Valentine has the matter in hand,'' Sir Edward said.

The men nodded, having a great deal of faith in the head of Intelligence, and then dispersed.

Castlereagh left the meeting with his doubts unresolved. He was naturally suspicious and like all aristocrats apt to view men in trade, even such an exalted trade as merchant banking, with contempt. Wilde had better watch his step, and keep a monitoring eye on young Lang.

If Castlereagh had heard the conversation between Wilde and Lang in the carriage returning to Wigmore Street, his misgivings would have been confirmed.

"I did not show the gentlemen a copy of the letter you wrote to Talleyrand about the Italian matter. It might have confused matters,'' Lang suggested slyly.

"Good Heavens, I had forgotten that. You probably should have showed it to them,'' Wilde replied, a bit taken aback. "It was a perfectly straightforward request that the Directorate pay the debt.''

Lang's expression was inscrutable.

"I am not sure Lord Castlereagh would have considered it in that light.'' he said.

"Yes, perhaps you are right. You have a good head on your shoulders, George. Tear up the copy of the letter, and we will forget about it,'' Wilde said peremptorily.

"Of course, sir," Lang said obediently. However, when he was once again in the office and unobserved, he quietly retrieved the letter in question. He handled it fondly, gazing at it with a crafty smile. Then he put it away again, very carefully.

Chapter Nine

It was perhaps unfortunate that Katherine's host that evening, after Peter Wilde's interview at the Foreign Office, was to be Prince Esterhazy, Austria's ambassador to the Court of St. James. Although the Esterhazys were well-received in London society—the Princess was a great niece of the Queen through her mother—Austria's miserable defence against Napoleon tended to make many Englishmen despise the country and view Austrians with suspicion. Whatever the Prince's political views, his Princess was considered somewhat of a "bon enfant", a woman unable to distinguish among the various ambitious pretenders to society's acceptance.

Lady Jersey, Lady Cowper and the Princess had prevailed against Mrs. Burrell in allowing Katherine admittance into Almack's where normally the vaguest hint of commerce was anathema, so now Katherine would be included in every important occasion on the social calendar. That the drawing rooms and ballrooms of London were the natural scene for much intrigue, of a political as well as a romantic nature, did not go unregarded by General Lucien Valentine and his aides in seeking out their country's traitors. Simon Stafford intended to keep a very close eye on Katherine's partners at the Esterhazy ball.

He could not fault either her appearance or her manner when he arrived rather late in the evening, long after the small, dark and animated Princess and her husband had left the receiving line. Katherine was dancing with Ronald Pemberton when Simon first spied her and he wondered not for the first time if she had any serious interest in the Wexford heir. She was looking especially enticing in a deep cerulean blue silk gown, rather a shocking choice, since debutantes were by custom regulated to wearing white or vapid pastels. But Katherine, with unerring taste, had decided that such insipid colors did not suit her vivacious brunette coloring. Simon could not repress a frown as he watched her step daintily through the paces of the dance. Surely she was exactly as she seemed, a young girl only recently graduated from the schoolroom, not a calculating adventuress conspiring as her father's tool to betray her country. He wanted to believe in her innocence, but Simon Stafford had learned not to trust appearances, especially where women were concerned. He joined the next set with a languid blond beauty, annoyed to find that Katherine's partner was Count Crespi, with whom she once again seemed on the most intimate terms.

Katherine found the Count's practiced flattery very soothing to her self-esteem, particularly since she had noticed Simon and his partner, who appeared to find delight in each other's company. Repressing her irritation at the sight of the pair she responded with rather more enthusiasm than she intended to Guido Crespi.

The Count congratulated himself that he was making great progress with the heiress. His intentions were to surrender his bachelorhood and bestow his somewhat tarnished title on a woman who was prepared to pay dearly for the privilege. Katherine, with her beauty and fortune, seemed an ideal choice. That she could be other than thrilled at the prospect of being his wife never crossed his mind. His success with the ladies was well known and he had no reason to think that Katherine would not find him irresistible.

At the conclusion of the dance he tried to persuade her to take a walk in the gardens.

"It is such a warm night, Signorina, you will enjoy the respite." He pressed her arm in a suggestive manner.

Katherine was not to be cajoled. "But Count, I am promised for this next set to Captain Ainsley. It would be most rude of me to abandon him. He might never ask me again," she teased, noticing the young Guardsman approaching.

"You intend to break my heart with your cruelty, bellissima" the Count complained woefully, but his eyes held an ugly look. He was not accustomed to being dismissed.

Katherine, tiring of the game, replied firmly, "I think you exaggerate, Count. You will excuse me now," and she turned her back on him to greet the Captain, resplendent in his regimentals, with a glowing smile.

Crespi had no recourse except to bow politely and surrender her to the captain. He vowed he would make the little madam pay for her cavalier rejection of his overtures. As he left the floor to seek a more obliging partner, he met Simon who was standing conveniently near.

"Ah, Count Crespi. You appear to be seeking a partner. Let me introduce you to Miss Winters." He steered the Count across the floor to the dowager's corner, and toward a platter-faced miss wearing an atrocious cream satin gown which did little to disguise her bony figure or sallow complexion. The Count, was about to wrest himself away from Simon's tight grip but Simon headed him off by remarking, in a low voice, "Miss Winters is the fabulously wealthy granddaughter of the Duke of Hertford. I am sure you will find her most entertaining."

Having summarily disposed of the Count, Simon repaired to the wall to watch the glittering scene before him. Despite himself he found his eyes following Katherine and the young Guardsman as they went through the paces of the country dance. Damn the girl. She was taking up entirely too much of his time and thoughts. The girl fascinated him, despite everything.

By the time the supper dance came round Simon had worked himself into a thoroughly disgruntled mood. But no shadow of his irritation showed when he presented himself to escort Katherine. She greeted him with the disingenuous smile she felt appropriate to the occasion.

"I wondered if you had forgotten your request, my lord. I was about to yield to the protestations of Viscount Pemberton." She indicated a flushed and stubborn Ronald who stood somewhat defiantly by her side.

"That would have been most unkind, Kate, when I have been waiting with great anticipation for our dance. After all, I only came this evening to claim you for supper," he added with an audacious grin. "You will excuse us, Pemberton," he said to the young man, and offered Katherine his arm. As they walked away Katherine gave Ronald a placating smile, not unregarded by her partner.

"I wish you would not call me Kate," she said with irritation. It denotes a familiarity I have given you no cause to assume."

Simon laughed at her indignation. "You remind me of a nanny I had who spent most of her time admonishing me for ungentlemanly conduct."

"And quite right she was too," Katherine agreed, but could not repress a smile. "I am sure you were a most aggravating charge."

"And I have not improved with age. But come, let us join this set to work up an appetite for the Esterhazy's lavish buffet. I understand that there are lobster patties," he said rather drolly.

"You are impossible, Simon. But since I fancy lobster patties, I must accede to your blandishments," she said and entered into the figures of the dance.

Later Simon rejected all attempts to lure them toward supper tables where he might have to share his partner with other importuning young men, and steered her toward a private corner. Returning with the promised patties and other succulent treats, he adopted his most courtly manner, hoping to beguile her into confidences under the influence of the champagne cup. But Katherine adopted a light social air and chatted of insignificant matters, asking him about the various guests and laughing at his scandalous tales.

"I saw you dancing with Count Crespi. And after all my warnings, Kate. Was that wise?" he asked softly.

"As I told you before, I choose my own friends," she answered sharply, though secretly rather pleased at his proprietary attitude.

"He is viewed with some suspicion not only for his womanizing but for his other activities. I would not want you to be hurt, Kate," Simon said quite sincerely, discovering that he really cared what she thought of the Italian.

"Count Crespi is no more than a delightful dancing partner, Simon. I am not such a flat as to be taken in by his extravagant compliments. And I would like to know about these mysterious 'other activities' which place him out of bounds," she asked, her curiosity aroused.

"Take my word for it, Kate. He is not a proper object of your interest. And now, I fear we must return you to the ballroom or I will be called out by Pemberton or another of your swains."

Before he surrendered her to her next partner, he insisted on securing another dance which she reluctantly gave him, but he was aware that he had annoyed her with his peremptory demand that she abandon Count Crespi. Why was she so determined to pursue that relationship? Was it just stubborness or had she some darker scheme with which the Count was involved?

Katherine considered Simon's remarks as she twirled through the figures of the dance with her stolid new partner. She suspected that Simon was more than he seemed—a personable young peer with little on his mind but balls, horses and gaities of the season. Why had he been in the garden of the Pantheon that night? He had seemed to be expecting the unknown Titania to deliver something. Information, perhaps? She choked back an exclamation. Could Simon Stafford be an agent for the government? It was definitely beginning to appear that he suspected her of being involved in some nefarious scheme. In addition, he obviously entertained suspicions of the count. Was Crespi a spy for Napoleon?

As she chatted with Ronald her mind scurried busily over the possible permutations on this idea. She decided to encourage the Marquis, for then she could achieve two aims, unmask the Count if he was indeed a traitor to the country which had generously offered him asylum, and even more satisfying, she could prove to Simon Stafford she was not some gullible fool enamoured of every man who paid her fleeting attention.

Her determination to give Simon Stafford his comeuppance was strengthened by watching him in animated conversation with a luscious brunette beauty. The lady must have been a late arrival for Katherine had not noticed her before. She was not easily overlooked, dressed in a brillant red gossamer silk gown which revealed far more than it concealed, and wearing the most lavish of diamond necklaces. Unable to restrain her curiosity she asked Ronald for the lady's name.

"Oh, that is Contessa Francesca Fontenelli, a lady who

has recently arrived in London from her estates in Lombardy. No doubt another indigent victim fleeing from Napoleon," Ronald informed her with a worldly air.

"Not very indigent, I think," Katherine responded and watched as Simon escorted the lady toward the gardens. He seemed on surprisingly intimate terms with the lady, which only increased Katherine's resolve to get to the bottom of all this intrigue. She was as capable as Simon of serving her country, if that was what he was doing, chasing that well-endowed Contessa. If there should be danger in such a doubtful enterprise it only whetted her appetite for the scheme and with that end in mind she greeted Count Crespi eagerly when he appeared to claim the final dance of the evening.

"Count, you are obviously a man up to every rig. Do tell me what you know of Contessa Fontenelli. She is a most beautiful lady," Katherine asked disingenuously.

"She lacks your fresh charm, cara," the Count answered, his eyes glowing with admiration as he led her skillfully down the floor. "She is supposedly from a distinguished Lombard family who have lost their estates, and has come to London as a refugee from the Corsican. She is being sponsored by Princess Esterhazy, I understand. I have not made the acquaintance of the Contessa," he said a bit shortly, causing Katherine to wonder if he was telling the truth. Surely he would have rushed to meet a compatriot, and such a lovely one, if he had not known her before.

Crespi soon returned to paying Katherine the extravagant compliments she found so tedious and insincere. But it was not part of her grand design to depress the Count's interest so when, at the conclusion of the dance, he invited her to drive with him the next afternoon, she agreed prettily. The Count was much too clever to ignore Mrs. Basingbroke; he improved his relations with that good woman by exerting all his Latin charm with the result that she sighed happily to

Katherine on the way home that Count Crespi was indeed a gallant gentleman.

"Do you find him attractive, my dear?" asked Mrs. B., leaning back against the squabs of the carriage with the knowledge that her charge had been well launched that evening.

"Oh, he is that, if a bit effusive. But so much more exciting than staid English gentlemen, don't you find ma'am?" Katherine teased, knowing that the Count had captivated Mrs. Basingbroke.

But she did not allow for that matron's font of common sense. "Oh, yes, Latin men have so much charm, but I doubt if they make very comfortable husbands, always chasing after some new amour. And, of course, Count Crespi's estates have been sequestered, which makes his need for a wealthy wife paramount. I would not want you to be taken in by a gazetted fortune hunter no matter how charming," Mrs. Basingbroke warned. She was about to put a good word in for Simon Stafford, but then thought better of it. For some reason she felt Katherine would not receive her kind words about the Marquis with enthusiasm.

Chapter Ten

Katherine had decided to investigate the mystery surrounding Simon's suspicions of her, but that gentleman's ellusiveness prevented her from acting on her decision immediately. Strangely, after pursuing her with such ardor before the Esterhazy ball, he now ignored her. For three days after the ball Katherine heard nothing from the Marquis of Staines, which convinced her that he no longer found her worth his time or trouble. However, his absence was more than welcome to Ronald Pemberton and Count Crespi, both of whom were assiduous in their courtesies.

In assuming that Simon had abandoned her, Katherine was doing him an injustice. New developments in the investigation occupied him. On orders of General Valentine he had traveled to Folkestone on the Channel to track down a report on the Contessa Fontenelli. Valentine was not convinced of the Countessa's bona fides, and since she was reported as having entered the country through that Kent port, her arrival demanded further investigation. The Marquis de Lisle was commanded to quiz Princess Esterhazy about the lady for she must have some pretensions to respectability or she would not have been welcomed by the Austrian Ambassadress, no matter how careless the Princess was about the Contessa's credentials.

For some inexplicable reason Simon did not confide his doubts about Katherine's relationship with Count Crespi to his chief, but he did agree that the Count also deserved surveillance.

"If there is some contact, of a secretive sort, between the Count and the Contessa, it would be a strong indication that they are intriguing on behalf of Napoleon," Valentine said. "Of course, this could all be a hum, and the two could be indulging in a romantic affair rather than leakage of money across the Channel." Valentine knew all too well that appearances were often deceptive and he hated to be led, along with his colleagues, down the wrong path.

"I am inclined to think that Wilde is still the man on whom we should concentrate," Valentine concluded. "Have you any further indication of his involvement with the Italians, Simon?"

"Only Castlereagh's sense that Wilde was not completely open at the Foreign Office." Although he was reluctant to bring Katherine's name into the conversation, duty forced him to reveal a certain matter that was worrying him. "One rather unusual occurance. Miss Wilde asked me what I knew of Sir Richard Overton, whom she seems to have met casually in some way."

"Indeed. How curious, considering that Sir Richard does not go about in society, and has spent little time in England in the past years." Valentine's brow furrowed in concern. Sir Richard was the repository of many state secrets and if he should prove vulnerable to a woman there might be trouble, but then Valentine shrugged off his worry. No doubt it was just an idle question by Miss Wilde. Lady Valentine told him he dreamt of spies and imagined every stranger in London had some nefarious traitorous purpose. He had laughingly agreed that sometimes he went too far, but experience had often proved that his wildest suspicions came to pass. His painstaking investigations had done much to stop the leaks of information and money across the Channel where they could do grievous harm to His Majesty's government and armies.

Valentine, Castlereagh, and other high-ranking government officials were well aware that the truce of Amiens was not likely to last, and that it allowed foreigners of dubious credentials entry into England. Valentine kept a wary eye on those he suspected of conspiring with Napoleon for the sake of fortune and rank, or to regain confiscated estates.

He was convinced that the Countessa was bogus, but had no proof of his suspicions, so for the moment he could only ensure that she was watched, straining his already attenuated man power. That was why he had to rely on volunteers in the business, dedicated men like Theron de Lisle and Simon Stafford.

It was Theron de Lisle who noticed the Contessa's frequent trips to Hatchard's bookstore. His wife, the delectable Melissa, a great fan of novels, had seen her there several times and mentioned it to her husband. Since de Lisle had informed Valentine of the Contessa's visits to the Picadilly store, Valentine had set a man to watching her movements. De Lisle had observed, in his cynical fashion, that he doubted the Contessa was a dedicated reader.

Two mornings after the Esterhazy ball Valentine's agent was in attendance when the Contessa arrived quite early at Hatcherd's. He took up an unobtrusive observation post, but was disappointed to find that she only wandered about the shop, picking up and discarding various books. And speaking to no one.

He lost sight of her as she moved to the back of the store where the more weighty tomes were shelved. His orders prevented him from following her further into the store, where she might notice him.

Katherine, in an effort to distract herself from the many matters on her mind, had decided to make an early trip to Hatchard's in search of the newest Sir Walter Scott opus of which she had heard glowing reports. As she entered the store that morning, her maid trailing properly behind, she inadvertently brushed against the Contessa, who was leaving. She apologized prettily, and said a few words to the lady, who seemed abrupt, almost rude. Katherine gave no further thought to the encounter, only conceding that at close quarters the Contessa was as lovely as she had seemed across the dance floor. She had not noticed the watcher who made an entry in his notebook about the mishap, and duly reported it to his chief.

Katherine, unaware that she was the object of scrutiny, continued on her way to the table where Sir Walter's books were prominently displayed. Joining her within a few minutes was a distinguished gentleman who eyed her narrowly and then raised his hat politely.

"It is Miss Wilde, is it not? Sir Richard Overton, if you remember, our meeting in the Park," he greeted her tentatively.

"Of course, sir. I remember you well, the victim of my carelessness," Katherine replied, delighted to meet again this kindly man, with whom she seemed to have some rapport.

"Have you had any other impetuous encounters lately, Miss Wilde?" he teased, equally pleased with the meeting.

"No, I am happy to say. I have been most prudent. Are you interested in Sir Walter Scott, sir?"

"I am a great admirer. And may I recommend his lays of the Scottish border, just the romantic tales which should appeal to a young lady such as yourself," he offered with a whimsical twinkle.

A bit put out by his assessment of her character, Katherine responded, "Thank you, but I should mention, Sir Richard, that I am not really very romantic. I am actually quite practical and unsentimental."

Her words seemed to amuse him. "Ah, I beg your pardon. I have made a grave error and incurred your displeasure. Perhaps I can redeem myself by inviting you to take a cup of chocolate with me, or would you be offended considering the informality of our meetings? Perhaps I should secure the good offices of an intermidiary who could make the proper introduction."

"That is not necessary, Sir Richard. I have been assured that you are a man of utmost probity, and I would be honored to take up your invitation."

Sir Richard insisted on purchasing the Sir Walter Scott volume for her and then escorted her from the store. Valentine's agent, whose brief had been to follow the Contessa, was long gone when they emerged, talking animatedly, in search of the promised chocolate.

While Katherine and new found friend were improving their relationship, George Lang was laying plans to further his own designs toward his employer's daughter. He stepped very cautiously, knowing that his scheme would receive little encouragement. In the Wilde offices in Lombard Street he and his employer had a meeting to go over the day's business, which did not include any reference to the outstanding Italian loan. However, the Earl of Wexford's affairs offered an opportunity to direct the conversation in the direction which Lang intended.

"It might be necessary to forclose on Wexford's town house if he falls any further in arrears, sir," Lang suggested. "We cannot afford another bad loan at this juncture."

"I don't think that is necessary at this point, George. I have a particular reason for allowing the Earl great latitude."

Wilde did not want to discuss his hopes of an alliance with the Wexford family with his young associate. His private business was no concern of Lang's, although George was privy to every nuance of his financial empire.

"I understand sir, that you are expecting a closer connection with the Earl and naturally you would be lenient in the matter of his debts," George answered with an understanding smile. "Is an announcement to be expected soon?"

"I do not wish to discuss a matter of such private concern, George," Wilde began brusquely, but then relented. "Young Pemberton has requested Katherine's hand, but she has not made up her mind. Girls are apt to be skittish and cannot be forced to the altar. But she will come around," he finished with more confidence than he felt.

"I am sure there are many candidates for Miss Wilde's hand. She is an exceptional girl," Lang said, careful to reveal nothing but the most humble interest.

"I suppose so, but she is damnably reticent, and has the most ridiculous notions about falling in love," Wilde replied, unable to repress his irritation at Katherine's attitude and relieved to have a sympathetic ear.

Lang nodded in understanding, and feeling that he had learned all he could for now, rose to leave and go about the day's business. But Wilde recalled him as he reached the door.

"About that Italian affair, George. Do you think we will hear anymore about it from the Foreign Office? It would not do to have our clients feel we are under investigation by the government."

"I think it has all been resolved, sir. It is most unfortunate about the Talleyrand note, but I have that in train."

Lang bowed himself out, leaving Wilde to wonder just what he meant. Was that a threat in Lang's tone? If so he must be summarily discouraged from thinking that the Talleyrand letter could be used to Wilde's disadvantage. It might be prudent to send George to Sheffield on a matter of bank business and get him out of the way for a while. Peter Wilde wondered for the first time if he had allowed his rising assistant too much license. The young man appeared a bit too self confident, and needed to be taken down a peg or two.

Wilde was certainly wise to have judged George Lang as capable of ambitious plans to further his fortune. What he could not suspect was the method which Lang had plotted to secure that fortune, an alliance with the Wilde family which would put him in an unassailable position, whether Peter Wilde approved or not.

Unwittingly Katherine added to the nebulous fears Peter Wilde entertained by telling him that evening at dinner about her fortuitous meeting with Sir Richard, and how charming she found the gentleman.

"If you have romantic notions about Overton, Katherine, forget them. He is much too old for you, and not a man it would be wise to encourage," Wilde said angrily, cracking walnuts with unwarranted ferocity.

Katherine looked askance at her father. Why did the mention of Sir Richard put him in such a temper? "Don't be ridiculous, father. He is just a kind new friend with whom I enjoy conversation. And I understand he does not go into society and is considered a determined bachelor. It is quite gothic to think I would entertain romantic notions about a man old enough to be my father," she reproved, noticing that her father's knuckles whitened and his brow furrowed.

"I do not think he is a proper friend for you, and his attentions could be misconstrued. I want to hear of no further meetings between you. Surely you have enough men dancing to your tune to satisfy you, Katherine. I am trying to understand why you want time to consider Pemberton, but I will not wait indefinitely while you pursue your fanciful ideas. And I have the means to force you," he threatened, thoroughly arousing Katherine's temper, making her even more determined not to accept Ronald Pemberton. She would not be coerced into a match.

Her father went on with a sneer. "And I have seen no more of the Marquis of Staines. You over-reached yourself there, I think. Obviously, he was not seriously épris,"

He threw down his napkin and stalked from the dining room, putting a definite end to any conversation.

Katherine pondered her father's odd reaction to Sir Richard Overton. There was some mystery here. In fact, since she had come to London her life appeared to be burdened with mysterious happenings. And she had not liked her father's contemptuous reference to Simon Stafford. She was feeling especially vulnerable about his disaffection, although she told herself it was all for the best, for she was in danger of spending too much time thinking about that enigmatic gentleman. What could be more dispiriting than to entertain a tendre for a man who treated one in such a negligent fashion?

If Simon was aware that he had lost ground in his apparent pursuit of Katherine, he did not consider it of any moment. He had discovered enough about the Contessa's arrival in Folkstone to endorse Valentine's suspicions of that lady's appearance in their midst. She had sailed from Bologna to the Kent port aboard a small packet with a few English travelers who had been on holiday in France since the Truce of Amiens. Having been immured in their island fortress since the beginning of the war with France, adventurous Englishmen had taken the first opportunity to travel to the Continent, but the Contessa had given everyone the impression that she had hurriedly crossed France to elude the persecution of Napoleon's minions. In fact, Simon had learned from a fellow traveler that she had spent some time in Paris, certainly long enough to receive instructions from Fouché, Napoleon's wily chief of his secret police, and the man who directed all the attempts at spying on France's erstwhile enemy. The Contessa had evidently not covered her tracks too well, and there was even some reason to suspect that she was not really of the Italian aristocracy. Among her fellow passengers had been that experienced diplomat, Sir Richard Overton. Simon's questions to that gentleman had strengthened his belief that Francesca Fontenelli was not all that she seemed. Sir Richard had been very wary of offering an opinion but he had admitted that the Contessa had been escorted to the packet by a man alledged to be in Fouché's confidence.

"Had you heard of the Contessa before her arrival in London, sir?" Simon asked the statesman.

"No, but that is of little account. What was most disturbing is that when I mentioned several friends in Lombardy that she should have known I was not satisfied with her answers, and she was very eager to escape any further conversation with me on the voyage. Surely, if she were what she claims she would be anxious to discuss common acquaintances. If she is a spy, she is not a very well briefed one, and relies on her undoubted fascination to carry off the deception," Sir Richard concluded shrewdly.

"It's rather difficult to flush out these traitors when we are, on the surface at least, at peace with the Corsican."

"Frustrating, I agree," Sir Richard agreed, rather amused by the young man's dilemma. "I have learned in long years as a diplomat that ladies often play games which baffle us men. But perhaps you will be able to win her confidence. Whatever her motive she is a very attractive woman."

Sir Richard was too adept to suggest that making love to the Contessa might produce results, but Simon wondered if that was what he meant.

Ignoring any further implications of his future relationship with the Italian, Simon suddenly changed tack and asked Sir Richard the pressing question which had been bothering him.

"Sir Richard, I understand you have a slight acquaintance with Katherine Wilde. Have you any reason to think she engineered your meeting for some particular reason?" he asked, almost fearing to hear a confirmation of his doubts.

Sir Richard raised his eyebrows in surprise. "Not at all. She appears to be a well-bred young woman, if a trifle impulsive. But she's hardly out of the schoolroom. Surely, you do not entertain suspicions about her?"

"Her father, Peter Wilde, has certain business connections which cause the Foreign Office alarm," he admitted carefully.

"You mean the Italian loan," Sir Richard replied, cooly acknowledging his grasp of the problem. "Wilde is a banker, and occupied thoroughly with business, but I doubt very much if he would enlist his daughter in any dubious enterprise. She would make a very poor conspirator, for by my reckoning, she appears a very forthright and honorable young woman." Sir Richard had abandoned his tactful suave diplomat's role and seemed intent on portraying Katherine in the most innocent light. Simon could not help but wonder if Sir Richard had been bemused by the lady.

Sir Richard appeared able to read Simon's thoughts without a great deal of difficulty, and surmised that the young man was caught in the age-old dilemma of attraction toward a woman he did not believe worthy of his admiration, an attitude which irritated Sir Richard as much as it amused him. He did not want Katherine to suffer at the hands of the marquis nor did he want Simon pursuing her for the wrong reasons. He felt very protective toward Katherine.

"I think, Lord Stafford, that you must look for your traitors in another direction. Miss Wilde is not a member of that despicable society," Sir Richard concluded with asperity.

He had obviously had enough of this discussion, and Simon, took his leave. He left behind a troubled and angry Sir Richard, who decided he would have to take a hand in Miss Wilde's affairs. He owed it to newly stirred memories he thought long forgotten.

Chapter Eleven

While Sir Richard, Simon, General Valentine and Count Crespi had been occupying themselves with Katherine's affairs, Ronald Pemberton had made up his mind to settle his relations with that young woman once and for all. Girding himself for what he hoped would be a felicitous resolution of his hopes, he dressed in his best black superfine Weston coat, and drove his valet to distraction over the tying of numerous cravats until he found one that met his approval. Then he took himself off to Wigmore Street, with the requisite bouquet of yellow roses clutched in a damp hand. He was successful in finding Katherine at home on this fine June morning and relieved that she received him with some charity.

"Good morning, Ronald. How kind of you to call. I was quite in the mopes and now you have appeared to cheer me up," Katherine greeted him sunnily. She looked very appealing in her crisp yellow muslin morning dress, her blue eyes unshadowed and her glowing face reflecting her pleasure in the day.

"I am so relieved to find you at home, Katherine, and alone for once. You seem always to be surrounded by admirers or protected by Mrs. Basingbroke,'' he chided, feeling that lately Katherine's new acquaintances were absorbing too much of her time.

"Dear Mrs. B. takes her duties as my chaperone very seriously. But today I am having a holiday, and there are no pressing appointments or engagements until a visit to Drury Lane this evening.''

She indicated that Ronald should sit opposite her on a plesant chintz sofa in the sunny morning room where she had received him, then thanked him graciously for his floral offering. He waited impatiently while she gave instructions to the butler to put the roses in water.

"Perhaps I can join the theatre party this evening,'' he said nervously, delaying putting his chances to the test. "Although Shakespeare is not always to my taste, I understand that Mrs. Siddons' Hermione is not to be missed. But don't you think she is getting a little long in the tooth for these romantic roles?''

"We are to be the guests of the Seftons, so you must appeal to them to be included,'' Katherine said quite lightly as if it did not matter to her one way or another.

Unable to postpone his declaration any longer, Ronald rose to his feet, pacing nervously back and forth, coming at last to rest before Katherine who looked up at him questioningly. Grasping his courage, he plunged forward.

"The other evening at Almacks you reproved me for trying to make a declaration, but this morning you can have no such inhibitions. Will you do me the honor of becoming my wife?'' he said formally, and then burst out with: "I do want awfully to marry you, Katherine.''

Touched by the rather endearing if ingenuous proposal, Katherine tried to tender her refusal gently. "I am honored that you would wish me to be your wife, Ronald, but I do

104

not feel I can accept. I am not sure of my feelings for you," she offered kindly.

Ronald would not accept such a tentative rejection.

"You may not love me in that way now but I would earn your love after we were married. Your father is quite in favor of the match, you know."

"I know, Ronald, but I am the the one who must decide, and right now I am not sure it would be the wisest decision," Katherine tried to explain, feeling confused and unhappy. She liked Ronald well enough, but enough to take him as husband? She thought not.

"It's all because of this damnable season! All these rubbishy fellows are turning your head. But none of *them* has made you an offer yet, I'll wager!" Disappointment was not putting Ronald in the best light.

"Ronald, I will not be pressed into making a decision which will affect my whole life, and yours." Surely he could see that a reluctant wife was not to be desired.

But Ronald was not to be reasoned with. "If you expect me to wait about for months for you to decide, I do not deserve to be treated in such a shabby fashion!"

"You are right, Ronald. If you feel that way, I suggest you look elsewhere for a wife, if you are so determined to be married. I do not think your desire for me is founded solely on a sincere affection." Katherine avoided putting the bald thought into words. Ronald wanted her, but he wanted her marriage settlement as well. And she would not be courted for her father's money.

Realizing that he had overstepped the bounds of propriety, Ronald hastened to retrieve his error. "It is not the money, Katherine, or not entirely. Of course, I could not marry a poor girl. My father . . . ," he broke off wretchedly, conscious that he was not improving matters.

Katherine, touched by his honesty, hurried to reassure him.

"I know, Ronald, and I cannot fault you for that. If I loved you that would not be a stumbling block, but it is just that I need time. It's too soon," she explained, aware that she was managing this whole business badly, hating to wound Ronald yet determined to hold firm. "Why cannot we just continue as we are—unless you would prefer to end our relationship? I will understand if that is what you want. I am sorry I cannot offer more, Ronald."

"If that is your final word, I cannot argue against it. But you cannot stop me from trying to change your mind," he said, returning to his usual sang froid. Ronald Pemberton rather fancied himself in the marriage stakes and could not believe that he would not win out in the end.

"Thank you, Ronald, for being so obliging, and we will still be friends, won't we?" Katherine pleaded, anxious to end the disturbing interview on a pleasant note.

"Of course, Katherine. And I will try to see you at the theatre tonight. No doubt women are inclined to balk at the first proposal. Perhaps when I ask you again I will gain the answer I seek," he said with an engaging air of humoring a recalcitrant if mistaken nitwit.

Katherine decided not to take issue with his attitude and to leave him with his amour propre entact. She bid him a warm farewell. But she had found the interview painful and upsetting, and she wondered if she had been too hasty. Ronald would make an unexceptional husband. She knew her father would be furious that she had turned down the Earl of Wexford's heir and somehow she must try to make him see her reasons for the rejection, a task she faced with some apprehension.

However, Peter Wilde did not quiz her on Ronald's visit although he must have known of it. He appeared abstracted when Katherine met him over the dinner table that evening before leaving for the theatre. Mrs. Basingbroke was dining with them, and her presence helped ease the tension between father and daughter. Katherine marveled at Mrs. B.'s deft management of Peter Wilde. She had a gentle touch to which he responded, an ability to soothe him with inconsequential talk to which he reacted with as much animation as Katherine had ever seen in her aloof parent.

"And what is the plan for this evening, Mrs. Basingbroke?" he asked her as the escalopes of veal were removed for some braised squab and cabbage.

"We are joining Lady Sefton's theater party at Drury Lane to see the remarkable Mrs. Siddons in 'Winter's Tale'," she responded chirpily. "It should be a most entertaining evening and evidence that I am introducing Katherine to some of London's more cultural treats. Not that I would wish her to be a blue stocking," she added as if such an idea was anathema.

"You seem to have the entree to all the best salons and are certainly giving Katherine a memorable season," Wilde approved. "Is she having a success, do you think?"

"Oh, yes. Everyone agrees she is an Incomparable," Mrs. Basingbroke replied brightly.

Katherine, who wished they would not discuss her as if she weren't there, could not repress an ironic comment. "And that is what you want, is it not, Father?"

Before Peter Wilde could make some hurtful reply, Mrs. Basingbroke entered the lists. "Your father has been most generous in providing you will all the necessaries to enjoy the season, Katherine. I am sure you are grateful." Mrs. Basingbroke smiled at the girl, but Katherine could not ignore the admonition in her chaperone's eyes.

"Of course, Mrs. B., you are right as always."

Peter Wilde gave Katherine a frigid glance only remarking very mildly. "You are fortunate to have Mrs. Basingbroke

107

to guide you, Katherine, but I do not think you should refer to her in that casual way.''

"Oh, but Mr. Wilde, I enjoy it, although I have asked Katherine to call me Cecelia, as my friends do," she said gently.

"And a very attractive name it is, too. I hope I may be numbered in that company." Peter Wilde replied, surprising Katherine with his gallantry.

"I should be most pleased," Mrs. B. responded, with what Katherine privately thought was an arch air.

"And you must call me Peter. We cannot stand on ceremony, you and I, Cecelia," he said jovially, to Katherine's amazement. Obviously Mrs. B. knew how to bring out the best in her father. She wished she had her touch. She must study her example.

"Why don't you join our party this evening, Peter? I am sure lady Sefton would be delighted to welcome you," Mrs. Basingbroke invited with sincerity.

Peter Wilde was tempted, but realized that his sudden appearance in the Sefton's box might appear encroaching. "Perhaps another time, but thank you for including me. I must admit I rarely go into society and perhaps I should alter my habits," he conceded.

"I will do my best to persuade you."

Later, as the two rode toward Drury Lane, Katherine teasingly reproved her chaperone for her cleverness. "You really are a sly one, Mrs. B. How did you manage to get around my father? He was almost pleasant at dinner tonight. What is your secret?"

"Katherine, I am not sure you understand your father. He is a man of enormous influence and tremendous responsibility. I find him most gracious, and he certainly denies you nothing," she reproved.

"Alas, I do not have your gentle touch, Mrs. B. Father

finds me frivolous and unappreciative, I fear. I have tried to be the kind of daughter he wanted, but I have failed miserably,'' Katherine admitted.

"I believe he sincerely wants your happiness. That is why he asked me to introduce you to society. He wants you to meet a young man who will make you a comfortable and affectionate husband,'' Mrs. B. said, although she was too astute not to realize that Peter Wilde hoped to further his own ambitions through an advantageous marriage of his daughter. Mrs. Basingbroke, unlike Katherine, did not fault him for that. She had experienced enough vicissitude during her widowhood to sympathize with one who feared the snobbery of London's haut monde. As a poor relation she had endured society's pinpricks to her self-esteem often enough to understand the desire for acceptance.

But Katherine was not so charitable. "He wants to sell me off to some aristocrat to further his own ambitions. That is not a regard for my well-being,'' she insisted rather stormily.

"Oh, Katherine, it is not that simple. You are too young to realize that men are a mixture of many motives and we females must learn how to manage them to secure our happiness,'' Mrs. B. advised, laying her hand on Katherine's and giving her a reassuring squeeze.

"You are a dear, Mrs. B., and I am fortunate to have you as a friend,'' Katherine returned warmly, wondering, how her chaperone had learned such kindly wisdom and what price she had paid for her hard-won serenity. But such thoughts were banished for the moment as their carriage pulled up in front of the impressive entrance to Drury Lane Theatre, where Mrs. Siddons' portrait was prominently displayed, advertising the evening's playbill.

Unknown to Katherine, Simon Stafford had been invited to join the party that evening, and he had given a tentative acceptance, explaining that he might be out of town. He had almost decided that his suspicions of Katherine were unwarranted, leaving him with little excuse to pursue the relationship and as a result, mixed emotions. But, then Valentine had informed him of Katherine's apparently casual encounter with Contessa Fontelli outside Hatcherd's and his doubts surfaced again. That meeting could have been planned for Katherine to slip some note to the Contessa, some notice of future meetings or information which her father wanted forwarded safely.

The girl hardly seemed an experienced adventuress, but every time he found himself leaning toward believing in her innocence, some damning evidence appeared to illustrate that he must guard against trusting her. So when he arrived at the Sefton's box that evening he gave her the curtest of greetings.

His dark mood was further exacerbated by the arrival after the first act by the ubiquitous Count Crespi, who bent over Katherine's hand with that Latin courtesy which set Simon's back up. Damn the fellow. Was there no avoiding him?

Katherine, meanwhile had been hurt by Simon's indifference and compensated by welcoming the Count with more enthusiasm than she felt, a reception the Count took full advantage of. He invited Katherine to stroll about the halls before the next curtain and she eagerly agreed, wanting to get away from Simon's suspicious and cynical gaze.

Simon eyed their departure with barely concealed disgust. Short of following them and trying to intrude on their conversation, he had little recourse but to seek his own diversions. Looking out over the stalls and across the audience to the boxes opposite the Seftons, he noticed the sultry gaze of the Contessa Fontenelli, who appeared to beckon him. When he did not respond, she turned her back and began an animated conversation with one of the men accompanying her party. Intrigued, Simon decided cynically, that if one of his suspects was unavailable at least another promised to be more accommodating. Excusing himself from the Seftons he made his way to the Contessa's box and within moments was successful in persuading her to stroll about with him.

"And are you enjoying the performance, Contessa?" he asked as they wandered slowly down the stairs.

"But, of course. Mrs. Siddons is quite the thing although I do not understand the English passion for this Shakespeare. So prosy, but then Englishmen lack the fire and passion of my countrymen, is not that so, my lord?" She gave him a smouldering look from her dark eyes.

"You have not met the right Englishmen, Contessa," he answered.

"A cold race, the English, more interested in sport and the gaming tables," she challenged, tightening her hand on his arm.

"You must allow me the opportunity to redeem my countrymen's reputation in your eyes, dear lady," Simon countered, playing her game.

"I would enjoy that," she agreed.

It was at that moment that they encountered Count Crespi and Katherine, convincing Katherine that Simon Stafford was the veriest flirt, who had now abandoned her for a more likely target for his attentions. The two couples stopped to greet one another and Simon was forced to introduce the two women, who appeared charmed to meet one another.

"I believe it was you I so clumsily joggled at the entrance to Hatchard's yesterday morning," Katherine suggested, surprising Simon with her frankness. She was not at all reluctant to mention that meeting which Valentine and Simon had viewed so suspiciously.

"Ah, yes, Miss Wilde. We share a love of books, I think," the Contessa replied carelessly.

Before Simon could digest this comment, Count Crespi offered casually, "I believe we are fellow countrymen, Contessa. How strange we have never met before. Perhaps I may call upon you and we can commiserate over our common exile."

Katherine, disgusted at both her cavaliers so eager to fall under the spell of this experienced woman, abandoned any pretensions to good manners. "I believe the next act is about to begin. Should we not return to our box, Count?" she asked abruptly.

Before the Count could agree, Simon interceded. "Allow me to escort you, Miss Wilde. I am sure the Count and Contessa would like to pursue their Italian memories." And before either could demur he had deftly whisked Katherine from the Count's grasp and steered her ruthlessly toward the stairs.

"Really, my lord, aren't you behaving rather highhandedly?" Katherine protested, but secretly pleased that he had extricated her from the distasteful encounter.

"You are the most maddening girl, Kate. The Contessa is not a fit person for you to meet," he said with some asperity, guiding her with a hard hand up the stairs toward the Sefton box.

"You appeared to find her most acceptable, my lord." Katherine pointed out sweetly.

They stopped in the deserted corridor outside the box, and Simon placed his hands on Katherine's shoulders, within an ace of shaking her in his frustration. "What am I to do with you, Kate? You are entirely too impetuous!"

"I haven't the least idea why you should have anything at all to do with me!" Katherine retorted.

"Alas, I cannot seem to help myself," he admitted ruefully, and before she guessed his intentions he had taken her into his arms and was giving her a most disturbing kiss.

112

Conscious of her response and furious that he could evoke such an emotion, Katherine wrested herself from his arms—just in time, for the box door opened and Ronald Pemberton looked out, obviously searching for her. He could not help but notice her flushed cheeks and general air of confusion. He looked hard at Simon, but that gentleman returned his accusing stare blandly.

"Has the curtain gone up yet?" Simon asked as if he had no other concern in mind but the beginning of the second act."

"Yes, and I was looking for you, Katherine, so you would not miss the first entrance," Ronald answered, annoyed without knowing exactly why.

"Thank you, Ronald. We must not miss it." Katherine refused to look at Simon and walked with straight back into the box to take her seat. She indicated that Ronald should sit beside her, and Simon obligingly retired to take a chair next to Mrs. Basingbroke. Count Crespi quietly entered the box, looking with some distrust at Simon, then subsiding into a seat on Katherine's other side.

The Second Act began, but from several members of the Sefton party, Mrs. Siddons did not receive the full attention she deserved.

Chapter Twelve

Katherine spent a disturbed night, the memory of Simon's unexpected kiss causing her to toss restlessly, and recollect endlessly his outrageous conduct and her reaction. Was he coming to care for her? And if he was, what did he have in mind? Somehow she doubted that the distinguished Marquis of Staines had marriage as his goal. He thought her an adventuress, an easy mark. Well, she would show him she was not to be used in such a fashion.

Rising from her troubled slumbers in a recalcitrant frame of mind she rang for her maid and hurridly munched a roll and drank some chocolate before donning her riding habit. What she needed was a brisk ride in the cool of the early morning to dispell her uneasiness. Certainly London life was proving to be more complicated than she had ever imagined, what with Ronald's proposal, Count Crespi's false flirtations and Simon Stafford's advances.

However, she was destined to receive an even more shocking assault on her senses that morning. As she rode with her attendant groom down the raked paths of the Park she unexpectedly met the very lady who had caused her such discomfort the night before. The Contessa Fontenelli looked impressively competent on a black mare, chosen, Katherine thought spitefully, to match her elegant black riding habit. She pulled the horse competently to a stop and viewed Katherine with a cool assessing glance.

"How fortutitous, Miss Wilde. We also share a love of the early morning gallop to blow away the cobwebs of last night's dissipation," she suggested archly. "Or are you on your way to a rendezvous with some lovelorn swain?"

"Not at all, Contessa. Like you I prefer to ride before the paths are cluttered with equestrians. Or are you, perhaps, expecting to meet someone and I am keeping you from your assignation?" Katherine returned with irony. Unlike herself the Contessa was not accompanied by a groom.

The Contessa laughed, "Oh, no, Miss Wilde. I am as aware of the proprieties as any English miss," but her eyes narrowed. She had misjudged this apparently docile English girl. She was capable of the sarcastic retort, and not at all impressed with the Contessa's attempts to dominate her with the worldly air she had previously found so effective with rivals.

Still, she had no time for her now. She had more vital matters in hand. She was about to reply with a quelling setdown, when from the trees bordering the path came a shot, hitting the Contessa in her shoulder, forcing her to slump sideways over her horse's mane, and causing the mare to rear.

"Oh, my Lord, miss—someone is shooting at us!" exclaimed Katherine's groom as he ran to restrain the startled animal.

Katherine, appalled by the sudden attack, lept from her own beast.

"Careful, miss. The attacker may strike again," the groom warned, trying to hold the frightened horse and see to the wounded Contessa.

Katherine, unheeding, was about to run toward the sound

of the shot, when another rider galloped up to them, taking in the confused scene with one encompassing glance.

"What has happened, Kate, are you all right?" Simon asked, dismounting and running to her side.

"Yes, of course, Simon. It's the Contessa. Someone shot at her from those trees. He might still be there."

Seeing that she was unharmed, Simon boldly entered the shielding trees, intent on apprehending the villain who had dared to fire on the women. If his quarry had determined on another shot, he had changed his mind and made his escape. All Simon found was the evidence—flattened grass and a crumpled cheroot—that indeed a man had hidden there. He decided against following the trail since Katherine remained unprotected.

He returned to the horses and helped the groom lift the Contessa from her horse. She was unconscious, and bleeding from a widening wound in her shoulder. Simon loosened her habit and looked at the wound, satisfied that it was not fatal, although quite serious.

"We must get her to a surgeon immediately. Can you escort Miss Wilde home?" he asked the groom. "I will take care of the Contessa."

"Of course, Governor. I will see to it," he responded, reacting to orders, retrieving the bridle of Katherine's horse and the stolid animal he was riding.

"Good man," Simon approved brusquely. "I will have to carry her on my horse. Lift her carefully after I mount and hand her up to me."

Katherine stood helplessly by, not knowing what to do but determined not to act in a missish fashion.

Simon looked down at her, holding his burden. "You will be all right, Kate. Not feeling faint, or sick, are you?" he asked, concern in his eyes.

"Of course not, Simon. I am not such a ninnyhammer.

George will see I get home safely. At any rate, I don't believe I was the assassin's target. See that the Contessa receives help as soon as possible." She turned away, aware of an entirely irrational pang that the Contessa deserved Simon's first consideration. Then she turned back and laid a restraining hand on his arm. "Do let me know how she goes on, please?" she asked, grateful to him for appearing so suddenly. Only later did she wonder if he were the man the Contessa had arranged to meet surreptitiously.

He smiled down at her, hoping to reassure her, and promised, "I will call on you later this morning, and perhaps you will remember more about this distressing episode. But, I must not linger. The Contessa needs attention," and with a last reassuring smile he cantered slowly away, intent on sparing the wounded woman as little jarring as possible.

Katherine had no recourse except to mount her own horse and ride off with her groom, who spent the interval to the Wigmore Street house exclaiming over the episode. "Bold varmits, coming up from the stews, looking for an easy touch. But I don't hold with shooting," he grumbled.

"Quite, George, but I do not think the attacker planned on robbery," Katherine replied, musing over the assault on the Contessa. There was more here than met the eye. The Contessa was obviously on her way to some rendezvous which she wanted to keep secret. And did the sniper hope to prevent the meeting, or was there some other reason for the attempt on her life?

Not for a moment did Katherine believe herself to be the target. She was of no interest to any plotter or co-conspirator; but the Contessa, with her rather mysterious background, her emigré connections, might have indeed inspired the attack. But why was Simon so prompt to come to their aid? She had thought for some time that his work at the Foreign Office entailed intelligence, that he was involved in unmasking conspirators, but did that include paying court to the Contessa during clandestine morning rides?

Now that she had become involved she was not content to ignore all these mysterious happenings. Could Simon's interest in her be connected with her father's business, with this investigation into the Italian loan? She could not think of any other circumstance which would make her worthy of Simon's suspicion. He could not realize that the last person her father would trust with his confidence was his daughter.

She wished she had paid more attention to George Lang's sketchy explanation of his financial responsibilities. She knew she could expect little cooperation from her father if she had the temerity to quiz him about the intracies of the loan or the Foreign Office examination. But George Lang was another matter. He might be persuaded to tell her what she wanted to know if she went about it in the right way. And she was sure she could discover more than Simon, who would have little hope of wresting any details from Lang, whose loyalty to Peter Wilde seemed absolute, though whether that loyalty was based on feelings of gratitude or self-interest, Katherine could not decide.

Katherine became quite excited as she planned a campaign to get to the bottom of all this mystery, and waited with increasing impatience for Simon to call and tell her what he had learned about the attack on the Contessa.

Her father did not come back to Wigmore Street for luncheon. Katherine's restlessness increased as the hours crawled slowly by. She should be putting her scheme into effect, not waiting idly here without any news.

At last Simon was announced. She rushed impetuously to greet him, full of questions.

"How is the Contessa? Is she seriously injured? And why was she attacked?" Katherine asked after the most perfunctory of greetings.

He ignored her questions and paced around the morning room as if unsure how to deal with her questions. Finally, he came across to her and placed his hands on her shoulders, forcing her to look up at him. She met his gaze candidly.

"Katherine, you could have been killed today, if that bullet had gone astray. You are meddling in things that are none of your concern, or at least I hope they are not. You are placing yourself in considerable danger. This is not some romantic game for your amusement, but a deadly serious affair. The Contessa will recover, but that does not excuse your involvement."

Shrugging off his grip, she sat down in a chair near the window and indicated he should take a seat opposite her.

"What can I do to persuade you that I am not involved in any havey-cavey business?" Katherine asked angrily. "I was innocently riding in the Park when I met the Contessa, and we stopped to exchange a few polite words. I know nothing about her errand there or why she was shot. I think you are investigating my father because of his dealings with the Italians. I know he is worried about collecting the money he loaned them before Napoleon's conquest. But that is *all* I know. He does not tell me the intricacies of his business affairs. If the Contessa is conspiring against us I have no knowledge of it, and I greatly resent you pursuing me because you hope to learn something to my detriment or my father's!" Katherine became more heated as the words poured out of her, and Simon thought her flushed cheeks and flashing eyes became her.

His own impatience turned to amusement. "You misjudge me, Kate. I am investigating the Italian business. I cannot hide that from you after all this, but it has been no unpleasant task paying you attention, you know. You are a very taking girl."

"I think you are despicable, making up to me in order to

119

ferret out my father's business secrets, like some loathesome toad," she stormed, not one bit mollified.

"Oh, dear. I have been called a great many epithets in my life, but loathesome toad quite tops them all. And I was not making up to you for that reason alone. My duty to my country does not entail that I sacrifice my personal life to such an extent," he said, then leaning forward to gaze at her, his dark eyes troubled and searching.

"You must be aware, Kate, that despite the truce between France and England, hostilities have not ceased; they have just gone underground. There are many emigrés who have accepted our hospitality with genuine gratitude, but there are others, here in the guise of exiles from Napoleon's tyranny, who will betray us either for personal greed or some idea of loyalty to their homeland."

"And is the Contessa of this number?" Katherine asked, impressed despite her annoyance with Simon.

"There is some evidence pointing to her being in league with our enemies. Our hands are rather tied since we are ostensibily at peace with the Corsican. But the truce is falling apart, and we are particularily vulnerable to intrigue now."

"Well, I just met the Contessa for the first time at the ball the other night and today was just an inadvertent encounter. I am not concerned with her, but with what you think of my father. I know the Foreign Office called him in the other day. The men there seemed satisfied with his explanations and I see no reason why you should not be," she protested haughtily, not at all mollified by his explanation. "And that still does not excuse your attitude toward me!"

"My dear, Kate, I have been in this game a long time, and I have learned that appearances are often deceiving. One of the worst villains I knew was a respected general in His Majesty's forces. You and your father could be clever intriguers, although I must admit it would pain me to put you in the Tower," he teased.

"You would probably enjoy it. I think it is ignoble of you to spend your time luring innocent girls into your toils in order to spy on their fathers," she insisted in some confusion.

"Are you in my toils? How fascinating. The idea fills me with excitement," Simon responded, vastly entertained by her response. "But all this delightful sparring is not settling the issue. I want you to promise me, Kate, that you will avoid any compromising situation. Perhaps you were guiltless this morning, but if you continue to meddle you will be in danger. These villains have no compunction about removing any obstacle to their plans, and you are no match for them." Even as he tried to persuade her, he found himself, distracted by the provocative rise and fall of her bosom, partially exposed by her low cut mauve muslin morning gown. Gad, she was a lovely thing, and much too enticing, for her own good—or his.

"You have not said that you think my father is innocent. Until you do I can make no promises. I must protect him from you and your your insulting accusations," Kate said with some heat, but aware of an electric current between them which was making it difficult for her to concentrate.

"Your loyalty is admirable, Kate, and I wish I could feel the same way. Then we could confine our exchanges to more pleasant matters. But I do promise you that I believe you personally are not involved in any wrong doing," he said, realizing that he was speaking the truth.

"I wonder if I can trust you, Simon. From the beginning you have suspected me of intriguing. It all began so disastrously," that night at the Pantheon. Katherine reddened as she remembered the finale of that meeting when he had kissed her.

"Not disastrously, Kate. I have the fondest memories of that interlude," he said, his eyes lowering to her mouth.

As if wishing to distance himself from his wayward desires, Simon abruptly stood up.

"I wanted to hear more about the Contessa," Katherine reminded him, "but you have fended off my questions."

"I know little more than the obvious, that she was attacked by some secret adversary. We don't know the reason, and she is not now in a condition to tell us. I am warning you, Kate, to keep well out of all this, or I will take measures to see that you do."

He might at least have asked her, not commanded her, Katherine sniffed. Really, Simon Stafford could be almost pleasant one minute, and the next—why, he was little better than her father!

"Like you, Simon. I make no promises," she retorted.

He took her in his arms before she could devine his intent and kissed her. His lips were warm and seductive, causing tremours of sensation. The kiss deepened as he felt her surrender, her arms creeping up around his neck. He was within an ace of taking advantage of her compliance, of pressing her to the sofa, when suddenly the door to the morning room opened and the butler, Saunders, appeared. If he was appalled by the sight of his flushed and disheveled mistress in the arms of the notorious Marquis of Staines, he gave no evidence of it.

"Viscount Pemberton has called, Miss, and awaits you in the drawing room with Mrs. Basingbroke," Saunders announced solemnly.

Simon stared at the man haughtily, while silently damning the interruption, aware of an anger that Ronald Pemberton was engaging Katherine's time and interest. Really, the girl was a minx, stubborn and flirtatious, interfering in affairs which could lead her into danger, and then defying him.

Ignoring his own ambiguous role in their interchanges, he turned a unreadable face to Katherine, and bowed.

"Do not let me keep you, Katherine. I understand you have other committments," he announced coldly. "Your servant," and he strode from the room, leaving behind a girl angry and confused. How dare he use her so, kiss her and then, without apology, stalk from the room as if she were the one at fault? It was just as she thought. He viewed her as a frivolous, amusing wench, available for light entertainment but not worthy of serious involvement. Well, the mighty Marquis of Staines would learn she was a formidable adversary, one who must be treated with respect. Patting her hair before the mirror, and straightening her bodice, Katherine marched from the room behind the disapproving back of the butler. If Simon was unavailable to suffer her wrath, other parties would bear the brunt of her displeasure. Katherine had decided she would no longer meekly follow orders, from her father or from Simon Stafford.

Chapter Thirteen

While Katherine was plotting retaliation on the men she felt were deceiving and using her for their own dubious purposes, other more dangerous intrigues were reaching a climax.

In Lombard Street George Lang contemplated the letter which he felt, if used judiciously, might bring him the reward he sought—marriage to Katherine, whose beauty, wealth and style would ensure him the place he desired in a society hitherto closed to him. That his employer would not welcome him as a son-in-law, and that Katherine herself might take him in dislike, he considered of no account.

In his own way, George Lang was as ambitious and greedy as the man to whom he owed his allegiance. Once Katherine became his wife Peter Wilde would have no choice but to include him as an equal partner in the brilliant coups which marked the banker's financial rise. No longer would he be considered just a useful clerk dependent on his employer for his livelihood and whatever sops Wilde threw his way.

In a Bruton Place mansion off Berkley Square, the Earl of Wexford brooded over his correspondence in his shabby if well designed library. His mahogany desk was crammed with dunning bills. This latest request from the bank reminding him that the quarter's interest on his loan remained unpaid was the final humiliation.

He was close to losing his London mansion, his Somerset estates, which had been in the family since the Conquest, and denying his heir his rightful due. Well, that young man must do his share in retrieving the family fortunes, and a damnned poor job he was making of the business. By now, the announcement of the engagement should have been in the Gazette, and Wexford's solicitor could have been negotiating the settlements with that Cit. What was a man to do, when these Cits ran the show, evidencing no respect for their betters, and gulling men into bad investments? The Earl conveniently forgot that his own solicitor had warned him against this latest series of disasters, and that he had ignored the wise advice tendered to him. His mistakes had multiplied until now he was deep under the hatches. But Ronald would save him. Then he could abandon his less admirable schemes to win out over the money changers.

In a shabby boarding house off Lower Thames Street, two somber men discussed the results of the day's events.

"I had to get out of there mighty quick when that cove rode up on his big black horse. No time to see if I done the trick on the lady. There was another one there with her, too. I weren't expectin' her," the scruffy looking ruffian explained in a whining tone. "I never planned on that."

"But you believe that you hit your target," his questioner asked sharply. "I hope you did not bungle the job." His companion did not like the menacing look in the gentleman's eyes.

"Oh, yes, I am sure. They took her off and she was

bleeding, but I could not wait for more. Much as my life's worth,'' the villain insisted.

"Your life will not be worth much if you have failed,'' the other said in chilling tones. Then, he threw a bag of coins on the table. "Here is your payment, but ten guineas less for a job botched.''

If his companion thought of protesting he changed his mind. He contented himself with a muttered, "Well, I ain't too eager to kill women. What had the jill done anyway?''

"That does not concern you. Take your money and be satisfied, that is more than you deserve. We might need to avail ourselves of your services again, but next time, depend on it, we will not tolerate failure.'' Although the gentleman did not raise his voice, there was a warning in his words which impressed the hired killer, who decided he had best leave while he was ahead of the game.

Clutching his bag of coins he ducked his head in a gesture of assent and scampered out of the room, leaving behind a much troubled conspirator. Whatever the reason for the order to kill the Contessa, the man who had made the arrangements did not feel any compunction for his part in the matter. With the stakes as high as they were someone was bound to suffer retribution for trying to betray the cause. He settled at a deal table and began to write his report, wondering how it would be received and if his own head would soon be on the block.

If he had suspected that the attack on the Contessa was engaging all the resources of General Valentine's intelligence corps his fears would have doubled, but he was unaware of the measures being taken to apprehend him and his cohorts. General Valentine had called a meeting to discuss this latest development with his trusted lieutenants. Both de Lisle and Stafford were convinced that the attack on the Contessa meant they were getting close to the conspirators, rattling their nerves.

"You seem sure that the lady tried to betray her principals and they decided to do away with her before she could reveal damaging facts," Valentine summed up succinctly. "How do you know she was not just the victim of a random attack or even the target of a jealous lover?" he asked the two men.

"Why would she lie about her stay in Paris?" de Lisle pointed out. "If she were there innocently she would have no reason for deception. Our sources lead us to think that she made contact with Fouché and received instructions to rendezvous with some traitor in England."

"There's the rub," said Simon, dissatisfied. "We might unmask the Contessa and some of her associates, but still not apprehend the master mind of this group, or learn the plan behind it. Certainly it must have something to do with the Italians—which makes Peter Wilde even more suspect." Simon frowned, not at all happy with the idea.

"When can the Contessa be questioned?" de Lisle asked. "And will she tell us anything? She may very well be too afraid to squeal."

"I wonder where you pick up these vulgar terms, Theron," Simon asked, amused by his colleague's cant phrase.

"My licentious life, alas, now a thing of the past." Theron sighed, his saturnine grin hinting of untold escapades. In his bachelor days he had been known to visit the stews of London in search of excitement and no doubt learned a shocking amount of such language.

"Yes, well, I wish your licentious past could dredge up some contact with these persons," Valentine said. "We do not seem very forward in our attempts to thwart their plan, or even have a hint of what they might be."

"Instinct tells me it has something to do with money, which is why we must refocus our attentions on Peter

127

Wilde," Simon offered, reluctantly. He despised the role he was playing, having promised Katherine he believed her innocent of any wrong-doing, and would bend his efforts to clearing her father. Instead he was embroiling the banker even deeper in the matter. Was it possible that Peter Wilde, who already possessed a tidy fortune, would risk his social ambitions, his comfort, his reputation, even his daughter to gain a few more millions? It would appear doubtful, but man's greed was legend. And his envy and disappointment might lead him to entertain traitorous ideas as a revenge against the society which barred him from its inner portals.

"There are other financial men who might have an equal interest in betraying their country for wealth. Financiers are not noted patriots. Money crosses all barriers," Valentine explained unwilling to abandon Wilde, since he had no other suspect in sight.

"Well, what is our immediate plan, Lucien?" de Lisle asked, eager to get to grips with the problem.

"I think Simon here must quiz the Contessa, while keeping in with the Wildes where he seems to have an entrée. Disagreeable, I know Simon, to spy on one's friends in their own drawing room, but the situation is urgent, you agree?" he asked, having all the reluctance of a well brought up Englishman for this type of deception.

"If I must, I must, but I tell you I find it a damned uncomfortable ploy," Simon agreed. "What dirty task do you have for Theron here, or am I to be the only scapegoat?" he asked ruefully.

"Theron has agreed to go to Paris, where his mother's connections should enable him to do some useful ferreting. And he will take Melissa. His wife's shopping and desire to see the sights will be a useful cover for his investigations. Will she consent to go?" Valentine asked, certain that the Marchioness de Lisle would eagerly accept the challenge. "Of course, you will tell her what you must," Lucien concluded, knowing that Theron would not deceive his wife, or even attempt it, for she would have the matter out of him in a trice.

"Melissa will be thrilled. Her adventurous nature has been thwarted lately, and the chance to do a little delving into a nest of traitors will have great appeal. At any rate, I could not leave her behind. Who knows what she would get into in my absence, and I could not contemplate a long separation," de Lisle admitted, leading Simon to think wistfully that the rakish Marquis had been fairly caught by his passion for his wife. He could only envy him.

"We are agreed on how to go on, then. And Simon, take care. I would not want you to suffer the Contessa's fate. Guard your back as well as your front. We cannot know where the villains will strike next. And I will wait with some impatience for the results of your interview with the Contessa." He hesitated a moment, lost in thought, and then chuckled. "You will have to charm the lady into confidences, not a task beyond you, I vow."

Simon stood up, making a gesture of disgust. "I would much prefer to be fighting Napoleon's soldiers then to chasing spies about London, but since that alternative is denied to me, I will do what I can," he said with resignation.

Leaving Valentine to his paperwork. Simon and Theron walked down Pall Mall together, saying little, busy with their thoughts, until de Lisle finally shook off his unease and turned to Simon as they entered St. James Street.

"And what of this Count Crespi? Is he the master-mind of the cabal or is he just what he seems, the dependent of the Duke of Ryland and acceptable to the ton?" de Lisle asked cynically. His tendency was to distrust all emigrés, an attitude shared in some degree by Valentine and based on long experience.

"Like you, Theron, I can't like the beggar, but my reasons may be personal rather than professional," Simon admitted ruefully. He knew his suspicion of the Count lay as much in his dislike of the Italian's pursuit of Katherine as in his doubts as to the man's probity.

"Ah, I gather the Latin's gallantry has impressed *la petite* Wilde," Theron replied with some precipience, his amusement at his friend's predicament overriding his concern.

Simon had to laugh at his friend's raillery, and concede that he might have scored a touch. "You are a devil, Theron, but I must admit I don't like to see the popinjay beguiling Kate with his insinuating ways."

"I warned you, Simon, you were in great danger of being caught in the toils of the alluring Miss Wilde, who I now see has become Kate. I had no idea you had made such progress," Theron could not refrain from teasing his scowling companion, who realized he had expressed more than he intended about his reactions to Katherine.

"Not at all. I am still very suspicious of Peter Wilde, but I have some evidence to support Kate's innocence, although she is damned hot in hand and flares up at any suggestion that her father may be embroiled in nefarious dealings," Simon confessed a bit shamefacedly. He quickened his pace as if to throw off his unease.

"Such loyalty is commendable, mon brave, but remember the female of the species have many weapons in their armory. You will find yourself at the altar before you know it, and then your position viz a viz your father-in-law will be ambiguous to say the least," Theron spoke in jest, but beneath his careless words Simon heard a warning, one that only strengthened his own feelings that he was becoming much too involved with the provocative Katherine.

"I must yield to your greater expertise in the matter of females, Theron," he said with a mock bow. "It's a wonder to me how Melissa every brought you into parson's mouse-trap. You're a wily, cynical devil to be caught by such an innocent, charming though she is.''

But de Lisle was not a bit abashed. ''She was clever enough to make me do the running, and I greatly fear you have encountered just such another naive miss,'' he admitted. ''But matrimony has its advantages, you know.''

Simon, well aware of the Marquis de Lisle's devotion to his young wife, only commend his friend. ''Well, Melissa is a rare one. You are deuced fortunate, and have more than you deserve, Theron.''

''True. She should have boxed my ears and sent me about my business. But, perhaps, she thought a better punishment was entrapping me in her toils, a happy choice for me,'' Theron conceded then added a bit whimsically. ''Perhaps you had better embrace the inevitable yourself, Simon.''

Not to be drawn Simon insisted, ''Well, I have no time to worry about my personal affairs while this intrigue consumes us. I must be off to call on the Contessa and discover what I can learn from that mysterious lady.'' Since the two men were nearing South Audley Street where the injured Contessa lodged, they made their farewells, and Simon wished his friend good hunting in Paris.

Simon was received by the Contessa's hostess, a Lady Ramsford, who was revealed to be an old schoolmate of her guest. They had attended a seminary in Brussels together, and the years had not been as kind to her as to her erstwhile schoolmate. She was comfortably plump and her once guinea-bright hair had dulled to a mousy brown, but she was an obliging woman of good county stock, and her very presence did much to assure Simon that she would not willingly entertain a traitor. His request to see the Contessa was received with some reluctance.

''I don't really know if she is in a state to see callers, but certainly she would want to thank you for rescuing her from that villain who attacked her. I don't know what we are coming to in London when a lady can be set upon in the midst of the Park. Shocking,'' she fulminated, obviously not understanding the real motive behind her guest's shooting.

Simon, who did not intend to enlighten her, agreed and pressed in his most charming manner to be allowed to assure himself of the Contessa's welfare. Finally, after much conversation and the acceptance of a rather indifferent Madeira, he was allowed to mount to the upper story and follow his hostess into the Contessa's boudoir. Evidently her wound had not been as serious as the loss of blood had suggested. She looked pale and drawn, with deep shadows under her dark eyes, but for all that she was made up cleverly to enhance her pallor, and attired in a most fetching bed jacket of cream silk accented with a lavish amount of Valenciennes lace. She greeted Simon with a languid smile and indicated that he should draw up a chair beside her bed so that they could have some conversation.

Lady Ramsford hovered about, fussing over the bedclothes, raising a pillow behind her patient's back and generally driving both Simon and the Contessa into the fidgets with her solicitude. Finally, when Simon felt he must take matters into his own hands and order the woman from the room, the Contessa managed more adroitly.

"Dear Lucy, you are so mindful of my health. And I do appreciate all you are doing, but I feel I am keeping you from more important duties. I think you can safely leave me in the capable hands of the Marquis of Staines,'' she suggested gently.

"But, Francesca, it will never do to leave you unchaperoned in your boudoir with a gentleman,'' Lady Ramsford protested, shocked at such a transgression of the proprieties.

"I am hardly in a case to offer much temptation, and the

Marquis is the most circumspect of men, I vow," she replied, hiding her irritation. "Now don't be a goose, Lucy, I have something of a private nature to discuss with his lordship. Do be a dear and leave us alone."

Lady Ramsford could hardly insist when Simon rose with alcarity to open the door for her. Tutting to herself she left the room. Simon only hoped she was above listening at doors. He returned to the Contessa's bedside and looked down at her quizzically.

"That was well done, my dear lady, for I was at my wit's end as to arranging private speech with you. It is reassuring to see you in such fine fettle. I do hope you are not in too much pain. You lost a great deal of blood," he said with every evidence of concern.

"It could have been worse, but for your intervention, sir. And I feel most secure, convalescing in the safety of this bed. But, although I am flattered by your inqueries as to my health, I am sure you have questions for me," the Contessa said, correctly divining that Simon's concern was not entirely for her recovery.

"You are too astute, Contessa. And it is true that I do not believe your attacker was the usual villain intent on robbery. I greatly fear he intended to dispatch you permanently, and I think I have some idea of the reason," he replied smoothly, noting that she was not at all surprised at his bald suspicions, showing neither outrage nor denial.

Finally she smiled, her natural instinct when closeted with an attractive man not affected by her invalid status. In fact, she was well aware of the fetching picture she made, languorous, pathetic, in need of protection. "I suppose you have caught me out, checked my story of fleeing from Napoleon's minions and found some discrepancies," she admitted, at the same time giving the impression that by throwing herself on

133

his mercy she would emerge from the interview in a favorable light.

"How clever of you to admit it, Contessa. And am I correct in believing that after landing in England you had second thoughts about cooperating with Fouché's band of cutthroats and intended to betray them?" he spoke in a level voice as if such devious action was not at all remarkable.

"I must plead your indulgence. I had to leave the Continent, and the only way to save myself from a tribunal was to agree to spy on the English. Believe me, I had no intention of following the Corsican's orders. In fact, as evidence of my good faith, I had made a tentative approach to your officials before this frightening occurrence," she confessed, trying to look abashed.

"Ah, yes. You are Titania, who failed the rendezvous at the Pantheon," Simon said with assurance after a lightening analysis of the situation. "What kept you from the meeting?"

"Lady Ramsford had a dinner party that evening, and I could not get away, but I intended to contact your Gen. Valentine today. Only the incident in the Park prevented me," she explained in a small voice, looking appealingly at her questioner. He was not impressed with her attempts to beguile him into accepting her innocence.

"You realize, of course, that your employers arranged for that attempt on your life? You are still in great danger. We will arrange protection for you, but the price is high. I want the name of your English contact," Simon urged sternly, not sure that even now she was telling him the truth. It was evident that she was frightened, and hoped to be shielded by the English authorities. That too could be an act, designed to win their confidence while she still worked for her French masters.

"But I don't know it, really, you must believe me. I was

134

to receive my instructions in the Park yesterday morning, just beyond the entrance to Rotten Row, by a large birch tree. I never reached the place, as you know, having been interrupted by meeting Miss Wilde," she pleaded. "And, of course, I intended to make the rendezvous so that I would learn something of value to give you when I threw myself on your mercy," she explained, as if that condoned her previous duplicity. Simon was not sure he believed her rather suspicious tale of strange meetings and mysterious contacts.

The Contessa was an experienced, sophisticated woman with a reputation which bore scrutiny. That she was also a skilled actress and seductive in the bargain, only added to Simon's mistrust. She was trying to captivate him now as she moved insinuatingly against her pillow, allowing him a view of her veiled bosom, and gazing with artless expectation at him.

"What can I do to assure you, my dear Marquis, that I am innocent of these grave charges? Do you think I would risk all, my safety, my acceptability, my fortune, my English friends, to aid those miserable French canalle who have robbed me of all I hold dear," she demanded, dabbing at her eyes with a bit of cambric, as though Simon were a brute badgering an ill and helpless woman.

Simon could not help but admire her performance. "I really don't know what your motives are, Contessa, but I suggest that you remain sequestered here where you are safe, not only from your French contacts but from any other rogues who might decide you are expendable. You are not in an enviable position, distrusted by both sides. I think you could tell us more, and let me assure you that your safety, even your life, would have a better chance if you did so. If you remember more than you have thought prudent to tell me, a message will bring me immediately," he said decisively, eager to remove himself from the cloying atmosphere and the attentions of this woman, whom he suspected had told him, if not a tissue of lies, then a tale with just enough of the truth to ease her path. He bid her a rather curt farewell with only the briefest hopes that she would recover her strength shortly. If the Contessa was disappointed in his reception of her story, she did not show it, giving him a seraphic smile and thanking him again for the rescue.

Simon left the Ramsford house with his misgivings multiplied. The Contessa could be playing a clever double game, but if so she had certainly carried the deception to the utmost lengths, allowing herself to be attacked, even if the shot had done far less damage than originally thought. And, he admitted ruefully, he was no further along in unmasking her English contact.

Chapter Fourteen

Determined to settle Simon Stafford's doubts about her father's loyalty, Katherine decided her first move would be to question Count Crespi, try to discover if he were really the dispossessed emigré he claimed to be. Her ability to prove her father's innocence would win his gratitude and affection and put Simon to rout. She dressed for her afternoon drive with the Count carefully, intent on charming him into revealing his motives. Her redingote of lime green Levantine over cream silk was the latest stare and her flat crowned gypsy hat made a perfect frame for her piquant face. That the Count was fully aware of the attractive picture she made was apparent in his extravagant compliments when he arrived to escort her with a lavish nosegay of migonette and yellow rosebuds in hand. As they prepared to leave the Wigmore house Peter Wilde and George Lang emerged from Wilde's library and introductions were made. Katherine, aware of her father's interest in pedigrees, mentioned lightly, "The Count is a connection of the Duke of Ryland's, father. Alas, he has been forced to flee his Piedmont estates because of Napoleon's incursions."

Wilde narrowed his eyes in speculation as he greeted the

Count, barely hiding his satisfaction that Katherine had managed to snare such a distinguished cavalier. He failed to heed his assistant's irritation, for neither Wilde nor the Count paid much attention to the young man. Lang did not fail to observe the omission.

"Are you finding your stay in England to your taste, Count?" Wilde asked.

"Your countrymen have been most sympathetic and hospitable, sir. And your ladies are so attractive and forthcoming, they quite spoil one," the Count replied with a smug, satisfied air.

Giving a cheerful nod to George Lang, whom she imagined could not be impervious to her father and the Count's indifference Katherine greeted him with a kindly word as to his work. Lang, sensitive to slights, read her charitable attempt to put him at ease as a definite interest in him, since his appreciation of his own worth assured him that he was attractive to most females he met no matter what their station in life.

Finally, the Count and Katherine made their adieux and departed on their drive, leaving George and Peter Wilde both prey to reflexion. Wilde was not sure he liked the idea of an impecunious Count as his daughter's suitor, but his sponsor, the Duke of Ryland, had impeccable lineage.

Lang had cleverly ferreted out that Viscount Pemberton's courtship of Katherine was not entirely successful. Her obvious reluctance to follow her father's wishes and accept the young peer's proposal could mean there was yet a more impressive rival. Perhaps he would have to accelerate his plan, before the Count made his claim. He decided he would plant the seed with his employer.

"Miss Wilde appears to be enjoying a most successful season," Lang offered with an obsequious smile. "May I presume to ask if she has decided to accept Viscount Pemberton, as you hoped?''

Wilde disliked personal questions but felt enough charity toward his young assistant to make an exception to his usual brusque repulse of such a liberty.

"Katherine has not yet made up her mind. The Season is apt to turn a girl's head, give her foolish notions, but I think she is sensible enough to see where her real future lies. The Count is only one of her many admirers, but she will come to see that Pemberton is her best option, I am convinced,'' Wilde said with some complacency.

Lang was ready. "I wonder, sir, if I could discuss a matter of some interest to us both before we return to the office. The atmosphere there does not lend itself to concerns of a more personal kind,'' he suggested ingenuously.

"Of course, my boy,'' Wilde replied. He was in an expansive mood after the meeting with the Count and inclined to be generous with Lang, believing the young man had some announcement to make about his own marital plans, perhaps. It was time Lang made a judicious union and set up a household that would insure his steadiness and his identification with Wilde's merchant bank, in which he had a bright future. If there were two attributes Wilde appreciated beyond social prestige and noble ancestry they were industry and financial acumen, both of which he believed Lang possessed in abundance.

Settled in the library, Wilde folded his hands and indicated he was prepared to entertain any confidences Lang wished to impart.

"You see, sir, I am thinking of marrying. Of course, I would wish your approval on the match,'' Lang came out boldly. His suggestion received an avuncular acquiesence from his employer.

"Capital, capital. I have been thinking you are of an age

139

to take this step. Who is the young woman?'' he asked, hoping that Lang would make a judicous choice, perhaps with some tradesman's daughter.

''I want to marry your daughter Katherine,'' Lang answered smoothly, prepared for the outburst he knew would follow. He was not disappointed.

Wilde, as he had expected, showed both anger and surprise, His austere features deepening into a ferocious frown. ''You must be out of your mind. I would never consider such a match. I have told you of my plans for Katherine, and that does not include an alliance with someone not of her station,'' he shouted arrogantly. Lang's presumption raised his hackles and he was within an ace of losing his temper and railing furiously at the young man.

''I think you will, sir, when you consider the alternative. I have it in my power to cause you deep embarrassment over the Italian loan, reveal facts that you might find it difficult to explain to the government,'' Lang replied, folding his hands together complacently. He had expected opposition but was convinced his employer was too astute not to see the invidiousness of his position once it was laid out for him. He chose his words carefully. ''You see, I did not destroy the Talleyrand letter copy. A very ambiguous letter if you recall, and the authorities might look with disfavor on your approach to that wily gentleman.''

''Have you the audacity to try to blackmail me, Lang, and after all I have done for you?'' Wilde protested, with a sinking feeling that Lang had just such a ploy in mind.

''Oh, no, sir. I would not call it that. Just an agreement that it would be wiser to accede to my courtship of your daughter.'' Then he continued as if his outrageous demand was only sensible. ''Come, sir, surely such an alliance would put to rest any fears you might have that I would betray your indiscretion to Castelreagh or Sir Edward at the Foreign

Office. I would not want to jeopardize my father-in-law," he ended, as if that sealed the matter.

Wilde grew red with rage. "You are out of your mind. Katherine would never entertain your suit when she has some of the most eligible men in London prepared to offer for her. I will not stand for this, Lang," Wilde said tightly, struggling to recover his aplomb. He would not be threatened by this clerk, and the audacity of the man's request amazed him.

"I realize that you would wish a more advantageous match for your daughter, but when you think about it you will see that this decision might benefit all concerned. I am sensible that you have furthered my career, but I have given you good value for your patronage and would continue to do so as your son-in-law. I have your best interests at heart," Lang insisted with assurance. "When you think about it, such a marriage would be to both our advantage."

"I admire your nerve, Lang, but you are omitting Katherine's desire in this matter," Wilde explained. "And I might see my way clear to approaching the authorities with the letter myself," he threatened, now convinced he could handle this encroaching clerk.

"I think Miss Wilde might be persuaded to entertain my suit with some encouragement from you, and you would be wise to give it. I do not think you want the government to interfere in your business," Lang replied, not one whit overcome by Wilde's defiance. He was sure his employer would not take such a desperate measure which might destroy all he had built.

Peter Wilde had not achieved his enormous success by submitting to vague menaces of retribution, but he was clever enough to see he would have to buy time. He had been gravely mistaken in his assessment of Lang's loyalty and obsequious attention to his business. But he was not so stupid as to ignore the danger the young man posed.

"I will not put any rub in your courtship if you are determined to aim so high, but Katherine will not be coerced into a match. I have tried to persuade her to accept Pemberton but she is adamant that she must have her Season. You have a formidable rival in that young man," he said with confidence. "And do not put much emphasis on that letter. *I* discount it." He believed that an outright refusal to entertain Lang's suggestion would be foolish, and Lang had correctly divined his uneasiness at the thought of the letter being offered to the Foreign Office investigators. He would have to discover some means of discrediting Lang before that happened and he would do so. What disturbed him most was his gullibility, his mistaken analysis of Lang, and he would take care he would not be placed in so vulnerable a position again.

"Well, we will leave it for the moment, sir. But I take it you will not cast a rub in my way of winning the young lady," Lang said, unaware that he had made a formidable enemy.

"You must follow your own inclinations, Lang, as I will," Wilde replied ambiguously. "And now, I think I must return to the office. Several important decisions await me there." His tone was soft and subtle with a hint of menace, but Lang was too pleased with himself and his conduct of the interview to realize he had put his future at risk.

If her father's welfare was very much on Katherine's mind, she did not evidence her concern as she rode into the Park with Count Crespi. He had a very smart equipage, a gleaming black phaeton with silver accents, drawn by a pair of showy chestnuts, but Katherine soon saw that he lacked the driving expertise of Simon Stafford. Annoyed with herself for making odious comparisons, she smiled sweetly at Count Crespi and began her campaign.

"It must be unsettling for you, Count, to be exiled from your homeland, your estates. I commend your cheerfulness under these difficult circumstances. And most of the emigrés in England now are Frenchmen, so you do not have the comfort of your countrymen in any great degree," she said sympathetically.

"You forget, Signorina, that I have several English relations, and indeed, spent some of my youth at your excellent scholastic institutions here. Of course, I miss my home in the Piedmont, and must put up with a more stringent mode of living here. And then there is the atrocious English climate," he explained with a slight grimace.

"Well, you can't complain about today, a lovely summer day," Katherine countered.

"No, indeed, and I can't complain about the beauty of English misses, so open and friendly, too, not at all like our very strict Piedmont ladies," the Count ventured, implying a license which Katherine was not sure she found acceptable, but determined to pursue her scheme, she decided not to take offence.

"You find our manners too free, Count?" she asked pertly.

"Not at all, bellissima, very refreshing. The English have been most kind to me and I could not be such an ingrate as to criticize their manners," the Count replied with every sign of amiability. "I only regret that my countrymen have shown themselves to be so lack-luster in facing our common enemy, that wretched Corsican."

"Napoleon seems to be set on mastering all of Europe. A dreadful prospect, don't you think?" Katherine asked, widening her eyes in innocence, a gesture she knew would would appeal to the Count.

"I think the English dragon will slay him before long, cara. We must just possess our souls in patience," he answered with a careless air, removing one hand from the reins to squeeze hers in a suggestive manner. Katherine found this not to her taste, but restrained her natural inclination to repulse his flirtatious encroachments.

"I am so relieved you feel that way. It is so comforting to discuss these grave matters with a man of your experience, Count. I have led such a sheltered life I know so little of politics, and Englishmen won't discuss these affairs with women," she said, flattering his conceit.

Katherine had realized that the count, although he seemed impervious to affront, could not help but notice that many Englishmen found him too fulsome, too Latin, and treated him with a certain amused contempt, not at all soothing to a man with his pride. He relied on his success with females to maintain his consequence, and Katherine did not intend to antagonize him.

Katherine continued her interview. "I am naturally concerned with my country's safety. And I am not sure this truce is a genuine one. There still appears to be a great deal of intrigue and treachery abounding in London. Look at what happened to the Contessa Fontenelli! Katherine said, as if appealing to his wisdom and experience to explain that frightening event.

"Do you think the Contessa is a spy, cara?" he replied, rather amused than irritated by her innocent observation.

Katherine repressed a startled reaction. She had not expected such a forthright question. She wondered what would be the most suitable reply. Boldly she came out with her suspicions.

"Well, it was the most unsettling affair. I could have been injured myself. And I hardly think the Contessa, or myself, were the objects of robbery. There must be some reason she incurred the attacker's wrath, a falling out among conspirators, perhaps,"she ventured, watching him closely. But the Count, if he was involved in shady undertakings, was too skilled to show any emotion but melting sympathy for his disturbed companion.

"I know, Signorina, it must have been a most distressing episode, and you are an unusual girl to have reacted so bravely. But the misadventure with the Contessa cannot really concern you," he said, a tone in his voice Katherine could not decipher. Was it a warning?

"Well, it does concern me, and I would like to know more about the lady. After all, I was nearly a victim of her enemy and have some interest in discovering what was behind that attack," she said sharply, forgetting for the moment to play the role of an admiring acquiescent, gullible young girl.

"I wish I could reassure you, dear lady, but I know nothing of the Contessa, if that is indeed her real name. Piedmont and Lombardy are neighbors, yet I have heard nothing of a noble family called Fontenelli. Strange, for most Italian aristocrats know each other or have some connection, yet she is a stranger to me," he explained as if dismissing the matter.

"Perhaps she says the same about you, Count," Katherine said boldly, and then wondered if she had been too revealing. It would never do if the Count felt she suspected him of any chicanery. Her course was to soothe his ego and wrest confidences from him without him suspecting her purpose.

"Touché, Signorina. You have a clever tongue. But I assure you that my credibility is well established by my uncle, the Duke of Ryland. He would never sponsor a charlatan, and he has been most generous, although I fear the dear Duke does not really approve of me," he confessed with a most apologetic air.

Katherine wondered how long it had been since the Duke

had seen his nephew, and how the Count had established those claims on his noble relative's bounty. Really, she saw evil motives on all sides, but recent events had promoted such suspicions, and the Count had not satisfied her doubts as to his innocence. In fact, he had raised other, more pressing questions, but was now the time to ask them?

"I understand the Duke is rarely in London," she said demurely, as if to change the direction of the conversation, but she mistook the Count's shrewdness.

"No, he dislikes town life, but he will be arriving this week to see his doctor and his tailor, so you may have a chance to quiz him then, cara. And you will decide if I am a fit person to escort you, I hope, after he lays your fears to rest." Divining her mistrust, the Count, had circumvented further probing by carrying the skirmishing into her arena. Katherine realized she would get no further information from him and contented herself with platitudes for the remainder of their drive. She did not like the knowing looks the Count gave her, nor the spark of amusement in his treatment of her. She feared he knew exactly what she had been trying to do. The results of her attempt had neither satisfied her doubts nor exonerated him from suspicion. She found him enigmatic and worthy of further investigation, although how she was to arrange that she had not decided.

Chapter Fifteen

Katherine spent the next twenty-four hours chiding herself for not pursuing the suspicions she had formed of the various actors in this drama of conspiracy. She would have liked to consult her father, confide in him, ask him to tell her honestly if there was any basis for the rumors about his involvement with Napoleon's men over this Italian loan. But he had shown himself to be uninterested in her opinions, unwilling to hear her anxieties. She had accepted the fact that he did not love her with the kind of affection she craved from him.

For some reason, the name of Sir Richard Overton came to her mind. Now, there was a gentleman with vast experience of diplomatic maneuvers, of the secrets of state, and he appeared kind. If only she knew him in a more intimate way she could confide her doubts, her anxieties about the coil in which she found herself. She had this strange conviction that he was a man on whom she could rely, who would listen to her problems and advise her with compassion and acumen. But how was she to arrange a meeting with Sir Richard?

To banish her worries she decided to visit Hatchard's again. Perhaps a new novel would distract her from the frustration of her position. On arrival at the bookstore it appeared that fate was on her side, for the first person she met was Sir Richard. He was conferring with a salesperson over some Russian tomes he had ordered which had not been delivered. Katherine waited impatiently for the discussion to end, determined to speak with him. Finally he turned away to meet Katherine's beseeching eyes.

"Ah, Miss Wilde, how fortunate that we meet again," he greeted her warmly, leaving her in no doubt that he really hailed this chance encounter with pleasure.

"Yes, Sir Richard, this is an unexpected treat. I was hoping to run across you again, for I have a favor to ask of you," Katherine pleaded, her mind made up that she would lay her problems before this wise and tolerant man.

"I am at your disposal. Perhaps we might repair to a nearby cafe and discuss your favor over some coffee or chocolate," he agreed, noticing her agitation and wondering what could possibly be causing her such distress. He wanted to help her, for she appealed to him for a variety of reasons. He felt drawn to this attractive young girl who stirred memories in him which were haunting and disturbing. He wished he could tell her why he found her presence so evocative of his youth, but he hesitated to burden her.

Katherine accepted his invitation with relief, sure that she would receive a gentle hearing, and they left the bookstore together, her search for a novel forgotten.

Over their coffee and cakes she chatted brightly of her experiences of the season, strangely reluctant to begin the conversation she so desired. He was not slow to notice her hesitation.

"Come, Miss Wilde. I am sure that the on-dits of London society are not causing you pain. What was it you wanted to discuss? I promise you any confidences you give me will be held inviolate," he suggested, aware that shyness and some other emotion were preventing her from coming out with what disturbed her.

"I have tried to approach my father with my concerns, but he is not an easy man to talk to," Katherine began, soothed by Sir Richard's manner and his attitude that he had all day to listen to whatever she had to discuss.

A fleeting frown passed over Sir Richard's face, but whatever his reaction to Peter Wilde he was careful not to be censorious. "Your father appears to be a bit aloof, perhaps too occupied with financial matters to be bothered, is that it?" he asked.

"Not only that," Katherine blurted out, twisting her napking in some nervousness. "But he doesn't seem to really care for me. It's as if I was a necessary incumbrance, only suffered for what I can do to satisfy his ambitions. He wants me to make a brilliant marriage," she confessed, her luminous blue eyes shadowed with her unpalatable thoughts.

"Surely he is concerned for your future happiness," Sir Richard offered gently, unwilling to go further into any criticism of Peter Wilde.

"I would like to believe that, but the evidence convinces me otherwise. He wants me to marry Viscount Pemberton," she disclosed with a frankness which Sir Richard found endearing.

"He appears to be a likeable young man, from the little I know of him," he offered.

"Yes, I like Ronald, but I am not sure I love him," Katherine confided, "but that is not the problem." How easy it was to lay all her worries at Sir Richard's shoulders. Before she could continue he smiled at her eager to calm her fears.

"Is there someone else?" he asked.

"I am not sure, and anyway, I doubt the gentleman in question returns my feelings. He suspects me of dark doings," she said with a mild grimace. "You see, he thinks I am deep in some conspiracy to aid my father in deceiving the government. That is what I want to tell you about," she said decisively, banishing all thoughts of Simon Stafford. Then, marshalling her arguments and suspicions, she told Sir Richard about the rendezvous at the Pantheon masquerade, her encounter with the Contessa and the attack upon that mysterious lady. She went on to disclose the Foreign Office suspicions of her father and the matter of the Italian loan.

Sir Richard, not revealing that he knew all about that investigation, listened quietly, not interrupting her tale. How young and idealistic she was, how like her mother, with none of the artifices and silliness often seen in debutantes. His sympathies were engaged, and he was eager to settle her doubts.

"You have unwittingly become involved in affairs which should not concern you. I regret that, but I must warn you it is best to let the authorities discover the real truth. I doubt if any of the gentlemen involved suspect you seriously of any chicanery. You are so obviously an innocent," he reassured her. The past, which Sir Richard had thought firmly banished, now rose up, urging him to help her.

"I want to clear my father, earn his respect and gratitude, even if he feels little affection for me," Katherine insisted.

Sir Richard hesitated, wondering if he should tell her the reason he cared so deeply what happened to her. She had been honest with him. Could he do less than honor her confidences by an equal disclosure, one that might cause her pain? Sir Richard was not a man to shirk the hard choice, to avoid danger. And there was danger that if he told her the truth she would hate him, find his actions cowardly and inexplicable. He sighed. Well, he must take his chances that his revelations would not turn her against him in disgust.

"My dear, I have listened to your concerns, and am honored at your confidences. But I must tell you that we share a bond that you might find puzzling. Years ago, when I was little more than a boy, I loved your mother and I think she returned my love. Stupidly I insisted on going into the army, trying to win glory, I suppose. I was a romantic, foolish young man, eager to throw away the gold for the dross," he began, noticing that Katherine hung on his every word.

She remained silent, intent on what was coming, unwilling to interrupt with the questions which were crowding her mind.

Sir Richard continued, "I took my commission and went to the colonies to fight in American rebellion. It's too long a story but in the end, I volunteered for an assignment on the frontier. I was captured by the savages and held for more than a year and believed dead by my relations. When I was finally released and returned to civilization I learned that your mother had married Peter Wilde. I was heartbroken and angry, cursing the false promises of women, and determined never again to fall into the snares of love." he confessed ruefully, ashamed now of that illogical reaction.

Katherine waited, expecting further revelations, and Sir Richard knew he could not disappoint her. "Our parents had not favored the match, for I was a younger son, and my father had great hopes of my following a diplomatic career, for which I would need a well-dowered wife. Your mother's people, although well-born, were not wealthy. When I heard of her marriage, I was only too willing to follow my father's wishes. And soon after I was sent abroad by the government, only to learn on my return three years later that your mother had died. I never made any attempt to see her, to hear her reasons for abandoning me, and that I deeply regret," he finished, an expression of pain crossing his face. "So you see, my dear, you could have been my daughter, if I had followed my heart and married your mother before going into the army. She was of a constant nature, sweet and loyal, and no doubt I did not deserve her. Your father was a fortunate man, even if he had her for such a short time.''

Katherine, too moved to speak, was silent. Sir Richard's story explained so much. No doubt her mother had taken her father as a husband because she believed her real love was lost to her. Before she could offer any sympathy, Sir Richard suddenly surprised her with a fierce question.

"How long after their marriage were you born?'' he asked obviously stunned by a sudden shocking thought.

"Almost immediately. I believe I came early and my mother had a difficult time, so an old housekeeper told me. She never really recovered, and died when I was a small child,'' Katherine admitted, not seeing the import of Sir Richard's probing.

"I wonder . . . Oh, My God, if it were true, I will never forgive myself. Why did I never realize. . . .'' he groaned, his usual composure destroyed at the agonizing idea which had occurred to him.

Katherine, although innocent, was not ignorant of the facts of life. She gasped, understanding what was gripping Sir Richard with such a passion of regret and anger. For a few moments her sympathy for his self-loathing was paramount, but then the wider implications of what he had haltingly suggested struck her. Did he mean that he and her mother had anticipated the wedding, that he had left her pregnant when he went off to fight in the colonies? But he could not have known, that she understood. He would never have abandoned her mother so callously. Katherine was convinced that Sir Richard was not of the careless, arrogant company of womanizers who took their pleasure as they saw fit, never caring for the women they used. He loved her mother, and obviously he had been faithful to that love. Why had she not told him? In her concern for her companion's distress, Katherine did not at first comprehend what this startling news meant to her own position.

"She could not have known before you left. Surely she would have told you, and then, suddenly it was too late, and she had to contrive the best solution to her dilemma . . . marriage to my father," she said then gasped with the sudden realization that the man who had sheltered her, supported her, for so many years might not be her natural father at all. This suffering and shocked gentleman across the table from her very likely was her true parent.

Sir Richard, who despite his anguish, was perceptive and noticed at once that Katherine had grasped their situation, that this casual interview between two strangers had now become a drama of painful intensity. Putting aside his own unhappiness he hurried to assuage Katherine's distress, wanting to offer whatever comfort he could.

"Your dear mother, Amelia, must have been desperate, and turned to the only way out, a quick marriage. And your father, Peter Wilde, whom I have always despised for taking her away from me, must have loved her greatly to have made such a gesture," Sir Richard said, determined to give his erstwhile enemy the benefit of the doubt.

"Perhaps he was deceived, and did not know," Katherine suggested scornfully, upset at the dishonesty involved. She hated the thought of her mother behaving in such a manner. She should have faced her parents, suffered society's obliquity, held to her first love. Katherine believed that she herself would have been willing to face the sniggers and scorn rather than to be false to the man she loved.

Sir Richard smiled a bit wistfully, able to read the emotions on her face, reluctant to spoil her illusions, although he could not allow her to keep such an unflattering picture of her mother.

"No, Katherine, my dear, she would not have done that.

153

She would have told him. He must have loved her a great deal to have accepted another man's child as his own" he admitted with some charity.

"Yes, it must have been dreadful for him. That is why he has never given me the father's affection I craved. He could not help it, I suppose. And how galling to lose the woman he loved and be left only with her offspring, sired by another, for whom he must be responsible until some other unfortunate man took her off his hands! No wonder he is so eager to marry me off, and to the most eligible party, as some recompense for his sacrifice," she concluded bitterly.

"That is not fair, my dear. He has done his best by you, given you a good education, supported you in luxury, insured your place in a respectable society. If he could not love you as his own, I cannot find it in my heart to blame him, although I envy him the opportunity. It should have been mine, the privilege of watching you grow up into the lovely young woman you have become," he smiled at her. Katherine noticed how moved he was, with what effort he repressed the strong emotions which threatened to overwhelm him. But he managed to throw off his own grief and shouldered the responsibility of cheering Katherine, helping her to an acceptance of her new situation.

"Although I decry the long arid years of separation, I cannot but be pleased to have gained a daughter to lighten my later years, but I will quite understand if you do not want to reveal the true situation. Your father might find it humiliating, and then, too, you are his heiress. I would do nothing to endanger your position, cause you embarrassment or threaten your future. Believe me, my dear, we will go on exactly as we are, mere strangers, if that is what you decide," Sir Richard explained, feeling that he had no right to make claims on this lovely young woman whose whole life lay ahead of her.

"No, no, that will never do. If you are my father, I will be proud to acknowledge it. I care nothing for Mr. Wilde's pretensions. Perhaps that is unfair, and I should honor him for assuming an unwanted obligation, as you suggest, but to me this news is a great relief. I have always seen the lack of true feeling in our relationship. I am evidence that my mother never really cared for him as he wanted. But any announcement of our changed status would surely cause you as much embarrassment, more even, than to us. You have a sterling reputation and a distinguished career. I will not put that in jeopardy," Katherine insisted fiercely.

"So like your mother, dear girl. I can hear her saying the same thing and meaning it as resolutely as you do, but this time I will not be so irresponsible and selfish. Perhaps, for now, we must keep our silence, until you decide what is the best plan and believe me, I will abide by whatever you think best. I only want your happiness, Katherine." Sir Richard's sincerity and concern could not be doubted. After the arid fruitless years of Peter Wilde's guardianship, Katherine was at last loved by her father.

With all the harsh judgment of youth Katherine felt that once he had agreed to marry her mother, adopt her child, he should not have visited the sins of the parents on the hapless offspring. She gave no thought to how galling it must have been to a man of Peter Wilde's temperment to know that he was second best. And the noblest gesture withers under the numbing pinpricks of daily living. But if Katherine could not understand such a reaction, Sir Richard, more experienced, more tolerant, could.

"I pity him, Katherine, and I feel I must acquit him of intending cruelty when he must have suffered painful reminders whenever he looked at you."

"You are more generous than I am, sir. I cannot forgive Mr. Wilde, which is what I must call him now, if not in public at least to myself. I would have respected him more even if I could not love him, if he had told me the truth,"

"He could not do that, Katherine, and what would your response have been, noble renunciation of the luxurious life he had given you? He justified his demand that you make a fine marriage as payment for all he had done for you, although he could never explain that to you."

"Well, we must just agree to differ about that. I am not feeling charitable toward him right now," Katherine admitted. "It is quite pleasant to have a new father, one who will listen to all my problems and give me sound advice," she said more cheerfully, intent on lightening the atmosphere which had become heavy with emotion.

Sir Richard smiled "Alas, I come as a stranger to the role, but must study to do the best I can. Now I can take some steps to relive you of this latest burden, your worries about Peter Wilde's handling of the Italian loan. I will speak to some chaps I know in the Foreign Office immediately," he replied briskly, then more somberly offered a suggestion. "Think carefully about our relationship, Katherine, before you challenge Peter Wilde. We must honor your mother's decision and insure that her sacrifice was not in vain. I would love to claim you, but others must be considered. Do nothing in a sudden temper. Sleep on it, as my old nanny would advise," he suggested, hoping to bring Katherine about to a more equitable state of mind. Then he added, "Here is my direction. You must contact me if you need me for anything at all. I have a small manor house in Wiltshire where I sometimes repair when the vacuity of Whitehall becomes too tedious. But normally I am in my rooms on Curzon Street. No doubt we will meet, too, at events during this Season. I rarely accept invitations, but will do so now, to keep an eye on my daughter," he assured her, with an intimate smile that warmed Katherine.

"Thank you, sir, or should I say, father. I believe I will have to save that appellation until we are private, but just knowing of your existance has lightened all my burdens. What a fortuitious meeting at Hatchard's," Katherine said, standing to pull on her gloves and collect her reticule.

Relieved that her spirits appeared restored, Sir Richard marveled and was grateful at the resilency of the young. For himself the dilemma Katherine posed was not so easily dismissed, and he saw stormy times ahead.

Chapter Sixteen

Sir Richard's prophesy of awkward days ahead for Katherine reached fulfillment more rapidly than he could have estimated. Upon leaving Hatchard's he had secured a hackney for her, determined to escort her home since she had dismissed her maid in order to have their private conversation. When they embarked at Wigmore Street they were met by Simon Stafford, just taking his departure. He greeted them both stiffly, to Sir Richard's secret amusement. If this were the young man Katherine preferred to Ronald Pemberton he could not fault her choice, and her hint that Simon found her not to his taste seemed ill-founded. It was evident, as Simon made his bow, that he disliked the sight of Katherine's escort, although his manners were frigidly correct.

"Good morning, Miss Wilde. Your servant, Sir Richard," Simon greeted the pair, ranking them with a glance which implied he would like to send them both to the devil.

Sir Richard was gratified to see that Simon's censorious glance only set Katherine's back up, and her reply was equally cold.

"What an odd time for a call, my lord. Was there some particular matter you wished to see me about?" she asked, her blue eyes frosty and her whole demeanour one of outraged propriety. She had no difficulty in reading Simon's suspicions about her arrival with Sir Richard. Well, if he preferred to believe her a designing minx, casting out lures to a man twice her age then, he must be allowed to let his wild fancy have full rein.

"A trifling matter, of no account," Simon replied curtly, aware that he was behaving in a churlish manner but unable to help himself. "You are out very early, Miss Wilde," he added as if he hoped for some explanation.

"On such a lovely morning, I felt the need for some exercise," she replied blithely. "And I fortunately ran into Sir Richard, who has kindly escorted me home. Will you not come in, sir, and take some refreshment?" she turned to her silent bystander, pointedly excluding Simon from the invitation.

"Thank you, my dear, but I have a pressing appointment. I will call on you again soon, to see how you are going on," he promised, with a roguish twinkle in his eye which disgusted Simon and won a pretty smile from Katherine. Giving Sir Richard her hand she insisted, "I will look forward to that, sir. Thank you again, I so enjoyed our chat," she said as he bowed and bounded into the hackney with an agility which earned another frown from Simon who thought, "The old fool, acting like May when he is verging on December."

Katherine, turning a stiff back on her visitor, walked determinedly up the steps to the door, not according Simon the civility of an invitation. She knew she was behaving childishly, but was thoroughly disgruntled with his attitude. He had no right to jump to conclusions about her friendship with Sir Richard. If she could tell the truth he would feel a fool, and no more than he deserved, she concluded.

Simon, aware that Katherine was unwilling to accord him any more conversation, turned away, marching down the street to where his tiger was walking his horses and phaeton. Whatever purpose he had in calling at this early hour, he abandoned it. Katherine, although she did not turn to watch him leave, felt a pang of regret at her treatment, but then continued on her way. If Simon Stafford believed her to be a hussy, on the catch for an old, rich and indulgent husband, she would not dignify his suspicions by denying them. She gave a bitter laugh as she thought of what Sir Richard would say about this picture of him, but trusted his good sense would see the ridiculousness of Simon's belief. Well, she had no time for the arrogant Marquis. She wanted to gain the sanctuary of her room and reflect on this newest dramatic change in her life.

Simon cursed both Katherine and himself all the way to the Foreign Office where he had been called to discuss an urgent turn of events. Normally his mind would be filled with questions and curiosity about this latest concern of the government, but he was so enraged with Katherine,'s behavior after he had decided that his mistrust of her was ill-founded, that he could barely concentrate on his driving. His tiger recalled him to his duties.

"You near brushed that carriage, My Lord," he said sharply, surprised that such a notable whip could have caused an accident.

Simon growled, "Inches to spare, Richter, and I don't believe I asked your advice," he said, but he realized the reproof was merited. Damn that girl, she was driving him mad and taking up entirely too much of his valuable time. He would banish her from his senses and tend to more important business. With noble resolution he stalked into the Foreign Office prepared to volunteer for some dangerous assignment which would take him far from London and the irritating Miss Wilde.

When he entered the conference room he was disgruntled

to see that among the gentlemen gathered there to discuss this latest crisis was Sir Richard Overton. He nodded briefly to the assembled committee, headed by the Permanent Secretary, Sir Edward, and took an empty seat next to his chief, General Valentine.

"Now that you are here, my lord, we can get on with the meeting," Sir Edward reproved. He did not like using amateurs in this messy business of ferreting out traitors, but the seriousness of this current affair demanded he not make objections. He was prepared to accept any scheme which would solve the problem. Sir Edward had long experience in dealing with the intricacies of foreign affairs, and if he disliked the tools with which he must sometimes work, he was too skilled a diplomat to make his annoyance known. He put the problem tersely.

"The latest shipment of gold bullion from the Indies includes more than a score of counterfeit ingots. We have reason to think that Napoleon intends to flood the gold market with these false bars in order to depress the exchange and throw His Majesty's government into disarray. This scheme must be thwarted and the culprits brought to justice," he informed the shocked men about the table.

He waited for some comment but when none was forthcoming he continued, "This renews our suspicions of Peter Wilde. Only a banker would think up such a devious design to bring the government to point non plus," he concluded grimly. At the best of times Sir Edward distrusted financial moguls who often put expediency above patriotism. This latest scheme only deepened his gravest misgivings. He must turn to the Intelligence corps to solve the matter and that, too, went against the grain.

"What methods do you gentlemen suggest we employ to discover how this latest villany of Napoleon be frustrated?" Sir Edward asked, disgusted at being forced to such a pass.

Castlereagh, who disliked any reference to financial dealings which he did not understand, turned to Sir Richard, hoping he might throw some light on the matter.

"Overton, you have recently come from Europe. What do you think of this latest villainy?" he asked in deep perplexity.

"I think it was only to be expected that Napoleon would try some such ploy. While the truce prevents him from taking the field he has turned his attention to other methods of bringing his enemy to its knees. But I doubt that such a distinguished banker as Peter Wilde would have anything to do with such havey-cavey business. He has too much at stake," he insisted, mindful of Katherine's concerns and wondering if he had been prudent to assure her that her erstwhile father was not a traitor. "He has too much to lose if unmasked," he finished decively, although secretly wondering if his desire to save Katherine anguish was clouding his natural good sense. "What do you think, Valentine?" he asked, turning to the Intelligence chief.

"It revives all our suspicions of Wilde, there is no doubt of that, but we have to find some evidence to tie him into this dastardly attempt to bankrupt the government. There is no real proof that he is involved," he admitted.

"Do you think the governors of the Bank of England, a prosy lot to be sure, would connive at this chicanery?" Sir Edward said in a tone of mockery. "It has to be some man who has great influence on the Exchange and with the financial markets."

"What efforts have been made to discover how the gold was substituted?" Simon asked, seizing on the practicalities of the plot.

Valentine began "We have a man in the bank who is making a careful, secret check of outgoing funds, but this is a long tedious process. We need proof of Wilde's involvement. We are relying on you, Simon, with your special talents, to give us some concrete evidence. What was the result of your interview with the Contessa?'' he asked with a rather grim smile.

Simon, taken aback by this latest development, did not rise to Valentine's inference as he might have done, but answered soberly, ''She claims that she never knew who her contact was in London, and that she had no intention of doing the villains' bidding. She was gong to approach us and throw herself on our mercy. Whether we can believe her is another question, but I am inclined to think she is not a genuine conspirator. There is no doubt, from the little she told me, that there is a complicated network of Fouche's men conniving against England. Of course, she could be lying. She is terrified after this attempt on her life. I did not like badgering her,'' he concluded, realizing that his scruples would not sit well with Valentine.

He was right. Valentine summarized curtly. ''We have several other suspects besides the Contessa, whom I do not believe has the brains or stomach to plan such a complicated maneuver as upsetting the exchange. There is the mysterious Count Crespi, another whose intelligence does not appear up to the job. That leaves us with Wilde, or another of his type, a man who is au courant with financial matters. Depressing the market with counterfeit gold is a clever ruse and one that is difficult to combat,'' he finished with a sigh.

Sir Richard, listening to the options, offered his own analysis. ''I doubt that Wilde himself is involved. As I have said before he has too much to lose and little to gain, except the payment of his Italian loan, and I think he can stand to lose that. He is a very warm man. We have to consider that there is some eminence grise, a man of outward probity, even a member of the nobility, who has been seduced by the prospect of riches. And, of course, there are those who believe that Napoleon will triumph, a possibility that is not without merit,'' he said, ignoring the mutters of anger from his colleagues.

"And just how are we to winkle this traitor out, Sir Richard,'' Castlereagh asked smoothly, not at all appalled by the suggestion, for he held a very cynical view of his fellow men.

"I understand de Lisle is off to Paris. Perhaps he will be successful. He has some very useful contacts,'' Simon replied.

"Time, that's the problem. And we have this spurious truce to consider, too. His Majesty's government does not want to appear eager to break the truce, although, no doubt, that is on the cards,'' Sir Edward said. "Our ambassador, Lord Whitworth, reports that Napoleon is working himself into a calculated rage, implying that England is conspiring against him when all he desires is peace.''

"It's not an attractive idea, Stafford, but you must pursue your advantages with both the Contessa and Miss Wilde, hoping they will betray some valuable information. Not a pleasant assignment, but necessary, I think. We might not be so furtunate as to discover the next shipment of counterfeit bullion, and then there is the possibility that the French might try to flood the market with false notes, another frightening ploy,'' Valentine suggested.

"I doubt that Miss Wilde is a conspirator. She seems to be exactly what she appears, an innocent debutante engaged in the Season,'' Sir Richard explained, winning a frown from Simon, who wondered why Sir Richard was so eager to excuse Kate, and what his real interest was in the girl. Well, distasteful as it might be, he would wring the truth out of her at all costs.

The meeting adjourned with little accomplished, and the men dispersed at their various duties, Sir Richard walking out with Simon, who did not welcome his company. He could not ignore the man without appearing rude, but he did not want to hear about Sir Richard's interest in Kate. Still, it might lead to some revelations.

"Do you not share my belief in Miss Wilde's innocence, Stafford?" Sir Richard asked as they passed on the steps of the building. He was secretly amused at Simon's farouche expression, and wondered if the young man might care more for his daughter than he realized.

"I would like to, but the evidence favors her guilt, I believe," he growled, but then remembering his distaste of Sir Richard's interest in Kate, he could not forbear adding, "I was not aware that you were in Miss Wilde's confidence. Perhaps she has been more forthright with you than she has with me, sir." If Sir Richard has not suspected Simon's remarks sprang from jealousy he might easily have taken umbrage, but his only reaction was to smile sympathetically at the confused young man.

"I find Miss Wilde a very unusual young woman, with a rare talent for friendship as well as a superior understanding. "You do not share my view?" Sir Richard asked, unable to resist provoking his companion.

"She's a dammned annoying baggage," Simon answered, now thoroughly irritated, feeling that Sir Richard was laughing at him from a position of superiority. He did not like the idea which sprang to his mind, that in Sir Richard he had a real rival. Then dismissing this picture with scorn, for after all, he had no serious intentions toward the girl, he bade Sir Richard a curt farewell, aware that he had cut a poor figure before the older man.

Sir Richard, distracted by the inconclusive interview with the Foreign Office gentlemen, decided that any attempts to explain matters to Simon Stafford would have to wait for a more propitious moment, and took himself off to White's for a period of reflection.

Of more import to him, for the first time in his distinguished career, than the problems of the government, were personal affairs which needed careful consideration before he took any decisive action. A great deal depended on Kate's decision and he feared that she intended to confront Wilde with her new knowledge. That could create problems for them all and he did not need to discover that Wilde was implicated in treasonable activity to add to their dilemma. He doubted that Valentine and his men would unmask the traitors in time to influence his own reactions or help Kate. He would just have to take a hand himself, for he had some rather startling ideas as to who might have organized this plot against His Majesty's government.

Sir Richard was quite right to fear Kate's impulsive confrontation with Peter Wilde. She had every intention of facing him with her newly acquired knowledge. Fortunately he was not available, for in the first flush of her awareness that he was not her father, she might have behaved with more passion than wisdom. As she paced the floor of her bedroom, digesting her changed situation, she realized that she must approach him warily. She *did* owe him some loyalty, and was still convinced he was not part of the conspiracy which Simon Stafford was investigating. Of that young man she refused to think, for she had quite enough to digest already.

Sir Richard had left the decision to her, promising to support whatever she decided. Her initial instinct was to ride pell mell to Lombard Street and face Wilde in his place of business, but on more sober reflection she realized little would be served by that dramatic move. He might deny all knowledge of her true parentage. On the other hand he might be relieved and decide to wash his hands of her. But, then, what of her future?

Sir Richard's career would be ruined by a scandal, and he would find it difficult to suddenly take on the responsibility

166

of a daughter, no matter how willing he appeared. She must have some plan in the event Wilde cast her off, rid finally of a duty he must have found onerous. But did he know the truth? Despite what Sir Richard had claimed about her mother's honesty, Katherine was not so certain that she had told Wilde the truth before they wed. Such a confession would imply a courage few young women would possess.

Would she be cruel to tell him if he did not already know? But surely he did not know. What else would explain his indifferent treatment of her? Probably he had promised to raise Katherine as his own, in the full flush of his passion for her mother, although Katherine had difficulty in picturing the austere Peter Wilde in such a state. Then her mother died, and he was forced to continue the charade. Did he then decide to use her for his own ends? Did he so ardently desire a place in the ton? Perhaps this was a subtle form of revenge on the woman who took him as second best, on the father who would never know his child. What a tortutous scheme, but one not beyond Peter Wilde's contriving.

Kate realized she was being unfair. She owed her erstwhile father some loyalty, and if not love, at least some tolerance. However, she did not know him well enough to understand his motives or his possible reactions to a personal crisis. He appeared to be a man to whom deception came easily. Simon Stafford's imputations could have some basis. He could be a traitor, although that surely would put paid to his social ambitions. What was she to believe?

Her head was awhirl with conflicting emotions. Katherine usually had no trouble in making up her mind. But this crisis, the most serious in her young life, left her bewildered and unsure. She was relieved when Mrs. Basingbroke's arrival was announced. Her chaperone had arrived to take tea and preside over Kate's "at home" afternoon. Katherine must appear calm, play the role of a hostess with little on her mind but dancing parties and gowns. Kate straightened her shoulders, a glint of determination in her eye. She had forgone luncheon, spent fruitless hours searching for some solution to her dilemma. Well, she had decided on one matter. She would allow no man, no event, to guide her fate. Whatever lay in store, she would be the one directing her life, for good or ill.

Chapter Seventeen

It was a perfect summer day and the carefree party of young people who set out for a picnic in Richmond appeared to be in high spirits. The expedition had been Ronald Pemberton's idea, broached at Katherine's "at home", where Simon and Count Crespi had also been among the guests. Hoping that Kate might look favorably upon his suit in the sylvan setting of Richmond's Great Park, Ronald had invited her on the outing, but was quickly thwarted by the insistence of Crespi and Stafford that they be included. Katherine, believing there was safety in numbers, had agreed. Eventually, a few other couples had been asked to join the group, properly chaperoned by Mrs. Basingbroke, so that several phaetons and two closed carriage cantered in tandem down the turnpike to Richmond.

Katherine looked fetching in a riding dress of cherry red, faced in white with a froth of ruffles at the neck and sleeves and a dashing straw hat tied with cherry ribbons from which her dark curls peeped enticingly. If she appeared a bit pale, the ride soon restored color to her cheeks and banished the shadows beneath her blue eyes. She had chosen to ride with

Count Crespi, feeling unable to cope with Ronald's soulful glances and his intention of renewing his proposal.

Simon Stafford had invited a dashing blonde to accompany him and they were getting along famously, Katherine noticed as the couples made their dispositions. Although she found the Count's fulsome attentions rather wearying, she did not signify her irritation and smiled vaguely at his compliments in a manner both Ronald and Simon found bothersome. Ronald scowled at all and threatened to cast a pall of gloom over the proceedings, but by the time they had reached the picnic site, his spirits had lightened. Katherine, relieved to have temporarily distracted her cavaliers, hurried to her chaperone's side and insisted on sitting by that amused lady during the al fresco meal.

If she had hoped that Simon would make some push to engage her in conversation she was disappointed, for he distributed his favors generously among the other young women in the party and eventually wandered off with one of them to see if there were any fish in the pond. Count Crespi, a skilled campaigner in such matters, took his congé with good grace and entertained some of the company with the latest on-dits of society, causing some shocked exclamations and general delight. This abandonment of his target gave Ronald the chance he was waiting for and he insisted that Kate stroll with him away from the revelers. Seeing there was no help at hand, Katherine agreed with as good a grace as possible, but determined to depress his interest once and for all. She would not marry Ronald Pemberton, even if she went to her grave a spinster. That Simon Stafford had influenced this decision she was honest enough to admit to herself, although she was disgusted that she could care for a man who treated her so mercurially.

Out of sight of the party, Ronald Pemberton hurried to renew his proposal.

"Katherine, I have been most patient, you must agree, but I cannot see you luring all these other fellows into your net without feeling deuced jealous. Crespi is the veriest bounder, and I cannot believe you are interested seriously in him," he complained, squeezing her hand in an excess of emotion.

Katherine found Ronald more than tedious but smiled at him gently, unwilling to cause him more hurt. She wanted to spare him another rejection, but they could not continue in this fashion.

"Dear Ronald, you have been most faithful. And I am convinced you would make a good husband, only I am not the girl for you. I have given your proposal serious consideration, for I find you well mannered and generally a good companion, but that is not enough on which to base a lifetime. I would dislike exceedingly to lose you as a friend, but friendship is all I can offer you," she said in a pleading tone, hoping to avert a scene which would increase the burden of care she was shouldering. She did not need the responsibility of coping with Ronald's hurt and disappointment along with her other problems. If only he would accept her refusal as definite, but she knew he had made up his mind to press her.

"Really, Katherine, I cannot understand you. I have done my best to behave in a circumspect manner, courting you with all the courtesies young women expect. You have treated me badly, leading me on one moment, then turning a cold shoulder the next. You are in danger of gaining a reputation of a flirt," he answered angrily. He saw his last hope of winning this girl fading rapidly, as well as his last hope of soothing his father's rage and frustration with him. Somehow Ronald believed that gaining Katherine as a wife would settle all the Wexford's many problems, although he was

171

decent enough to admit that her money was not her only attraction.

"Ronald, that is not fair. I told you some time ago that I did not want to marry you, but you persisted in trying to force me to change my mind. Badgering me will not do the trick. Now come, admit we would not suit, that my rackety ways would soon annoy you. What might be attractive in a dancing partner would not do as the wife of the heir to the Wexford title. Your father would much prefer you to wed within your own circle, and I greatly fear it is Peter Wilde's assets rather than my charms which is the magnet. You would be much better to look at Mary Willoughby-Gore, for example. She is quite attracted to you, and a charming girl with impeccable breeding and heiress to her father, the Earl of Courtland. I noticed her sending you distinct lures today," Katherine teased, hoping to soothe Ronald's self esteem. she had noticed Lady Willoughby-Gore's languishing glances at Ronald, and thought she would do very well for him.

"She's a ninny, and has no conversation. How can you suggest I would even consider such a match when you know I am devoted to you," Ronald protested, a sulky but calculating look in his eye. Katherine rightly interpreted this as his considering Mary Willoughby-Gore's rent roll. Ronald liked his comforts and his position too much to sacrifice them for love. If he knew, that she might not inherit millions, she doubted that he would continue his pursuit with such ardor. She might be maligning him, but Katherine had little use for romantic follies and did not delude herself that he was uninterested in the Wilde fortune. His father would never consent to a match not to Ronald's advantage, no matter how violent his heart stirrings. He saw himself as conferring a great honor upon her, the daughter of a pretending Cit, and could not understand his rejection. She sighed. Why was it

172

the man she wanted distrusted her, while the man who wanted her was so unworthy? She turned away, signifying to Ronald that she wished to return to the company, but he would have none of that.

"By God, Katherine, you try my patience. I will not allow you to treat me so. You need a lesson in conduct, my girl," he said in what he believed was masterful fashion designed to display his power. Before she could argue, he had taken her roughly into his arms and was trying ineffectually to press a kiss on her averted face. She struggled against his arms, then seeing no other recourse but to give him a resounding box on his ears, forcing him to release her. Before he could recover himself he heard the sardonic drawl of his rival, Simon Stafford.

"It seems the lady is reluctant, Pemberton. Really, it's not the thing to press your embraces on a struggling female. But if you must, be sure to secure her hands so that she can not land a decisive blow," Simon mocked, looking at the pair in disapproval. And well he should. Katherine was trying to restore her disheveled locks and retie her bonnet while Ronald was only too aware of the sorry picture he made under the reddening effects of her blow.

"I fail to see that this contretemps is any business of yours, sir," Ronald responded in what he hoped was a haughty tone. Really, he was foolish to bandy words with Simon Stafford, that cool arrogant customer. Katherine did not know which of the two she disliked more at that moment, Ronald for placing her in this position, or Simon for viewing her discomfort. She tossed her head in anger.

"You are both impossible creatures, and I will remove myself before any further embarrassments occur," she said in a passion, turning her back on them and preparing to flee the scene of the disaster.

"Now, Kate, don't lose your temper. Poor Pemberton

here was only trying to reinforce his very honorable proposal, and my intention was not to cause you embarrassment but rescue you from an uncomfortable situation. And
what thanks do I get? You doubt my sincere efforts.'' Simon mocked, successfully masking the real anger he had
felt at glimpsing Kate struggling in Ronald's arms. What
he really wanted to do was to take the puppy by the scruff
of the neck and give him a good drubbing, but he could
not create that kind of a scene within earshot of the other
guests.

Katherine ignored Simon's offer of escort, aware that she
had behaved like a shrew. Furious with Ronald, Simon and
with her own handling of the situation, she wanted only
to consign both men to the devil and retreat to some sanctuary for a good cry. Of course, that was not possible, so
she marched back to Mrs. Basingbroke's side and remained
firmly anchored to that comforting lady for the rest of the
afternoon, refusing to glance at either of her recent tormen-
tors.

Ronald, with a defiant look in Katherine's direction
which she ignored, made a great play of flirting with Mary
Willoughby-Gore, who responded with flattering attention,
soothing his hurt pride. Simon, whatever his reactions to
the scene he had interrupted, gave no evidence that he was
not enjoying the party, chatting not only with the fetching
blonde but with all and sundry, angering Kate even more
by his imperturbability and the knowledge that she had
behaved in a hoydenish fashion sure to repell a discriminat-
ing gentleman.

It would have eased Katherine's chagrin if she had known
that Simon's apparent indifference to her hid a deep awareness and depressing realization that he had acted the veritable cad. He was not prepared to make a declaration yet
he disliked the idea of Kate accepting any other honorable

offer. This excess of possessiveness toward the vexing girl enfuriated him, but he could not decide whether his concealed anger was with Kate for luring other gentlemen into her toils or with himself for behaving in such an unexpected fashion.

As the party prepared to leave for town he had just about decided to try to make his peace with Kate when he was intercepted by Count Crespi. With insight gained through vast experience with women, the Count had noticed Katherine's return from her walk with Pemberton and was in no doubt that she had rebuffed the young man. He decided that it was the occasion to make his own move. He approached her with that caressing smile which had proved so effective in earlier conquests and urged her to make the return journey with him.

"I could not help but notice, cara, that you are more than a little distrait, perhaps annoyed with a certain importuning young man. It has been my experience that Englishmen lack the delicate touch. They do not treat ladies with the deference they deserve," he suggested sympathetically.

Katherine, throughly out of sorts, found the Count's understanding soothing. He might be a charlatan, a fortune hunter, a womanizer, even a conspirator, but at least he served as a distraction from her thoughts. If she had been tempted to rebuff his interest as he deserved she changed her mind. That her decision was affected by the sight of Ronald escorting Mary Willoughby-Gore toward his phaeton and Simon absorbed by the delectable blonde, she would not admit. Her other choice was to accompany Mrs. Basingbroke in the closed carriage, which would certainly increase her headache. Katherine accepted the Count's invitation with a defiant smile.

"How kind, Count. I would enjoy the ride. It is much

too delightful a day to be cooped up in a carriage. Thank you," she replied, allowing him to take her arm.

Mrs. Basingbroke, who had noticed the undercurrents developing, had seen Katherine return in a pet from her walk with Ronald, quickly followed by Simon, and felt it was time to intercede. Who knew what folly the impetuous girl might entertain?

"Perhaps it would be wiser to come with me, my dear. I don't think you are feeling quite the thing?" she suggested, tossing off the suggestion in a negligent manner while shaking out her skirts and looking about for her reticule. Charming as she found the Count, she did not entirely approve of him as an escort for Katherine.

"Oh, Mrs. B., all the ladies are riding back with their various escorts I am sure no harm will come to me with Count Crespi, unless of course, you require my company," she added.

"Not at all, Katherine. I am sure Count Crespi will take the utmost care of you," she answered, giving that gentleman an admonitory look which he returned with a reassuring smile. He was accustomed to dealing with watchful duennas.

"Of course, madam. I am honored by your trust in me," he replied gallantly, hiding his amusement. He had sensed the warning in the older woman's tone.

As the company prepared to make its departure, Simon, was not prepared to let his quarry escape so easily. He approached the pair just as they were departing.

"I do think it is unfair of you, Crespi, to have the pleasure of Kate's company on the homeward journey. You drove her out and must not be allowed yet another opportunity to enjoy her charms," he quipped, with a steely light in his eyes which the Count rightly interpreted as a challenge.

"I believe it is the privilege of the lady to make the choice of her escort," he responded, reluctant to cede his advantage, but somewhat intimidated by Simon's proprietary air.

"Not in this case," Simon said arrogantly, pulling Katherine toward his phaeton and leaving the rejected Count behind.

"Really, my lord, you are behaving in quite a gothic fashion, and quite rude to the Count besides," Katherine protested but somewhat curious as to what his sudden need for her company might portend.

"Not as rude as I would like to be. And you, my girl, need a stern talking to. What do you mean by encouraging that popinjay to make a cake of you? Mrs. Basingbroke surely has warned you of his ineligibility," he growled, throwing her up into his phaeton with a certain ruthlessness.

"Certainly. Just as she has warned me about you. Not that I needed that advice," Katherine replied curtly, prepared for a real brangle. Simon Stafford's attitude puzzled her. He did not appear to want her himself but he disliked the idea of her encouraging other, more amenable gentlemen.

"If we are going to fight, Kate, by all means I am ready to take you on, but at least wait until we have put some space between the rest of the company and ourselves. Surely you do not want them to see you raking me up?" he teased, in a much better mood now that he had gained his desire.

"I don't intend to say another word to you. You are completely out of bounds and deserve no other courtesy from me," Katherine answered, her cheeks flushing. She discovered to her dismay that she enjoyed arguing with Simon more than listening to the charming compliments of more obliging men.

"Ah, but if we all got what we deserved in life, how depressing it would be," Simon agreed, signifying that he quite understood the reason for her pique. He slanted a quick look at her, finding her stormy face and sparkling eyes quite enchanting. Kate in a temper was even more appealing than when in a more equable mood. None of the simpering wide-eyed admiration of the usual beauties, and certainly a challenge. But was it one he wanted to accept? As Kate's anger increased, Simon's lessened, and he was tempted to forget the scold he had intended to give her.

Her lips set in a line of disapproval, Katherine bit back whatever rejoiner she intended to make. She would not dignify this arrogant lord with an explanation of her behaviour, nor listen to his strictures. Who was he to give her lessons in deportment?

"I take it from your silence that you intend to sulk for the remaining miles home. Well, my charming termagant, you will listen to me at any rate. If you continue to play ducks and drakes with the likes of Count Crespi, Sir Richard Overton, and poor Pemberton, you will find yourself without a single decent offer. You might believe that your fortune excuses all but believe me, that is not the case," he fumed, furious that Kate should ignore him and unaware that he was revealing more than he realized.

Kate was not slow to understand that Simon Stafford might actually be jealous of her preference for other men. Well, it would do him good to feel that, and she continued to smile enigmatically and enjoy his frustration. Seeing that he would get no reaction to his lectures, Simon gave up, furious that Kate should treat him so when he had her reputation and well being at heart, or so he deceived himself. He had meant to apologize for his behaviour during the scene with Pemberton and gently advise her that her present actions could be misconstrued but somehow with Kate he always put the wrong foot forward. They rode the intervening miles in silence, both feeling misjudged and ill-used, and by the time they arrived at Wigmore Street seething with repressed emotions.

Katherine scuttled down from the phaeton, ignoring Simon's helping hand, gave him a black look from her wide blue eyes, and a cold thank you, marched up the steps of her home. She left behind a very frustrated gentleman, who had no recourse but to lash up his horses. If he hadn't been so conscious of propriety he would have pulled her into his arms and kissed her senseless. But some remmnant of sense prevented him from such an assault on the open street. He could not know that Kate might have welcomed that release of their common emotions.

Chapter Eighteen

George Lang had been biding his time. If Katherine accepted Ronald Pemberton's proposal of marriage, his own chances of achieving his ambition would fly out the window. There was a possibility that Peter Wilde, whose ambitions equalled Lang's own, would insist on this desirable match and ignore the threat of blackmail. However, as long as Katherine remained unable to make up her mind and resistant to her father's coertion his hopes remained alive.

Love was a foreign emotion to George Lang, and though he found Katherine attractive the considerable assets, both social and economic, she would bring to the union tempted him more than her beauty. As the days passed and Pemberton's suit did not seem to prosper, Lang was convinced he would win in the end. He believed that Katherine could be induced to look favorably upon him, and was careful to treat her with the most obliging courtesy. However, Wilde's fear of the letter exposing him to further investigations of the Foreign Office was his chief card.

Katherine's feelings did not really enter into his calculations. He was well aware that marriage was the only solution to young women in Katherine's position and flattered himself that he would serve as well as some decadent peer to fulfill that role. Normally a clever reader of men's motives and desires, he had no real understanding of volatile and independent females, so in his ignorance he did not despair. But he was not prepared to wait indefinetely. After several outings with Katherine and those assiduous attentions which marked his interest he decided to put his proposal to her.

He chose an afternoon when he knew Peter Wilde would be occupied with a meeting at Lombard Street and presented himself at the Wilde mansion. Katherine received him kindly, wondering why Wilde's assistant found it necessary to call. She was not long left in doubt.

"Good afternoon, Mr. Lang. And what can I do for you?" she asked, indicating that he might sit opposite her on a settee in the morning room, which she preferred to the more formal drawing room for receiving callers.

"I hope quite a good deal, Miss Wilde," he answered in an attempt at jollity which did not sit well on his stern features.

Katherine smiled, a bit impressed by his solemn demeanor but wondering why he was looking so grave. Was he about to confide in her about some suspect behaviour on the part of Wilde? She had been so occupied with her questions about her erstwhile father's complicity in treason that she had not given any attention to Lang's effort at developing a relationship. At first she barely heard Lang's preliminary address, but was recalled to the moment by his mention of Ronald Pemberton.

"Your father has told me of his ardent wish that you wed Viscount Pemberton, but I have not yet heard of any announcement. Have you decided to accept the Viscount?" he asked a bit baldly.

Katherine, startled and not a bit pleased by Lang's effrontry answered coldly, "I cannot see that my decision is any business of yours Mr. Lang. Unless, of course, you are here as an emissary of my father's, but even so . . ." she broke off seeing the expression on Lang's face.

"You cannot be so blind as not to see that I hold you in great admiration, Katherine," he began boldly, undeterred by her cold stare, "and I do have your father's permission to speak to you. I ardently wish you to be my wife, and hope that you will look on my proposal with some charity," he finished, with not quite the assurance he would have wished in view of her shocked response.

"I have not been mindful of any regard except that of friendship from my father's employee, Mr. Lang, and cannot understand where you have gathered the notion that such a proposal would be acceptable to me," Katherine said in her haughtiest tones. She did not scorn the young man for his humble background but she found his suggestion unwelcome and surprising. And he had stated that he had her father's permission.

What had happened to Peter Wilde's social ambitions, his cherished wish that she become the wife of Ronald Pemberton or some other notable sprig of London society? Suddenly, a wicked suspicion crossed her mind. Could George Lang be in a position to insist that Peter Wilde consent to such an outrageous marriage?

Lang appeared to lose some of his coolness, as he retorted, "You have to marry someone, and I would make a much better husband than one of these rubbishy peers that impress your father. They, no doubt, would spend your money, be unfaithful, and immure you in their country estates while they desported themselves among all the vices of town." He spoke agitatedly, seeing his chances of success fading before Katherine's implacable rejection.

"And do you have no designs on my supposed fortune?"

Katherine asked cynically. If George Lang had professed a hopeless romantic love for her she might have dealt more kindly with him, but he appeared to be no less interested in financial gain than Ronald or any other gazetted fortune hunter, and far less attractive than some of that company. She waited uneasily for him to make further explanations.

Thoroughly angered by Katherine's scornful appraisal of him, Lang lost his usual composure and blurted out the threat he had meant to hold in reserve. "I have it in my power to cause your father great embarrassment, if not criminal prosecution," he said smugly, as if that settled the matter.

"If you indeed have such a power, I suggest you implement it, *if* you can reconcile with your conscience such ingratitude to the man who has promoted your welfare and trusts you," Katherine replied in chilling tones.

So she was right. Lang had some hold over her father, and she was to be the victim of his blackmail. Whatever loyalty she might have felt toward Wilde, it did not include sacrificing her life to save him from justified prosecution. If he had behaved treasonably he must pay the price, she decided ruthlessly. Years of indifference and lack of affection from Wilde had now borne their bitter fruit. Katherine could only marvel that Wilde, so astute, so clever, had allowed himself to be deceived by this encroaching young man. She was furious with Wilde, with Lang, and with the situation in which she found herself. How dare these men believe she was a pawn to be moved helplessly upon their orders?

"Do you want to see your father in the dock?" Lang sneered, taken aback at the reception his words had received. It had never occurred to him that Katherine might defy her father and risk the loss of her inheritance.

Enraged, she replied, "If that is where he belongs due to improper conduct, then he will find himself there despite any efforts of mine to prevent it. And I only hope you will be beside him. I cannot imagine why you have made this outrageous attempt to compel me to do your bidding by holding such a threat over my head. You have my permission to withdraw, Mr. Lang, and I hope you will understand why you will not, in future, be welcomed in this house."

"As you will, Miss Wilde, but I suggest that your father might advise a more cooperative attitude and you would do well to heed his words," he replied, gaining control of his temper with some difficulty. Then, as if he could not restrain himself, "I would like the taming of you, my girl. You need some lessons in obedience," he growled, preparing to leave.

"But not from you, Mr. Lang. Goodbye." She turned her back on her hateful suitor, and heard the slam of the door with relief. But her mind was awhirl with questions brought about by this strange encounter. She would challenge her father that very day, for affairs between them must be settled, and if what Lang had threatened were true the sooner she knew where she stood the better.

She remembered with horror that her so-called father was her legal guardian and had certain rights over her person. He might try to compel her either to wed the odious Mr. Lang or some other equally repellant claimant. He might abandon her, throw her from the house.

Any of these actions were preferable to the state of indecision and cold antipathy she felt existed now. She did not want to hate Peter Wilde, but he was fast placing her in a position where she entertained the most heinous suspicions about him. If he was a traitor and intended to insure his own safety by giving her to George Lang, he was in for a battle, one which she had no intention of losing.

However, she must face Wilde with some ammunition, and her first inclination was to seek out Sir Richard and ask his advice. To invite him to call upon her here would incur Wilde's wrath, and would put Sir Richard in an embarrassing position. Although anger spurred her to take some pre-cipitate action she realized she must lay her plans carefully. She dashed off a note to Sir Richard, asking his permission to call upon him that very day. She doubted that Lang would inform Wilde of her rejection of his proposal but she must be prepared. As if summoned by her thoughts, the butler announced the arrival of the Marquis. He swept in and in-formed her that he had come to take her riding in the Park, and would accept no refusal.

"But I cannot go. I am expecting . . ." she began, think-ing of the desperate note she had just dispatched to Sir Rich-ard.

"Whatever, or more probably, whomever you are expect-ing will just have to wait," Simon said grimly. He was not pleased at his reception. In the few days since the disastrous picnic at which they had quarreled he had not been able to accomplish anything. Neither work nor an uncharacteristic resort to the bottle had managed to erase that exchange of bitter words from his mind. He had come to apologize and seek some sort of truce but her cool greeting did not promise well. Still, he refused to be dissuaded from his purpose.

"Come, Kate, put on your bonnet and let us go. It's a lovely day, just the tonic to banish your megrims," he in-sisted pleasantly.

For a moment Katherine resisted, but she yearned to put all her problems to one side, to revel in Simon's company and forget reality. "Oh, all right. You are most persuasive, my lord."

"And do stop calling me 'my lord' in that missish way. It is most off-putting," he replied, determined to get to the bottom of what was troubling her. If he could manage to discover that he suspected he might have the answers to his own dilemma.

They set off for their ride in charity with one another.

185

Simon apologized for his farouche humor at the picnic and Kate accepted his explanation, pleased that he had made the overture. With their past differences behind them they chatted easily, but behind their outward rapport lay all the questions which had caused their previous disagreements. Simon refused to quarrel, and Kate, exhausted from the recent encounter with Lang and his threats, was tempted to confide in him.

"Simon, I know you are involved in the investigation of my father," she stumbled a bit over the last word. With her new knowledge it was difficult for her to continue calling Peter Wilde by that name.

"Well, I suppose you would have discovered that. You have an uncanny ability to wrest my secrets from me," he admitted whimsically.

"Not all of them. I have just learned that you might have some basis for your suspicions of his transactions, but I do not believe he is the culprit. I have learned that George Lang is not the loyal employee I have believed him to be. I think Father puts too much trust in him," she confided a bit tentatively.

If Simon was surprised at this introduction of a new conspirator, he did not evidence it. He disliked probing, especially since Kate had adopted a softer mood, but he put his scruples behind him. "Has he given you some reason to think he might be involved in dark doings, Kate?" he asked gently, turning to look at her at his side. Her mouth drooped down in a sad expression which troubled him. He hated to see her so worried, so upset by events which should not darken her young life. Peter Wilde had much to answer for, he thought, drawing Kate into his torturous ploys.

"Well, if you can call a proposal of marriage a reason, yes, he has," she said, surprised at her wish to confide in

186

Simon, She felt the urge to have him as an ally in the dilemma which she faced.

"Have you given him any reason to suspect that such effrontry would be welcome?" Simon growled, furious that Kate should be exposed to the badgering of a mere counterjumper.

"Of course not," Katherine replied in righteous indignation. "He insists he had my father's permission to pay his addresses and further, I gather that he has some hold over him. I had no idea he was that type of man. I thought he was completely trustworthy. My father appeared to admire him exceedingly. I don't understand it. The only reason he could have entertained this outrageous idea is because my father fears him in some way," she concluded.

"When thieves fall out . . ." Simon murmured, deep in thought. This put a whole new complexion on affairs. Evidently Peter Wilde had to give his assent to a situation he must have deplored, for Simon was in no doubt that the merchant banker would not normally have approved of the match.

"You mean that father is embroiled in some nefarious plot and that Lang is his henchman and could betray him?" She was aghast at this revelation and her own stupidity.

But Simon, who knew a bit more of financial dealings than Kate, was not so certain than Wilde's agreement was based on treachery. There were other reasons for his eagerness not to antagonize his employee. He might have dodged too near the edge of legality in his dealings, affairs which had no connection with Napoleon's efforts to disrupt his enemy's economy. In building his financial empire Wilde could easily have committed some breach of the law; Lang knew of it and was prepared to use it for his own ends. Of course, the young man could just have easily have fallen in love with

Kate. Simon could understand that even if he could not condone the villain badgering her to assent to his offer.

"You refused him, I take it," he countered lightly, wishing to buy some time to think over this latest news.

"Naturally. I had thought he was an agreeable man, polite, and fairly personable. I rather admired his ability to rise from lowly status to a position of some responsibility, but I never dreamed he aspired. . . ." she broke off, unable to utter what his thoughts must have been.

"Quite," Simon agreed, stifling his anger at the thought of Kate being used in such a deplorable fashion. There was much here that was not explained. "What are you going to do?" he asked.

"Confront my father and discover what hold Lang has over him that would allow him to consent to be blackmailed, or rather allow me to be," Kate replied quickly. She was tempted to mention that she had enlisted Sir Richard Overton's assistance, but realized it would be wiser not to introduce yet another character into this drama. And she could not tell him of her real relationship with the diplomat without his permission.

"Do you think that is wise?" Simon offered, in deep thought. "Here, let us stop for a moment. I can't think properly while driving these mettlesome beasts," he said with little evidence that his horses were causing him trouble. But Kate was willing to dismount and continue their discussion under easier circumstances.

Simon tethered his cattle to a nearby tree and they settled onto a convenient bench. He had mastered his feelings of fury at the thought of Kate marrying Lang and was prepared to talk the matter over calmly, but he realized that underneath his facade of friendly concern he hated the idea of Kate marrying a jumped-up Cit to save her father from prosecution. Surely no right-minded man would ask such a sacrifice

188

of his daughter. That his own desires entered into the matter must be placed to one side for the moment.

"Look, Kate. Promise me you will do nothing for the moment. There is more here than you realize. And you could be placing yourself in some danger," he said seriously, taking her hand in his and pressing it gently to assure her of his concern.

"You have said that before. Why are you so certain that father is involved in treason? What proof do you have?" she asked, impressed with his sincere protestations. Her inclination was to trust Simon, but was that because she found him so attractive. Was she again making a mistake in her assessment of a man's character?

Looking into her beseeching eyes, Simon discovered he could no longer deny the strength of his feelings. She maddened him, fought him, and when suddenly all her defences were down, inspired in him a tenderness which disarmed him. All he was prepared to do was tell her of his affection, his willingness to help her in this current crisis which could affect her whole life.

"Listen, Kate, you must trust me in this matter. I promise I will protect you from Wilde or Lang and whatever they plan. You shall not be sacrificed to their dubious designs. Do you rely on me to discover just what their motives are, how deeply involved they may be in illegal activities? Even if they should be unmasked and you lose everything?"

Katherine wanted to trust Simon, to tell him that Wilde was not her father, but she hesitated. Confused, unhappy, she had reason to doubt every man now. And she would not be betrayed by her growing feeling for Simon if what he felt for her was a passing attraction. He, too, might wish to use her for her own ends.

"I would like to trust you, Simon, but I have discovered

189

I am not a good judge of character," she admitted sorrowfully.

"It is not my character which concerns me, Kate, but this unaccountable emotion you evoke in me," Simon said almost desperately, and then before she could move away from him, reject him, he took her roughly in his arms and kissed her with an unexpected passion. As she seemed to respond, his ardor increased, deepening the kiss when Kate appeared to welcome it. Mastering his desire before it could completely overset him, he put her gently aside.

"I did not mean to do that, Kate. Forgive me. You are in no case to receive the advances from yet another predatory male," he excused himself, inwardly cursing. Why had he kissed her? Now she would never trust him. But to his surprise she did not appear angry, only thoughtful. He could not know she realized she loved Simon Stafford and had no reason to expect he returned her feelings in the way she wanted. Suddenly she could bear no more.

"I must go home, Simon. Please take me, and speak no more of this latest problem. I will have to make some difficult decisions," she insisted, placing a pleading hand on his arm, her huge blue eyes begging him to forebear any argument.

Almost as dazed as Kate by the force of emotion, Simon nodded in agreement and escorted her to the carriage. Their ride back to Wigmore Street was made in silence, each of them busy with their thoughts, and neither ready for more confidences. Only when they reached Kate's home did Simon signify that he was not prepared to leave matters in this inconclusive state.

Belive me, Kate, I care about your welfare, and want to protect you. Send for me if you need my help," he said, looking at her with concern. He hated leaving her to what he knew was a situation which would try her to the utmost. But at least he had some evidence now to present to Valentine. He hoped she did not believe he had cozened her to reveal more than she meant. He was ashamed of his behavior and yearned to put their relationship on a different, more intimate footing. But caution surfaced, and he bid her farewell with no more than a reassuring smile.

street to behind. She was walking his horses and placated
whatever these two young ... as though they only now ...
on her horse? Yet with ... distraction these ... Dave
was in the window. Pat tucked ... so and in it, in the ...
was the picture of a young girl ...

Chapter Nineteen

Katherine decided She could postpone the confrontation with Peter Wilde no longer. Events were conspiring to force her into decisive action. On the return from her ride with Simon she was disappointed to learn that Sir Richard Overton had not replied to her urgent summons. Perhaps he had been called out of town. She could not believe he would not answer her plea for a meeting. Well, she would just have to handle this on her own. George Lang's proposal and her suspicions of his villainy demanded that Peter Wilde make some explanations. Whether she would challenge him with her knowledge that he was not her natural father would depend on how the interview developed. She was dining at home that evening, and for once, Mrs. Basingbroke was not joining them. It seemed the perfect opportunity to have this discussion, and Katherine prepared what she would say carefully, hoping that she would be able to present her case dispassionately, without losing her temper.

Dinner was a rather subdued meal. Obviously, Peter Wilde had a matter of some moment on his mind, and his replies to her polite conversation were brusque and indifferent. He did not ask her about Ronald, for which she was grateful, nor did he appear interested in her social engagements. After the syllabub was removed, barely tasted, for neither of them had an appetite that evening, Katherine took a deep breath and plunged into her request.

"Father, I would like to talk to you about an important matter," she said bravely, her large blue eyes serious, her chin determined. If he had any intention of fobbing her off with some excuse she would not entertain it. And, at first, it seemed as if he had just such an intention.

"Really, Katherine, I have no time to spare. I need to examine some important papers before tomorrow," he replied frowning. Katherine, having heard this excuse so often, was not impressed.

"I think you will find what I have to say more important than any papers, sir," she said tartly, causing Wilde to raise his eyebrows in surprise. This evening he noticed that Katherine's attitude had hardened. She no longer appeared concerned whether he was angry or not. Although he was in no mood for any vagaries, he saw no recourse but to listen to her.

He followed her into the library, noting the determined set to her shoulders, and a sudden premonition of disaster came over him. Seating himself behind his desk, a barrier which gave him the upper hand and an unwarranted feeling of confidence, he prepared himself to listen with the weary air of a man indulging a feckless female. Katherine did not appear impressed. The time had past when she would be thwarted by her father's mannerisms in dealing with her.

"This afternoon George Lang made me a proposal of marriage," she explained. "And I understand this peculiar offer has your approval," she stated in a firm voice, staring at her father with candid eyes which made him shift uncomfortably in his chair. Damn the girl. When she looked at him out of those questioning blue eyes, he felt guilty. Somehow, no matter how Peter Wilde tried to exonerate himself, he knew that he had failed to cherish Katherine as he had promised, and that failure haunted him now. He would not give in to this kind of emotional blackmail.

However, it was blackmail of a different sort that Katherine intended to bring to his attention.

"Have you nothing to say to this odious plan of your employee?" she asked in a forthright manner which would brook no refusal.

Peter Wilde, seeing there was no way to evade the truth, hurried into an explanation. "Lang has a letter, completely innocent which I wrote to Talleyrand, about the Italian loan. I saw nothing wrong in asking him to facilitate payment, but certain members of the Foreign Office might misconstrue the letter. It places me in a most delicate position because I did not mention it to them, when they were conducting that ridiculous investigation into my loyalty.

"Not so ridiculous that you considered selling your daughter to a blackmailer to prevent it becoming known," Katherine countered implacably. She would not allow her sympathy for his dilemma to blind herself to the wickedness of his effort to save himself at her expense.

Wilde replied with bitterness, "If you had accepted Ronald Pemberton's proposal George Lang would never have offered for you."

"My feelings did not enter into your calculations, I see," Katherine upbraided him in a disgusted tone.

Peter Wilde rushed into speech. "You refuse Pemberton because you claim you do not love him, a much overrated emotion, so I cannot see your justification for railing at me because I allowed another man to make you an offer. You might have come to care for Lang," he temporized, "After all, Katherine, you have to marry someone."

Katherine, thoroughly enraged by his efforts to put her on the defensive, rushed into battle, her eyes sparkling and a

194

flush on her cheeks. "You did not consider my feelings at all. You meant to use me to get yourself out of a disaster which was all of your own making. I will not stand for it." She was not prepared to play her final card, but he was rapidly forcing her into that situation.

"I might remind you, Katherine, that I am your legal guardian and could insist that you marry whomever I choose," Wilde insisted, uncomfortable and uneasy but reluctant to yield to her persuasive arguments. She was not behaving in a manner he understood. She held him in contempt and he did not believe he deserved that treatment from his daughter, and he would not endure it.

"If you encourage Lang to persist in his suit, then I will go to the Foreign Office and tell them the whole story," she threatened, infuriated by his use of her as a victim to save himself.

"Oh, come now, Katherine, aren't you being a bit hysterical? There is nothing so dreadful in Lang's behaviour. Perhaps you misunderstood him," he said, laughing a bit hollowly. "I doubt if he really meant to use that letter to my detriment, and he may genuinely care for you, and in his disappointment at your refusal, said more than he intended."

"If you wish to keep such a rogue in your employment there is nothing I can say, but I warn you that I will not be used in this fashion. I will decide whom I should marry and if you try to coerce me I will take steps to prevent it," she replied sternly. Then hesitating, not wishing to introduce the topic, but unable to help herself. "If mother were alive, I suspect she would be outraged at your treatment of me."

A grimace of pain passed across Wilde's face, to be replaced with a frown of anger. "That will do, Katherine. You are my daughter, and owe me some respect. This defiance will avail you nothing. I have the means to compel you to dutiful behaviour and if you resist my discipline I can have you punished. I have been much too forebearing and you are ungrateful. Haven't I provided you with all a girl could ask?''

"You do not care two pins for me, and I have some suspicion as to the reason. But that does not excuse your infamous use of me. Whether this damaging letter Lang refers to is based on any wrong-doing I have no way of judging, but this I do know, I will not marry George Lang to prevent some havey-cavey business coming to light," she replied scornfully, her eyes full of accusation.

Wilde, furious at being challenged but uneasy under her candid gaze, hid his disquiet. Why should he feel guilty? He had done nothing wrong, or at least he had not intended to deceive the government, but only save himself from some embarrassing explanations. Wilde was a practical man, who knew when to accept defeat, to retire and fight on a different front. He would deal with Lang and he would throw himself on the mercy of the Foreign Office boffins, explaining that he had completely forgotten the Talleyrand letter.

He spared little regret for Katherine's position, his mind occupied with how he would manage Lang. If the man was clever enough to have devised this scheme to feather his own nest, he might have taken liberties with some of the business which Wilde had entrusted to him. He was more concerned with his midjudgment of his associate than Katherine's contempt. Legally she had no rights and must abide by his decisions. Ruthlessly he pushed whatever guilt he might have about his treatment for her to the back of his mind, too occupied with the ramifications of Lang's treachery to care about Katherine's reaction.

She waited for some response, hoping he would confide about her mother, or at least try to make her understand how he felt about raising another man's child, if that was what he had done. But Wilde, skilled at handling financial adversaries, had little experience at manipulating women. He

196

found Katherine's defiance irritating, and unwomanly. He was not prepared to make the explanations she demanded, and she must accept his decision. What choice did she have? Restored once more to his usual confidence, he discounted the force of her emotions.

"I believe, Katherine, you may leave this matter in my hands. I will deal with Lang and his paltry intrigues. However, I greatly dislike your manner in threatening me. I have been much too lenient with you, and I tell you now, that if you do not accept an eligible suitor by the end of the season, I wash my hands of you. I am not prepared to spend good money on indulging your whims," he warned her sternly.

Katherine stood up, frustrated and furious, but determined not to give way to a fit of temper. Facing him bravely she gave her own warning. "You may think you have the power to compel me, but let me warn you, in turn. I am not to be coerced nor threatened. I will make my own choices, whether they do meet with your approval or not. I have other resources, another refuge. I owe you a certain amount of gratitude, but do not push that debt too far. I have lost my respect for you, and you have seen to it that there is little of affection in our relationship. You are a businessman accustomed to measuring profit and loss. Remember that I, too, can make that calculation. And do not rely on my future acquiescence in any schemes you may design.

Peter Wilde watched her go. Did the girl really think she could win in any duel of wits with him? Had she some ammunition she had not revealed. Suddenly he recalled her interest in Sir Richard Overton. Could she mean she would call on that gentleman to assist her? Wilde, ambitious and practical, doubted that Sir Richard would endanger his own position by admitting any damaging information to Katherine, and he had no real proof that Wilde was not her father.

His immediate concern was how to handle George Lang.

When that ambitious young man had first approached him, threatening to turn over the Talleyrand letter to the proper authorities if Wilde did not consent to his plans for Katherine, he had been astonished, but not really worried. He felt, after some consideration, that Lang had been carried away by his desire to further his career, for which Wilde could not entirely fault him. He might even have fallen deeply in love with Katherine and realized he would never win her by honest means. Wilde had acquiesced because he needed time to discover just what Lang was doing with the business secrets entrusted to him. Wilde accepted that his normally astute judgment had been at fault in promoting Lang, but the young man had reminded him of his own struggles. That was what came of allowing emotion to override common sense.

Wilde, looking back over his life of ledgers and figures, had to admit there was little on the personal side to cause him comfort. Perhaps the fault was his. His recent interview with Katherine had left him uncomfortably aware that he had not handled that relationship with the care and skill he had given to building up his financial empire. And now that opportunity was gone, for he doubted that any rapprochment was possible. He had failed with Lang and he had failed with Katherine, but at least he need not compound his errors. He could certainly prevent Lang from doing any more damage, either personal or professional.

Katherine, still smarting from the inconclusive meeting, could not settle to reading, sewing or any other task. The idea of sleep was also repugnant. She paced her room, wondering why she had not confronted Wilde with her conviction that he was not her natural father. Surely he would have been forced into telling her the truth, but Katherine sensed that the time was not right.

If only Sir Richard was available for counsel! She would

say nothing to Wilde until she had consulted him. For a fleeting moment she wished that she could have enlisted Simon Stafford's assistance, but the Marquis, despite his kindness and interest, was still an enigma to her. She sensed that he felt some emotion for her, but she feared it was not the abiding love she craved. Honest with herself, Katherine admitted that she desperately needed an ally, one she could trust and rely upon. Only Sir Richard appeared to fill that role, but wistfully she wondered if she would ever find a man who would give her the affection and support she needed in a husband. Her recent experiences had led her to believe that few men were capable of providing those rare commodities.

Only one result of her interview with Wilde seemed likely to bear fruit. Wilde would see to it that Lang's maneuvering would be investigated. He might be the traitor whom Sir Richard and his friends sought, but Katherine doubted that he was the master-mind behind this vile treason. He could manipulate figures, deal with the financial markets, but he had neither the entree nor the resources to direct a full-fledged conspiracy. Shrewdly she surmised that he had become involved in the matter by his ambition and greed. He craved the status that Wilde had achieved, but Katherine doubted that he was clever enough to have initiated a sophisticated scheme to bring down the government. As angry as she was with Wilde, she was convinced of his innocence in the larger matter. And she could trust Wilde to expose Lang. Where his financial empire was concerned he would brook no rivalry, nor would he excuse his assistant, whose power over him now rested on very dubious grounds. Lang had overreached himself and would pay the price. But she still had several pressing worries. What to do about Sir Richard? And could she in good conscience continue to live under Wilde's protection, accept the luxurious life he provided, when she had defied him and shown her contempt. What refuge was available to her? Those were her immediate problems. Of Simon Stafford and her reaction to him, and his to her, she refused to think.

Chapter Twenty

As their party alighted from the sculls which had conveyed them over the steamy river to the water-gate at Vauxhall Gardens, Katherine thought that this rather ostentatious choice of entertainment was well suited to Count Crespi. He had organized the party some days ago and inveigled Mrs. Basingbroke, who did not really approve of the pleasure palace, into chaperoning the group. They were an uneven number. The Count had invited three couples and an elderly clubman for Mrs. Basingbroke, intending to serve as Katherine's escort himself, but at the last moment Simon Stafford had begged to be included. With suave politeness Crespi had expressed his pleasure, but inwardly he had been more than annoyed. He had designed the evening as an opportunity to fix Katherine's interest in himself, and did not contemplate the inclusion of a formidable rival such as the Marquis.

Still, the Count's manner as a host could not be faulted as he shepherded his party toward the box he had reserved. Dusk was falling, which gave an added aura of romance to the groves of trees and shrubbery festooned with lights. In the main garden which spread onto a vast cleared sward, a pavillion lined with mirrors provided a lavish buffet for those who did not take their supper in their boxes. An orchestra played cheerfully in the rotunda where later in the evening performers—singers, rope dancers, jugglers, sword swallowers and the like would entertain the guests. Climaxing the festivity would be a spectacular tableaux and Vauxhall's famed fireworks.

As Katherine allowed the Count to place her tenderly in the box she noticed fountains gushing streams of water, reflecting the colored lights which glowed about the gardens. Beyond the lighted area various walks tempted couples toward shaded rendezvous where dalliance and worse was promised. Mrs. Basingbroke had warned Katherine of the notorious Dark Walk where impudent young men ambushed young women and inflicted shocking indignities upon them. In another mood Katherine might have relished her first sight of the popular gardens but tonight she found the aura of spurious romance tawdry and a bit vulgar. Still, she made an effort to enter into the occasion. After all it was not the Count's fault that her mood was somber.

Outwardly, however, Katherine appeared ready to enjoy herself. She was wearing a new gown of ivory silk over an apricot underdress with a light Norwich shawl over her shoulders to ward off the river breezes. She was rather surprised to see Simon Stafford among the party, and she suspected that the Count had reluctantly acceded to the Marquis' request to join them. Knowing his dislike of Crespi she wondered why he would want to be included in the party. Perhaps he had another assignation with a Titania. She could not help but compare this evening to the light-hearted rebellion which had impelled her to attend the Pantheon Masquerade that, in turn, had led her into such difficulties.

"You seem a bit distrait this evening, cara. And I had hoped my poor efforts at providing an entertainment might please you," the Count murmured into Katherine's ear.

"Not at all, Count. I much appreciate this opportunity to taste the pleasures of Vauxhall. It is my first visit. You were too kind to arrange it," Katherine assured him, moving slightly to put a proper distance between them. Really, she did not feel in the mood for the Count's gallantries, and rather suspected that he had more in mind than idle compliments. He looked a man with a purpose in his mind. Whether that purpose was to seduce her or propose honorable marriage, Katherine did not know, nor was she very interested. She wished, not for the first time, that she could have avoided this evening, but when she had suggested to Mrs. Basingbroke that they might cry off, her chaperone had protested that courtesy would not permit a last minute withdrawal. Katherine did not want to invite probing questions as to her reluctance so she consented with as good grace as possible.

Simon Stafford was watching the couple beneath hooded lids, while conducting a desultory conversation with a fellow guest about the latter's chances at Newmarket that season. He wondered if Katherine had challenged Peter Wilde about Lang's blackmail attempt, and what the banker had told her. With the information Katherine had given him about Wilde he had been able to inform Valentine of his suspicions of Lang, and the focus of their investigation turned toward Wilde's young associate. So far he had heard nothing of the results, whether any proof could be found of Lang's villainy. Valentine had been quite appreciative of this latest effort, but Simon had been in a dark mood all day, disliking his role. He had chivied the facts out of Katherine by acting the sympathetic friend and more, a position he found very uncomfortable. Watching that Italian bounder flirt with Katherine did nothing to improve his humor.

From the beginning of their relationship Kate had caused him nothing but trouble, defying him, challenging him, ignoring his offers of assistance, generally treating him with disdain. Except on the few occasions when she had, almost against her will, responded to his kisses, he had found her maddening and impossible. Of course, he had done little to improve his chances with her, doubting her, accusing her of all kinds of double-dealing, then warning her of retribution if she did not follow his advice. How much more flattering to be courted and complimented by Count Crespi or that young cub, Pemberton.

Certainly, if she were the adventuress he had at first assumed she would have leapt at the chance to marry Pemberton, but he knew she had refused the Viscount summarily. He doubted she entertained any but the mildest emotions toward Count Crespi. And she had rightly sent Lang about his business. That only left Sir Richard Overton, who appeared to stand high in her regard. Well, he could not fault her judgment. However annoying he found the older man's pursuit of Kate he had to admire the diplomat's career, his manners and general conduct. He was too old for Kate, but perhaps she was looking for a father figure to replace the arid relationship she had with Wilde.

Simon moved restlessly in his chair, wanting to take some action, to grab Kate and flee this contrived revelry. But before he could make any move toward that end, Count Crespi rose and took Kate's arm, inviting her to stroll about the gardens, taking in the sights. Mrs. Basingbroke, appealed to for permission, gave a reluctant nod. She did not like allowing Katherine to stroll about Vauxhall with an acknowledged womanizer such as the Count, but she felt, as his guest, she could not be so churlish as to express her disapproval.

As the couple disappeared in the direction of the Dark Walk, she looked appealingly at Simon Stafford, who was not slow to answer her silent request. Giving a polite excuse to his fellow guests, he strolled after the couple, pleading the sight of a friend glimpsed in a box across the pavilion. Vauxhall was crowded this evening and Simon had some difficulty in tracking his quarry, as the revelers included several brunette ladies dressed similarly to Kate. He suspected that the count would lead her toward one of the secluded nooks which gave Vauxhall its dubious reputation. Licentious behavior was expected and unremarked, so lax were the manners in the Gardens. Reputable citizens who normally observed every propriety abandoned much of their respectability under the influence of Vauxhall's special enticements. Simon passed several trysting couples and groups of slightly inebriated young men looking for an unescorted miss on whom to try their wiles, while he searched for Kate and the Count. Just what he would say when he found them he had not decided. He knew that every moment that passed he was becoming angrier, most unfair to be sure. He had no rights over Kate, but that was a situation he determined to change, and before this night was over.

Katherine, meanwhile, was fending off Count Crespi's blandishments with a light mockery which he found extremely frustrating and damaging to his amour propre. Accustomed to coy acceptance of his gallantry from the fair sex, Katherine's inability to take him with becoming seriousness annoyed him. She seemed distracted, giving him only a part of her attention. However, he persisted.

"You are unusually frank for a debutante, cara," he protested as she laughed at his latest attempt to cajole her into a more receptive mood.

"Oh, dear, I am sorry, Count. I do not have the proper manners, I fear. But so much of society is so meaningless, don't you agree?" she countered with a wicked grin, throwing off her disquiet. The Count did take his reputation so seriously! It seemed a shame to prick his self-assurance, but Katherine could not resist the challenge.

"Come, let us rest here for a moment," he suggested,

indicating a secluded bench shielded from the view of pass-ersby. "Then we can continue this discussion of your delight-ful character, Katerina," he urged, anxious to push her into a compromising position. Count Crespi's blithe journey through the sophisticated paths of the London ton had received a rude jolt that very day, and he had accepted that he must take steps to retrieve his position. Katherine would serve as an enjoyable counterplot to his uncle's harsh refusal to frank him any further. He needed a wealthy wife to insure his status, and overcoming Katherine's scruples would soothe his conceit. Once their engagement was announced his situation would improve considerably. Affairs were marching in a way that disturbed him.

"Come, cara, you must know how much I admire you," he cajoled, preparatory to making a declaration.

Oh dear, sighed Katherine to herself. The Count seemed intent on proposing. And she did not need this added irritation to her confused mind. Even if she were desperate, and she was fast attaining that state, he was the last man she would consider. He was too conceited, too dubious, too much of a womanizer and sure to be an indifferent husband once the knot was tied. And, of course, her affections were not engaged.

"I am flattered that you think so highly of me, Count. It is always gratifying when one is admired," Katherine replied with a certain irony the Count found puzzling.

"Are you toying with me, bellisima?" he asked, playing the injured suitor.

"I hope not, sir. I dislike flirts," Katherine answered a trifle wearily.

"You have been kind enough to honor me with your attention, and I would like to think you entertain warmer feelings about me," the Count continued, determined to pursue the matter, but not entirely liking Katherine's rather indifferent reception of his interest.

"You have been most entertaining and considerate, Count. We enjoy a fine friendship, I believe," Katherine parried, wondering how she could prevent him from making a declaration.

He was tired of fencing. "I wish to make you my Countess, dear lady." He expected her to be overcome by her good fortune, but Katherine did not seem to be aware of the honor he had just bestowed on her.

"That is very kind of you, Count, but I fear you would not make a very good husband, and I would be a most tiresome wife. I require fidelity, a quality you might find unacceptable," Katherine replied, thoroughly put out by his histrionics. "You would not ask for me if I was a penniless nobody," she finished a bit sharply.

"That is unjust, cara. I adore you," he persisted, grasping her by the shoulders and muttering a string of Latin endearments which were to assure Katherine of his passion but which only made her want to laugh. Count Crespi playing the devoted suitor was not a role which she found convincing.

But he was not to be put off with her objections. "If you do not want to live in Italy, after we have defeated the Corsican, we can settle comfortably in England, cara. I am not averse to staying in your country," he insisted with a certain pompous nobility.

"That is kind, sir, but not the main problem. I do not love you, and I doubt if you feel more than the most tepid affection for me. You must look elsewhere for a well-dowered wife. My father is not as generous as you require, I believe," she answered sharply.

"You wound me, cara. And you have trifled with me. I will not be treated so," he protested, giving her a look of pained surprise. Then, seeing she was not impressed, he tried to press a kiss upon her averted face. Furious at his license, Katherine responded by slapping him, a bit astounded at her own temerity. She rose to her feet, and he once again attempted to gather her into his arms, his own temper rising at this unexpected rejection.

"It seems to be my fate to be always rescuing you from assaulting some importunate suitor, Kate. Really, you should learn to manage these affairs more adroitly. It is such bad ton to resort to fisticuffs." Simon Stafford's interruption, although timely, did nothing to soothe Katherine's humor.

Count Crespi was equally annoyed by Simon's amused interference, but he was too poised an adversary to display his irritation.

"You forget yourself, sir, I think. Your presence is most unwelcome," he said stiffly.

"Not by Kate. She is obviously in need of assistance. I doubt that you mean to importune the lady against her will, Count," Simon returned smoothly.

"Certainly not sir, I am not a clumsy Englishman," the Count replied, resenting any attack on his fabled address.

"Too true, you are not, Count. Perhaps there is a lesson in that comparison. What do you think, Kate? Would your fellow countrymen benefit from some Latin chivalry?" he asked turning to Kate with a mocking grin.

"You certainly evidence little chivalry, my lord," Katherine replied grimly. Why was it that Simon Stafford always discovered her in some compromising situation that was not of her contriving? Then seeing the ridiculousness of it, her irrepresible spirits rose and she grinned, too. The Count, puzzled by the Anglo-Saxon idea of wit, frowned and complained. "Really, I do not see this intrusion as a cause for amusement." He felt foolish, his conceit endangered and was

208

about to stalk off in a huff, but he hesitated to surrender the field to his rival.

Seeing his expression, Katherine sobered. "I do apologize, Count. You are quite correct. It was unkind of me to laugh at you, but, although Lord Stafford lacks your gallantry, I have to admit that his interruption was most timely. It does not do for a respectable girl to be lurking about in secluded groves, entertaining the advances of gentlemen." She hoped to slide adroitly out of the uncomfortable position in which she found herself.

"How well you put it, Kate. Just what Mrs. Basingbroke believes and why she sent me to rescue you," Simon agreed aimiably. "Shall we return to the box?" he added as if the whole matter was not worth bothering about.

Katherine, only too happy to oblige, smoothed her dress with one hand and smiled forgivingly at the Count, who had no recourse under the ironic gaze of Simon Stafford but to consent. The trio walked abreast, Katherine drawing her cavaliers' attention to the glittering scenes spread out before them. On their return to the party they settled down to watch the entertainment and to dine on the delectable ham which was a feature of Vauxhall. Katherine had decided that she would remain close to the Count's other guests and not give either Simon or the Count an opportunity for private conversation. She ignored Crespi's burning reproachful glances, but could not help but notice that her efforts to ignore Simon went unregarded. Obviously he found his recent errand to return her to Mrs. Basingbroke a tedious chore.

Feeling both frustrated and ill-used, Katherine had to content herself with drinking more wine than was her wont, which only increased her bad humor and clouded her usual good sense. She felt the evening would never end. Several times she danced with the various gentlemen of the party, but Simon Stafford did not request a turn, which further annoyed her. He behaved very much like an admonishing older brother with the tedious duty of guiding a gooseish sister onto the proper paths. That was not at all the reaction she wanted from Simon.

Finally, after a spectacular tableaux picturing the glories of ancient Greece, several of the guests insisted on remaining for the grande finale, the display of fireworks. Katherine, who felt she would scream if she had to stay a moment longer mouthing inane platitudes, smothered a protest, but evidently Simon had noticed her unease.

"Come, Kate, let us stroll across the pavillon. I think I need to stretch my legs and there is a much better view of the doings from the higher ground there," he invited guilelessly.

Katherine, lulled by wine, and eager to put some distance between herself and the Count, agreed with unbecoming alacrity. She had decided to treat Simon with haughty disdain and here she was allowing him to lead her off tamely. As she accepted Simon's arm and they walked away, she was conscious of the Count's accusing gaze.

"Probably very bad manners for me to capture our host's target," said Simon. "Obviously, this whole evening was planned in your honor and I have spoiled it. But I have heard that it is considered bad form to accept a man on the first proposal, so if you are regretting refusing the dashing Count this evening, I am sure he will come up to scratch again, intrigued by your reluctance and even more determined to win you." He grinned at her in a way that made her want to shake him, but Katherine was determined to remain cool under his provocation.

He appreciated her self-control, raising his eyebrows as she refused to be drawn. "Ah, Kate, you are learning. I know you are yearning for a good brangle, but you won't give me the satisfaction of seeing you in a temper," he teased. By now they had vanished into the shrubbery, down one of the paths which crossed the gardens.

"I thought we were going to a better vantage place to view the fireworks. This direction seems far from advantageous," Katherine complained.

"Ah, but it is advantageous. Like the Count, I, too, have designs on you, my fair lady," Simon quipped, hoping to banish her sullens and put her into a more receptive frame of mind.

"And what do you mean by that remark, pray?" Katherine asked, resolutely stopping and prepared to turn back toward the company. They were completely alone now, masked by heavy shrubbery and beyond the glittering lights which shone over the more frequented parts of the gardens.

Simon did not answer immediately, but placed his hands on her shoulders and turned her toward his searching eyes. For once all mockery was absent from his expression and he looked desperate and determined.

"Listen, Kate. I had intended to await a more opportune occasion, but seeing that Count swarming over you, and knowing how many men find you irresistible I cannot give my rivals any more advantages. I have fought it too long, and now I surrender. I must have you for my own, and God knows, you need protection. You haven't the sense of a pea hen, embroiling yourself in all kinds of danger, trying to sort out problems which are none of your concern. You need a man who can control you, and who will love you as you deserve," he blurted out, hardly aware that his proposal could not be couched in more unflattering terms.

Katherine's heart soared for a moment but then plummeted. "Love me. Of all the arrogance. You care nothing for love, you are only interested in having your own way. You can't bear the fact that a woman could defy you, or reject your insulting offers. Well, I have had enough of London gallants, who appear all polite manners in public, and have no compunction in making the most improper suggestions to a girl in private. I think you are disgusting!'' She felt like weeping. Simon Stafford was offering her carte blanche and she could have died from the pain of it.

But he was a angry as she. "Disgusting? How dare you say that. You have not been disgusted in the past, I vow,'' he answered, now in a temper as furious as her own, and gathering her ruthlessly into his arms, his anger overcoming his best intentions.

Katherine, wanting to remain stoic under this assault on her senses, found herself responding to his kiss. She felt the heat rising in her body and had an irresistible impulse to surrender and give Simon whatever he wanted. But just when she had dropped her last defence she heard him say with satisfaction.

"Now, at last. You are mine and you will not fend me off again, Kate,'' he muttered, his hand moving under her bodice to stroke her breast.

Katherine, shuddering with the emotions he evoked, was not so far gone in ecstasy that she did not understand his meaning. He thought she had agreed to become his mistress, that she could not resist the sensual spell he was casting over her. With maddened strength she pulled herself from his arms.

"Never, Simon. You are worse than Ronald or the Count or any of London's worst roués. I will never submit to your disgraceful suggestions. How could you think I would be content to be your mistress?'' She was aware of what she was saying, so humiliated was she by Simon's apparent treatment. Before he could explain or protest, Katherine ran down the path as if the devil were at her heels, and disappeared into the night.

Simon, gathering his wits together, was totally bemused

212

by her reaction. Then, he realized his stupidity. Of course, he had not mentioned the word marriage. She thought he wanted her to become his love without the bonds of matrimony. How could she have leapt to such a conclusion? Easily, you dolt, he told himself. In your passion to claim her, you neglected to mention that your proposal was an honorable one. And now she had fled into the shadows and he would have a devil of a time finding her and explaining this royal misunderstanding. Well, he would find her, he would explain and he would get her consent, if he had to wring her delightful neck. And with such unloverlike sentiments, Simon set off after his elusive love.

Chapter Twenty One

Rushing along the dusky and secluded paths of Vauxhall, Katherine was scarcely aware of her direction, so deep was her shame and anguish. Exhausted from the storm of emotion, heedless of the tears which blinded her, she stopped, panting, to drop onto a convenient stone seat behind a clump of shrubbery. She had to regain her composure before facing the party and Mrs. Basingbroke, and especially Simon Stafford.

She mopped her streaming eyes and tried to bring some order to her appearance, all the while aware of a pressing unhappiness. Why had Simon thought she might entertain his infamous suggestion? What was even more shaming, for a moment she had even responded to his overtures. How could she have been so lost to all sensibility as to contemplate becoming the mistress of such a man? She had, for a brief while, abandoned all honor and had no excuse for her response except that she loved him.

What could be more pitiful than a woman who would consider such a future with a man who thought of her as no better than a light-skirt? Slowly her anger at Simon's presumption began to overcome her humiliation and she took several deep breaths, calming her pounding heart. She was in a vulnerable position, separated from her party and having lost all notion of her whereabouts. The dark lanes of Vauxhall were dangerous to an unescorted female. She must try to return to the pavillion.

The burst of fireworks startled her although she could not see the display well, the trees shielding most of the pyrotechnics. Rising trembling to her feet, Katherine chided herself for her timidity. The sooner she returned to her party, the better for her reputation. And she did not want to give Simon any reason to think she was so overset that she had lost command of herself. But before she could put her good intentions into effect she heard voices, muffled but nearer than she liked. She did not want to be accosted by some drunken reveller who believed her fair game. The voices rose and she thought she recognized the timber of one of them. Surely, that could not be Ronald Pemberton? About to emerge from her seclusion and face him, she suddenly realized that Ronald, if indeed it was he, was having an angry confrontation with some man. Not wanting to eavesdrop she had turned away, intent on making her escape, when she heard the other man shout in a furious temper.

"You will not leave me to carry the burden of suspicion. If I am apprehended and sent to the dock, my lord, you will be beside me," the man promised in a threatening tone.

Now unwilling to leave the scene of this puzzling meeting, Katherine edged silently around the shrubbery which concealed her and peered out at the rendezvous.

There was Ronald Pemberton standing in an uncharacteristic, menacing posture. Opposite him, looking both uneasy and defiant, was George Lang. That she had come upon a scene of two conspirators, she had no doubt. But what was the plot that drew two such unlikely allies together? Holding her breath, determined that not the slightest movement would betray her hiding place, she listened appalled at the confrontation between the two men.

Pemberton confronted Lang. "If you have been careless enough to have attracted the attention of Valentine's men, you must pay the penalty. You might hope to win some relief from transportation or the hangman's noose by naming me, but no one would believe you, and you have no proof. I would deny everything, and your accusations would be put down to spite or jealousy. I understand you had the temerity to aspire to Katherine Wilde's hand. If she did not accept me, she would hardly look with favor upon one who is so far beneath her touch. That was really quite insolent of you. And now you have the audacity to approach me to rescue you from your own ineptitude."

Katherine could hardly restrain herself from revealing her presence to the two men, so disgusted was she. But some inner prompting told her that it would be both ineffective and dangerous. She needed to know more. Could Ronald Pemberton, that polite, sociable, proper young man about town, be the notorious traitor that Simon and his chief were searching for with little success? It seemed impossible. But the Ronald she saw now was far different from the role he had adopted before the world. Before she could order her thoughts at this amazing revelation, Lang protested once again.

"I had reason to think Wilde would look kindly on my suit. She refused you, didn't she? Your fine background, your title, your position did not help you to find favor in her eyes. Perhaps she would prefer a more ambitious young man," Lang suggested with a sneer.

"You are a fool, Lang. You might have a certain financial acumen, but you are far from possessing the qualities to win a young lady like Katherine. But that is of no account, now. By your own admission you have endangered our plans, exposing yourself to suspicion. I am most annoyed with your stupidity,'' Ronald countered in chilling tones.

"It was not my fault that the false bullion was discovered, a mere fluke that Valentine's men came across the substitution. And I suspect the damned investigators have a man in the bank, thinking Peter Wilde is at the bottom of the whole affair. He might yet be called to explain his situation, and our involvement may remain secret,'' Lang excused, his tone apologetic, his stance less assured.

"For your sake, you must pray that is so. But your usefulness is at an end, and if you try to drag me down with you, you will find that I can deal most harshly with any attempt to implicate me. Your best plan is to sit tight and reveal nothing. Your greed and ambition has led to your plight. Fouché will be annoyed and will undoubtedly take steps to silence you before any more harm is done. Perhaps you would be wise to leave the country,'' Ronald said coolly.

Lang, blustered, but obviously was shaken by the warning. "It's not fair. You have as much to lose as I do. You should share the blame.''

"But I don't intend to expose myself to any suspicion. There is too much at stake to sacrifice my position for a paltry fellow like you. You took a grave risk in contacting me here, and you must not make any further attempts to meet me. I am more than capable of dealing with you as you deserve,'' Ronald concluded with a suave finality which Lang could not challenge.

"Perhaps I will take your advice and leave town for the moment,'' he agreed, his assurance gone.

"That would be best. And I will try to retrieve what I can from this debacle. My own fault for trusting the business to such an ineffective ally,'' Ronald said. "Now begone.''

Katherine watched, rooted to her hiding place, her mind aghast at what she had learned. She must somehow contact the authorities about this unbelievable disclosure. Should she tell Simon? She was not yet ready to face him in view of his recent shocking suggestion to her. Suddenly, she remembered Sir Richard. He would know how to deal with Ronald Pemberton. She sighed with relief as she watched Ronald and Lang melt away into the shadows. She must somehow return to Crespi's box and behave as if nothing had happened, a task which seemed almost beyond her. She was not foolish enough to discount her own vulnerable position. If Ronald suspected that she knew of his traitorous activity he would take steps to silence her—of that she had no doubt.

Katherine had her own reserves of courage but this was a problem she could not solve on her own, and her only refuge was Sir Richard. Smoothing her hair with trembling hands and straightening her dress, she waited until she had mastered her emotions and then made her way carefully back along the path which led to the pavillion.

Mrs. Basingbroke hailed her return with a lifted eyebrow but did not quiz her. Katherine avoided looking at Simon Stafford, and sat down next to her chaperone.

"Do you think we can leave soon, Mrs. B.? I feel quite fatigued, and the fireworks appear finished. It has been an agreeable evening but I really must seek my bed soon." She yawning with a convincing air of langour. Turning to the Count she expressed her pleasure in the evening, an attitude she found most difficult to sustain.

She ignored Simon, who viewed her with concern. Where had she been after she fled from him? And what maggot did she have in her head now? He repressed his first instinct to drag her off and demand an explanation, but sensibly realized that this was neither the time nor the place to explain the misunderstanding. Really, she was a most maddening girl with a very unflattering opinion of him. Still, she was the

218

girl he wanted—indeed needed—and he would persuade her of his sincere intention to make her his wife.

He had not been unmindful of her response to his kisses. She had not taken him in disgust then. What a suspicious mind she had, believing he wanted to make her his mistress. Simon was both offended and amused at Katherine's reaction, but in thinking back over their tempestuous interview he conceded she might have seen his proposal as an offer of a shocking nature. Accustomed to disguising his feelings, he behaved with nonchalant aplomb, further exacerbating Katherine's distress and strengthening her belief in his perfidy.

However, Katherine too could mask her feelings, and she displayed little of her worry and shock at the events of the evening. All she wanted was to seek the sanctuary of her chamber and reflect on her next move. To her relief, the party appeared ready to depart, and within minutes she was being escorted to the waiting carriage, avoiding Simon's inquiring look and giving her full attention to Count Crespi. Too conceited to accept that she might be encouraging him with another end in sight, he accepted her pretty expressions of gratitude with complacence and promised to call upon her soon, as he had a particular question he wished to ask her.

Distracted, Katherine barely heard his request, but had enough presence to accede with apparent composure. Her attitude did little to soothe Simon's irritation, but soon she was esconced in the carriage and was cheerily discussing the evening with Mrs. Basingbroke.

Thinking she would toss and turn all night with the burden of her thoughts, Katherine was surprised to find that she slept dreamlessly and well, exhausted by the disturbing events of the evening. And on her breakfast tray was the long-awaited note from Sir Richard, explaining that he had been out of town, and suggesting that he call for her that morning and they could ride in the Park which would allow them to talk privately. Katherine, relieved and cheered by his answer to her plea, dressed in a calmer frame of mind after sending a note of acceptance. She waited impatiently in the morning room for Sir Richard's arrival, pacing up and down, taking up a journal and then throwing it down in disgust, unable to settle to any task. At last she was rewarded with the announcement that Sir Richard had called. She barely gave him a civil greeting when he was ushered into the room, throwing on her bonnet and shawl, and shepherding him toward the door.

"Such haste is flattering, Katherine, but I suspect a pressing reason behind your eagerness to be private," Sir Richard teased as they walked toward the entrance. "But we will wait until we are well on our ride before we discuss whatever it is that is concerning you," he insisted, giving an admonitory glance at the butler's back as they followed that dignitary toward the front door.

"Yes, of course, Sir Richard," Katherine agreed trying for composure. She realized he was uncomfortable in Peter Wilde's house and wanted to quit it as the earliest moment. Sir Richard's prompt reply to her plea for an interview had somewhat soothed her agitation, but she was in a fever to tell him what she had learned.

She was so preoccupied with the information she had for Sir Richard she did not notice the phaeton which pulled into Wigmore Street as they cantered quickly in the opposite direction. But Simon Stafford glimpsed Sir Richard's equipage and his passenger as the vehicle moved out of sight. He cursed to himself, trying to decide if he should follow the pair. It appeared to be his fate to call upon Kate only to find that Sir Richard had been quicker. Would she confide in the older man, tell him that Simon had made improper proposals to her? He would not relish having to explain their misunderstanding to Sir Richard, although he doubted that the man would challenge him. Perhaps Kate would rashly make some decision about her future which would put his own hopes completely out of court. Did she intend to entertain an offer from Sir Richard, a man twenty-five years her senior?

He had awakened after a troubled night determined to face Kate and wrest an answer from her. He had supposed that once she understood that he meant marriage and not a liaison he would be accepted. Now doubts surfaced. Could she have taken him in such distaste that she would rush into a misalliance with the statesman? Well, she could do worse, Simon conceded ruefully. Sir Richard was a distinguished man, with tolerance and an experience of life which would enable him to shield and guide an impressionable girl. Not that Kate had ever impressed him as needing protection. She appeared well able to manage her life and still interfere in what should never concern her without the least trouble. She had been a thorn in his side since the first moment he laid eyes on her in the gardens of the Pantheon masquerade. If he had the sense he was born with he would have flown to the farthest reaches of the realm and avoided being caught in her toils.

That he was fairly caught, he accepted and in fact was eagerly marching to the very fate which de Lisle had prophesized for him. But he had to have her. Somehow she had insinuated herself into his life and heart, and he would not tamely allow her to be influenced by her gothic notions of his morals or by some aging gentleman with a kindly nature. Sir Richard did not need Kate, but he did, and he would win her. No matter what he had to do to carry her off to the altar he would manage it somehow. That she might not love him, or even like him, he did not entertain for a moment. She could not have kissed him, welcomed his embraces as she had if she found him repulsive. But, did she love him

221

enough to marry him? He wanted no tepid affection, no acceptance of his suit as desirable match. What he craved was a passionate avowal of her feelings but his hopes for that were now clouded by her preference for Sir Richard.

There was some mystery here and he determined to solve it. For some reason Kate felt troubled by her relationship with Peter Wilde, and in her unhappiness might easily be forced into a tragic choice which would blight her life. And his too, Simon conceded. He had never expected to fall headlong into love, to feel such intense desire for a woman that he could not contemplate life alone any longer. He had had his share of light romances, but he had never become so involved that it mattered greatly whether the lady in question strayed or stayed. He yearned for the domesticity, the stability, the joy she would bring him as his wife. And he would triumph, no matter what obstacles were put in his way. Simon's nature was not to admit defeat, either in rooting out his country's enemies, or in the matters of the heart. Well, he decided wryly, he would have to persevere. He was making little progress in either direction for the moment.

Chapter Twenty Two

Katherine would have been heartened to learn of Simon's intent, but as she and Sir Richard rode toward a secluded section of the Park she gave little thought to her romantic travails. Her whole attention was centered on what she would tell Sir Richard about the more pressing problem of Ronald Pemberton's treachery.

At last they reached a fairly deserted section of the vast environs of the Park and Sir Richard suggested they alight and pursue their conversation in a more comfortable situation. As they settled down on a convenient bench, Sir Richard having tethered his pair of chestnuts to a nearby tree, turned to Katherine and took her hands in his.

"Now, how can I help you, my dear? I dislike seeing you so at odds with yourself and life. Nothing is so serious that we cannot alleviate your concern," he assured her in the calm, smoothing manner she found so heartening.

Sir Richard, with long experience in dealing with trouble, found Katherine's obvious distress more affecting than he had believed possible. An unhappy love affair, perhaps, even an angry confrontation with Peter Wilde, could be worrying her, but neither of these should produce such anguish. Katherine was neither frivolous nor shallow, and she had a rare independent spirit, not easily quailed so her problem must be considerable.

Her first words enlightened him. "I think I have discovered the traitor, the man behind the financial conspiracy of which my father appears accused," she told him. "By the merest chance I came upon Ronald Pemberton and George Lang discussing the plot in the gardens at Vauxhall. At first I could not believe my eyes. That Ronald, the most affable and easy-going of men, should be a master spy! George Lang was not so much of a surprise, for I had reason to think he was using his position to feather his own nest. He is a cold, ambitious, ungrateful villain, using my father to protect himself," she explained, her voice quavering, but her chin set with determination.

"You were in considerable danger, Katherine. Now, tell me exactly what you overheard," Sir Richard insisted, taking her hands in his firm warm grasp, his voice encouraging and promising protection. Behind his serene facade he was appalled. Had the girl exposed herself to these men, her very life might have been threatened.

Katherine, marshalling her thoughts, gave Sir Richard a clear and concise report of what she had overheard. Sharing the secret with him relieved her of an overwhelming burden. When she finished her tale she felt only satisfaction that she had been able to assist in bringing two traitors to the attention of the authorities. Concluding, she wondered aloud, "Why would Ronald join forces with our enemies, betray his country? He will inherit a great title, and his position is unassailable. How could he behave so?" she asked in real perplexity. Horrified as she was by his duplicity, she also could not forget certain happy episodes in their relationship.

"The Wexfords are under the hatches. You know his father has been urging him to marry a fortune. But that alone would not account for it. There must be some weak strain in Pemberton's makeup, some impelling urge for power which he must implement. And many members of our aristocracy rather admire Napolean. If the Corsican devil has preyed on his baser desires, promised him vast rewards, he might have succumbed to such lures. I agree it is revolting and shocking, but I have learned in my long career that men's motives often defy analysis. What we must do now is bring him to justice while protecting you from danger. These men are ruthless. Look at what happened to the Countessa Fontenelli. I fear for you, Katherine, and will do what I can to see you do not suffer for your bravery.

"You will arrange matters so that Ronald will be apprehended and my father vindicated," she pleaded.

"Yes, I will do my best. I have no love for Peter Wilde, but he does not deserve to be used as he has been by these wicked traitors. There are a few problems. We have no proof of Pemberton's treachery, and as he rightly pointed out to Lang, even if that turncoat betrays him in order to save his own skin, he could simply deny the accusations. I will have to put this problem before Valentine. We must come up with a scheme to force Pemberton to betray himself." Sir Richard frowned, mulling over the possibilities, among them how to protect Katherine. For a fleeting moment he wondered what she had been doing hiding in the Vauxhall shrubbery, in a position to overhear the argument between the two traitors. But foremost was his eagerness to report to Valentine, to set matters in train for apprehending the men who had betrayed their country so heinously.

Katherine, observing his abstracted expression, suspected that he was impatient to put the business in hand. The responsibility for her safety was just an added problem for him. Her relief at sharing her startling discovery had been followed by a strange depression, a shattering emptiness. She should have been overjoyed, but in back of her mind lurked the oppression induced by Simon's cynical offer to make her his mistress. Unfortunately there was little he could do to solve the problem of Simon for her. She must deal with Simon herself.

"My dear," said Sir Richard, "you have done a noble service for your country, and repaid any conceivable debt to Peter Wilde. We will have to set about a plan to bring Pemberton to justice and that will take some contriving. I would suggest you remain at home today, cancel any engagements you might have made, until we have resolved our next move. I think you are safe as long as you remain secluded, perhaps give out a story of ill-health. And I might have to ask you to tell your story to Valentine, in case he needs more information. I will try to keep you in the background if I can, but you are a brave girl and will do what is required of you, I know," he said, then hesitating went on. "I have no right to ask obedience from you, Katherine, but I must tell you I am proud of your courage and intelligence, and I know your mother would expect no less of you. She had courage, too, if of a different sort," Sir Richard had abandoned his usual controlled manner, his diplomatic mask. His affection and concern brought ease to Katherine and for the first time in her short life she felt that her happiness and well-being was of paramount importance to someone.

Deeply moved, she said, "Thank you, sir. I knew I could rely on you to solve matters. I do wish you and mother could have married, and that I could claim you as my father to the world. You are a splendid man, and I will cherish your words always." Both of them remained silent, in the grip of powerful feelings, and his grasp of her hands tightened before he leaned over to kiss her on her forehead.

"Thank you, Katherine. Our personal affairs will have to await on these more urgent developments, but I promise you we will settle them finally to your satisfaction when this is all finished," he assured her.

"Dear sir, I knew you would help me resolve my worries.

226

And do not be concerned about me. I am sure Ronald had no ideal that I have discovered his infamy. And if I am the instrument of bringing him to justice I would be willing to undergo any temporary danger, although I suppose it is a remote possibility."

Sir Richard was not so sure, but he knew that apprehending Viscount Pemberton and proving his guilt would not be easy. The wily devil had covered his tracks well. However, Valentine would come up with a scheme, he was convinced, having every confidence in that clever and dogged spy-chaser.

"You have behaved with great fortitude and sense, Katherine. Now you must forget all about any further attempt to bring the culprits to justice, and leave the matter in the hands of those with the proper experience. Promise me you will not expose yourself to further peril?" he urged, suspecting that Katherine was not the girl to sit tamely at home while others acted on her information.

He showed none of his impatience to be gone, but escorted her back to Wigmore Street, talking of mundane matters, sensing that she had not told him all of her concerns, but reluctant to press her. He only hoped what she was concealing would not lead her into trouble.

Katherine dearly wanted to tell him about Simon Stafford, but shame and anger at that gentleman's cynical proposal kept her silent. She knew that Sir Richard would confront Simon and demand satisfaction for the insult to her, which would raise questions and scandal, and in no way soothe her raw feelings. She bade goodbye to her protector, begging that he let her know how the affair marched and the outcome of her revelations. She feared Sir Richard would have a poor time of it, persuading his colleagues of Ronald's perfidy, but she knew he would do his best to come up with a plan to apprehend the Viscount.

Katherine was quite correct in her surmise that Sir Edward and his committee would view Sir Richard's disclosures with scepticism, since he refused at first to reveal the source of his accusations. Finally goaded by Castlereagh, he explained that Pemberton's treachery had been discovered inadvertently in Vauxhall Gardens by a young woman, whose name he preferred to keep secret.

"Are you asking us to arrest a well-known peer, who has no stain on his reputation, on the unsupported word of some flighty chit who happened to misunderstand his rendezvous in the shrubbery at Vauxhall?" Castlereagh scoffed.

"I believe the girl is trustworthy, and since she identified Lang, there is every reason to think that Pemberton is the mastermind we are seeking," Sir Richard replied imperturbably, having long practice in dealing with Castlereagh.

Simon Stafford, who had accompanied Valentine to the hastily-called meeting, hid his reaction to the news, but he was in little doubt that the source of Sir Richard's damning information was Katherine, and he barely repressed an outburst. She had fled from him into a veritable hornet's nest, and now she had turned to Sir Richard for advice, not to him. He was deeply hurt by her lack of confidence. She must truly despise him, think him unworthy, and all because she misunderstood his honorable proposal.

Unable to see, in his own unhappiness, that Katherine would not have reacted so impulsively if she had not cared for him, he glowered at Sir Richard. He would not challenge the man, so many years his senior and a respected member of the government, but his temper rose at the thought of this man winning Katherine. Still, he had to commend Sir Richard for not revealing Katherine's name.

Valentine himself was persuasive in his arguments for investigating Pemberton. He had spent too many hours, and sacrificed too many good men, to allow the miscreant to escape if there was any opportunity of bringing him to justice. But the committee, unwilling to believe such treachery of a respected peer, wanted more information. They would not be satisfied with Sir Richard's anonymous source.

Sir Edward put the notion smoothly. "You must see, Sir Richard, that although we believe you, others might not be so easily persuaded. Pemberton has powerful allies. His father is well-liked, and a friend of the sovereign. To accuse him of traitorous activity without firm evidence would be disastrous. We must press you for the name of your informant so we can interview her ourselves." It was apparent that he found the idea of women becoming involved in intelligence affairs distasteful. Valentine was not so fastidious, having employed women in the apprehension of spies before and finding them in some ways far more devious and clever than their male counterparts. But the General knew that badgering Sir Richard would not serve. He needed to be gently led into cooperation. Sir Edward would only set his back up. Valentine approached the matter cautiously.

"I think we must honor Sir Richard's scruples, gentlemen. But perhaps we can approach the delicate affair in another direction. If you would leave the matter to our department I think we can work out a method of answering all the doubts about the Viscount. It does seem most unlikely that the young man could organize such a formidable operation as the counterfeit bullion plan. Not that I disbelieve your informant, Sir Richard, but there is more to be learned as I am sure you will agree. If it is permissible I would suggest that I huddle with Sir Richard and devise a plan," Valentine suggested.

Sir Edward appeared to be considering the matter, as if the choice were his alone, and then consented with a grudging, thin-lipped smile. "I am sure you will handle the unsavory business with your usual talent, General."

Valentine suppressed a sarcastic rejoinder, recognizing that

Sir Edward's reference to his talent had a certain barbed implication. But he was too eager to get on with the affair, and only nodded cheerfully as the Foreign Office contingent left the room. Castlereagh lingered. He liked knowing the details of these maneuvers, but if any disaster befell them, he denied all knowledge. Still, Valentine considered Castlereagh an ally and encouraged him to take an interest. Sir Richard, too, remained firmly seated. He was prepared to offer his cooperation and also protect Katherine.

"We appear to have a rather sticky situation on our hands. If we mount a campaign to entrap Pemberton and it goes wrong we could find our whole department in jeopardy. The Army does not look favorably, at the best of times, on what it so smoothly calls our 'irregular operations'," Valentine began. "What would you suggest, Stewart?" he asked, calling the Viscount by his family name. Actually, Castlereagh had no official standing, having resigned from the government in defence of Catholic Emancipation. But now he was about to accept another appointment and his interest in foreign affairs, especially all matters dealing with the French meant that Valentine would have a powerful friend in the circles which counted.

"Well, it appears we must persuade Pemberton to confess, if he is indeed the culprit, since we have no evidence except this girl's tale," Castlereagh said ironically. It was clear that he put little stock in Katherine as a witness of Pemberton's treachery. Sir Richard and Simon resented this assessment of Katherine's behalf, but wisely held their tongues.

"Quite right, sir," Valentine agreed, then waited politely for further suggestions. But it appeared Castlereagh had decided not to offer any scheme. He stood up, signaling that he had taken notice of the problem but had now decided to disengage himself from any active participation. Whether this was because he did not believe Katherine's story, or because e had graver matters on his mind, neither Valentine nor imon could fathom.

"I am sure you will get to the bottom of this sordid affair, General. These constant efforts at treachery against His Majesty's government are extremely trying, especially when they reoccupy ministers who should be weighing important issues of state." Castlereagh appeared to find traitors annoying but unworthy of his personal attention. That was not always he case, as Valentine knew, but the General was well versed n dealing with official contempt for spy catching.

"I must thank you for your interest, Stewart, and we will come up with some scheme, to either vindicate Pemberton or catch him out," Valentine assured him a bit wryly.

"Please keep me informed, Lucien," the great man asked, with one of those winning smiles which occasionally lightened his stern visage and won him allies despite his aloof manner. With nod to the others he strode from the room, obviously ready to ilt at the next windmill which impeded his path.

"Now to business," Valentine said, surveying his supporters, Simon and Sir Richard. It was to the latter he turned, he germ of an idea already stirring in his fertile mind. No riminal was more wily than Valentine with a quarry in sight, nd if Ronald Pemberton was a traitor he would apprehend im, for to the General's mind the home-grown conspirator was the most despicable of all spies. And for one, with a amily which dated back to the Conquest to behave in such fashion was most abhorrent. He had a certain sympathy for French patriots intriguing against their country's enemy, but none for England's aristocrats who betrayed their homeland.

"I do not think an outright confrontation with the Viscount would shake him. He is too clever to reveal any damaging evidence when he knows we have no proof. We must ust somehow trick him into admitting his guilt," Sir Richard suggested.

"Yes, and probably the only method is to taunt him int
boasting. Much the best if he confides in a woman. He woul
not be so on his guard. And the best tool for that task is Katherin
Wilde. Obviously Pemberton has a deep interest in her," Val
entine suggested, knowing he would meet with objection.

"He has already proposed and been refused. That will no
make him feel very charitable toward Miss Wilde, I fear,"
Sir Richard demurred.

Simon, hiding his surprise and anger that Sir Richard shoul
be the recipient of Katherine's confidence to this extent, had a
idea what was in his chief's mind and did not like it, but he hel
his tongue, hoping his supposition was wrong.

"This is what I thought might prove effective. We coul
ask Miss Wilde to request Pemberton call upon her, a hint
perhaps, that she might be having second thoughts abou
accepting his proposal. That should bring him running, com
pletely unsuspicious. Women are notorious for changing thei
minds about suitors. Then she could challenge him with wha
she had heard and seen in Vauxhall. If she is clever, she wi
goad him into a confession, a boasting of his exploits. An
we will be on hand, concealed, to hear the whole sorry story
Then we will have him," Valentine put his plan bluntly, b
he expected argument and was prepared to meet it.

"It's unthinkable," Simon stormed. "We have no righ
to ask Miss Wilde to place herself in a position of dang
because we are too inefficient to catch this damned fello
without her cooperation." He flushed with anger and wa
on the verge of refusing to assist Valentine with any suc
plot. He hated the idea of Kate being exposed to Pemberto
who might do her some harm before they could rescue her

"I thought you might prevail upon her to cooperate. Yo
seem to be on very intimate terms with her," Valentin
suggested smoothly, but Simon frowned and looked obdu

232

rate. Forestalling Simon, Valentine turned to Sir Richard, "Or perhaps, you, sir.

"I am not sure that I approve. I am inclined to agree with Stafford here that it puts an unfair burden on Miss Wilde. If you could guarantee her safety?" he left the question in the air. Valentine was quick to answer it.

"We will be nearby, to prevent Pemberton making any menacing move toward her. I know she had been most anxious to clear her father of any guilt in this affair of the counterfeit bullion. This would be her opportunity." Valentine wondered for a moment at the fleeting look of pain he thought he saw in Sir Richard's eyes. Could it be the man was seriously interested in the girl, caught at last by a mere child after refusing lures by the most determined husband hunters? And if so, where did that leave Simon Stafford?

"She is sure to make a mull of it, and end up warning Pemberton so that he can escape our net," Simon growled, determined to keep Kate from danger. Not that she would heed his pleas, and with her penchant for meddling she would probably enjoy the business while he agonized in the background.

"I don't think so, Stafford. I have great confidence in Kate. She is level-headed and mature beyond her years. I think she will help us, but Valentine, I want your guarantee that she will be well protected."

His concern was obvious, and the General reflected that there was some mystery here. Sir Richard appeared to care greatly for the girl, but not in the besotted way middle-aged men usually reacted when they were caught by some fledgling. Valentine had too much experience in reading character not to wonder about Sir Richard's interest in Miss Wilde. He was in no doubt about Simon's, nor about his aide's irritation that the older man stood in some closer relationship to the girl. Well, they would have to work all that out after Pemberton was caught. Now, there must be no divisions to threaten the scheme.

"Now, who will approach her? I think it had best be either you, Sir Richard, or Simon. She would hardly be impressed by my request, a stranger to her, and the man who has been chevying her father," Valentine proposed cleverly, knowing that each man would respond to his invitation, not wanting the other to be relegated to the background.

Sir Richard, having no trouble devining Simon's jealousy and suspicion of him, took pity on the Marquis. "I think we might both put the plan to her. I believe she respects your opinion, Stafford, and probably would be more influenced by your appeal than mine," Sir Richard offered generously, disarming Simon, who wanted to object more strenuously to the idea but found himself unable to resist Sir Richard's adroit maneuver.

"Then it is agreed you will see Miss Wilde. We must not delay long, for we have to coordinate the Pemberton confrontation with the arrest of Lang. In that case we need no further evidence, for our man at the bank has come up with some very obvious embezzlement on Lang's part. If he stole from his employer we can be sure that he was not above other treachery," Valentine insisted.

The two other men agreed that nothing would be gained by postponing the distasteful task and Sir Richard invited Simon to his club where they might further their plans for approaching Katherine. Sir Richard had another purpose, too. He wanted to learn more about the young man whom he thought might, before too long, become his son-in-law, although he was not yet ready to admit his relationship with Katherine to the Marquis of Staines.

234

Chapter Twenty Three

Katherine, impatient for Sir Richard's report of his meeting with the authorities about Ronald Pemberton, was taken aback when he was announced later that afternoon in the company of Simon Stafford. Although she had known that Simon was involved in intelligence work, she had hardly expected his visit. However, personal concerns must be relegated to the background in face of this pressing need to thwart the conspiracy. She greeted Sir Richard warmly but turned a much cooler countenance to the Marquis. She had neither forgotten nor forgiven their last encounter. He lifted an ironic eyebrow at her obvious discomfort, and bowed over her hand.

"Dear Kate, all is not as it seems. I see you are still not in charity with me, but I fear you have gravely misjudged me. When this latest business is cleared away I will accept your apologies in a most magnanimous fashion," he drawled, knowing she would find his remarks provoking in the extreme, but any tender remonstrances would be inappropriate at this delicate juncture in their affairs.

Kate ignored his words and asked the men to be seated. Sir Richard did so, but Simon propped himself against the mantel in the morning room, and gazed at her with disturbing intensity. She looked away, her face warm, and turned her attention to Sir Richard.

"I know you are anxious to hear about the reception of your news, Katherine," he began.

"Yes, dear sir. I hope your colleagues believed my story and are taking steps to apprehend Ronald."

"Well, much depends on you, my dear," Sir Richard continued in his calm, tactful manner. But even he, experienced in dealing with duplicitous and irritating heads of state without losing his aplomb, blanched before the prospect of asking Katherine to confront Ronald.

"I will do whatever you think wise, sir, but I cannot see how I can play any effective role," Katherine answered, puzzled.

"Those pompous fools at the Foreign Office will not move on Pemberton without firm evidence against him, and you have been selected to wrest that proof from him," Simon answered angrily. "It's a damn shame that we cannot do our job without placing some female in danger to save our own skins," he growled, for all Sir Richard's powers of persuasion had not convinced him that Kate should serve as a tethered victim to lure Pemberton into exposing his treachery.

"Such intemperate language, my lord. You are in a tizzy. Surely you cannot be worried about my safety in any scheme you have devised," Katherine taunted.

"Don't bandy words with me, my girl. You appear to like meddling and this will give you your best chance yet to stick your pretty little nose into affairs best ignored," Simon fulminated, forgetting his resolution to remain calm and unruffled by Kate's taunts. He really believed that what Sir Richard required of her would place her in dreadful peril, and he was afraid all their precautions to protect her could go awry. Cornered, who knew what Pemberton would do?

Sir Richard, rather amused by the byplay between the two young people, reflected that their inevitable union would be a stormy one, with neither willing to play a subservient role.

"You see, Kate, in order to arrest Pemberton, considering his status and influence, we must have a confession or at least some tangible proof of his infamy," Sir Richard explained carefully.

"Well, perhaps, George Lang will offer you that. Sneaky rogue that he is, no doubt he has secured some evidence against his co-conspirator," Katherine said with scorn.

"Pemberton would never have allowed any written proof of their designs to fall into Lang's hands, and as he said in that telling interview, if he denies Lang's accusations, he will probably be believed. Reasonable men will never consider a peer, whose family has given centuries of service to the Crown, could behave in such a miserable fashion. I find it difficult myself," Sir Richard explained.

"I do also," said Katherine, "except that I heard him with my own ears, and there was a menacing air to his dealings with Lang which also convinced me. The Ronald Pemberton I know played the part of a rather weak amiable young man about town, hiding his real interests and treachery with consumate skill." Katherine shook her head as she remembered that encounter in Vauxhall.

"So you can see we must tread carefully in order to bring him to justice," Sir Richard agreed.

"We will not be doing the treading, Kate will. He's a dangerous man to cross, despite his affable facade. Remember what happened to the Contessa Fontenelli. His hired assassin almost brought that off, and the thought of Kate in a like position does not commend itself," Simon objected.

"But we will be nearby. She will come to no harm if she follows our direction," Sir Richard argued, although he, too, was anxious at the thought of Katherine's exposure to such danger.

"She does not follow prudent advice, believe me, I know," Simon argued, casting a baleful look at Kate.

"Will you two stop arguing as if I were not present and tell me what I must do?" Katherine insisted, returning Simon's brooding look with a scornful toss of her head.

"Of course, my dear," Sir Richard agreed. He set out to explain what they required of Katherine, trying not to over-persuade or cajole her, but leave her free to make her own decision.

Simon turned his back on the pair as if wanting to wash his hands of the whole affair. When he and Sir Richard had discussed the interview before facing Kate he had agreed to let Sir Richard make the explanations, but his gorge rose now at what they were asking of Kate. At least, he had learned from the session at Sir Richard's club that the older man's interest in Kate was more fatherly than lover-like. Sir Richard had given Simon a brief outline of his relationship with Kate's mother, which did a great deal to allay Simon's distrust of him though he still felt that there was a great deal more that Sir Richard had not told him.

Katherine meanwhile listened carefully to Sir Richard's outline of the plan. It seemed easy enough to invite Ronald to attend her on the pretext that she had a matter of import to discuss. He would assume that perhaps she had changed her mind about his proposal. Of course, she mentioned wryly, Ronald might have changed his mind and transferred his affection to another girl, but Sir Richard dismissed this as a diversion. Pemberton would come if she insisted, he was convinced. What mattered was the coordination of Ronald's appearance and the secreting of the witnesses who would hear his explanations when he was challenged by Katherine.

"That's where the whole affair could go awry, Kate,"

Simon insisted gravely, his former irritation abandoned now that they had settled down to plot out the confrontation. "He could arrive betimes, before we were hidden, and place you in a very uncomfortable position. Or he could laugh away your accusations, which would leave us where we are now, with little reason to arrest him. And, then, we have to be sure that George Lang has not the opportunity to warn him," he argued, aware of all the barriers to a successful outcome of this scheme. He did not mention that Pemberton could attack Kate or threaten her in some other frightening fashion when he was not present to protect her. The whole business caused him great anguish, when what he really wanted was to carry Kate off to the country, wed her, bed her, and forget all about spies, jealous suitors, and unappreciative fathers. If he had suspected that Kate's desires were rather along those lines, too, he would have denied Sir Richard, Valentine, the whole government including His Majesty's most august ministers and done just that.

But as it was, Kate appeared delighted to become a part of unraveling this conspiracy and eagerly questioned them about the logistics of the plan. It was decided what form her note would take, the date and time. As soon as Ronald signified his acceptance, she would notify Sir Richard. That was the tricky part. Could Simon and Valentine's men install themselves in secret before Ronald's arrival? The three of them went over the details exhaustively—Simon dejected, Sir Richard cautious and Katherine excited—before Sir Richard finally acknowledged himself satisfied that all had been plotted to his satisfaction. Uncomfortable as a guest in Peter Wilde's house, he made his adieux soon after, leaving Simon behind to make his peace with Katherine.

Before Katherine could marshall her defences against Simon he had crossed the room and taken hold of her shoulders, abandoning his sardonic pose and holding her gaze with his dark eyes.

"I think before we go any further one thing should be clear. You completely misunderstood me the other evening at Vauxhall. I was not making you a dishonorable proposal, but for once I was trying to deal honestly with you, Kate. I love you and want to marry you."

Confused and overcome Kate blushed and stammered, not sure she had heard Simon correctly. "You never mentioned marriage, you talked about protecting me, and that meant setting me up in some hideaway, offering me carte blanche. I was furious," she admitted, unwilling to accept that she had misunderstood him.

Simon rolled his eyes. "Lord, give me strength. I have just made you a proposal, and you want to argue the sense of some words I said in the heat of an ungovernable passion!"

Kate relaxed and twinkled up at him. "Was it really an ungovernable passion? How intriguing. Then I suppose I will have to forgive your intemperate language and give your proposal my serious consideration." A glowing happiness was building inside her which she could not yet comprehend fully.

"I will love you desperately if I don't murder you first, you termagent." Deciding that stronger tactics were demanded, he pulled her fully into his arms and kissed her. For a long while there was not sound in the room but the labored breathing and inarticulate murmurs of two thoroughly aroused lovers. Simon, aware that Kate's innocence did not allow her to see the direction in which they were moving, removed his roaming hands from her bodice, and tucked a wayward curl back into her disarranged coiffure, before leading her to a nearby settee.

"Enough of that, my girl, or we will be anticipating our wedding night right here, not at all suitable for what I have in mind. I take it from your gratifying response to my kisses that you accept my proposal. And about time, too. Much more of this tempestuous courtship and I would be exhausted," he teased, trying to lighten the highly charged emotional atmosphere.

"I had no idea you were so easily fatigued, my lord. And let me tell you that if what we have been enduring was your idea of a courtship it is not to my taste. All you have been doing is raking me up, taking me to task, brangling and generally behaving like a scolding older brother, not at all like a man suffering from a desperate passion," she responded, remembering their past encounters and some of the heartache she had suffered.

"Soft words and a besotted stance would not work with you, minx. I need a hard hand and a cool head to cope with your vagaries. But enough of this. When can we wed? I will not wait the traditional six months for you. Neither my heart nor my head could endure it, not to mention other pressing wants," he said, suiting his action to his words by kissing her yet again and allowing his hands to stray toward the enticing glimpse of bosom displayed by her low cut cerulean silk gown.

Rather half-heartedly Kate stilled his roving hand. "We cannot make any plans until this business of Ronald Pemberton is finished," she insisted, coming back from the delightful dreams Simon had induced with his insistence on their early union, a resolution she desired as much as he.

"Damn Pemberton," Simon muttered as his lips traveled over her hair, and down toward her throat. Then, taking himself in hand, he stopped his assault on her emotions and recalled with a muffled oath the peril which faced his love. Taking her hands in a warm clasp he said earnestly, "I fear for you, Kate, in this plan of Valentine's, and if you are reluctant to go through with it, I will insist we come up with another scheme to capture Pemberton. I have never liked the idea from the beginning. If Valentine were not so desperate to settle the affair, he would see the iniquity of using an innocent girl as the bait to snare the villain. Be honest, Kate, and tell me what you really want to do,'' he pleaded.

"I want to go through with it, Simon. I owe my father this, and Sir Richard, too. But that is a long story which we need not discuss now. Also, I am as much a patriot as you. Women make much better intriguers, you know. We are so used to dealing with men it comes quite easily to us,'' she quipped, eager to distract him from his objections to the danger she faced.

"Yes, you are quite adept at manipulating us poor fools. You have had me on a string since that first encounter in the Pantheon Gardens, and now I am completely enslaved,'' Simon admitted ruefully.

"Oh, I would not say that, Simon. You gave me some very anxious moments before we came to this felicitous ending,'' Kate argued, pushing a lock of Simon's hair back from his forehead in a possessive gesture which symbolized their new relationship.

"I hope I will never give you any more such moments, dear Kate,'' Simon replied, thoroughly captivated by this enchanting girl, who had melted so deliciously into his arms, and who promised even more delights. Not for Kate the timid shrinkings and coy demurrals before an over-riding passion. He knew once she was won her response would be generous and warm hearted. If only they did not have this hazardous crisis to face, how ecstatic this first hours of acknowledging their mutual love would be.

But the coming interview with Pemberton shadowed the precious moments, and with difficulty Simon returned to reality, to the scheme which offered so much danger for Kate while he stood by in an agony of apprehension. Allowing his love to play the starring role in this drama was not a position he relished, but he felt helpless to prevent. So much depended upon the resolution of this treacherous attempt to subvert the country. Only when the plot had been circumvented, the rogues captured, and their enemies foiled, would Simon and Kate be able to enjoy their new-found happiness. They agreed that their personal plans must wait upon the successful outcome of Pemberton's apprehension. Reluctantly postponing their own desires they settled to composing the letter which would set events in train.

Chapter Twenty Four

Despite the excitement of the day, Katherine slept well that night, although she knew that the morning hours would bring the answer to her letter and the confrontation with Pemberton on which so much rested. Simon had wanted to approach her father immediately and gain his approval of their marriage, but she had urged him to keep their personal news a secret for now. Kate had assured him wryly that Peter Wilde would be more than willing to surrender his daughter to the Marquess of Staines, but that their talk would have to wait.

She had spent a quiet evening, for to attend any public gathering might enable Pemberton to press questions upon her when she was unguarded. Peter Wilde, conveniently, had not dined at home that evening, so Katherine had had the luxury of a some private hours to hug her happiness, and think of a blissful future.

At the back of her mind had been the coming confrontation with Pemberton, but somehow that had assumed a vague shadow in her mind, unreal compared to the prospect of becoming Simon's wife. However, when morning dawned and the abigail brought in her morning chocolate, reality returned. Today must see the resolution of this affair. Ronald would certainly reply to her note within hours and then events would move swiftly.

She was not mistaken, for a message was delivered by hand later that morning. Ronald agreed to meet with her at three o'clock that afternoon. He suggested they might ride in the Park, but Katherine had no intention of allowing him to lure her away from the house and the protection which Simon and Valentine had offered. She sent a footman around to Ronald's house with a measured acceptance of the hour, and then sent another message to Simon, who would notify his chief. Now all she could do was await the outcome. Simon had asked her how she meant to broach the subject of his treachery to Ronald. She had decided that she would have to let the conversation lead her, that to plan too minutely would not be sensible. Blithely she had assured Simon that she would handle the interview with dispatch and he was not to worry that she would allow Ronald to evade her questions.

Now Simon arrived to take luncheon with her, accompanied by his chief, General Valentine, whom Kate had met previously at one of the season's soirees. She found him a most sympathetic and intelligent man, appreciative of her demanding role in this scenario. Valentine had decided that he and Simon alone would be the secret witnesses to the interview, for employing less prominent listeners might cast doubt on the hoped-for revelations. He stationed two burly soldiers in the nearby garden in case they were needed to subdue Pemberton or to prevent any attempts to rescue him from his folly.

As the hour neared for Ronald's appointment, Kate found herself calming the nerves of her two guardians while she appeared cool and collected. Somehow the reality of the coming encounter had not penetrated the shield of happiness that Simon's confession of love had inspired. Before Valentine he appeared all that was proper and reserved, concentrating on the business at hand, but Katherine knew that yesterday's avowal was not a dream. He took the opportunity to press her hand and give her an encouraging hug when Valentine's attention was elsewhere.

"I believe you think this is all the most thrilling escapade Kate. Don't you have any fear of Pemberton?" Simon asked as the hour neared. Indeed, Kate was looking exhilarated, dressed in a peach silk gown scalloped at the low neckline which lent both a demure and provocative air to her appearance.

"What can he do with you and Gen. Valentine within shouting distance?" Kate answered, stilling the small quaver of panic she felt, for it would not do to let Simon know she felt any anxiety about her own safety. Somehow it was difficult to envision Ronald as a desperate traitor, prepared to embezzle, threaten, even murder in defence of his nefarious ends or his own life. He had certainly played his role skillfully with a talent which any actor could envy. But she doubted he would attack her.

"No doubt you will manage him as skillfully as you do all poor hapless males who cross your path," Simon reassured her in a teasing tone.

"Do I manage you, Simon? What a delightful prospect," Katherine replied, more than willing to encourage his light-hearted mein, for to fret about the interview in advance would serve no purpose.

"For the nonce, baggage, you have me in your toils, but when I have you tied to me securely by sacred vows, we will see who will do the managing," he promised, pleased to see she was treating this affair as an adventure.

But as the hour neared for Ronald's appointment, Simon could see that Kate was hiding her apprehension with a brave face, reluctant to show any fear although she knew how much depended on how she handled this confrontation. At the quarter hour, the scene was set in the morning room, with Valentine and Simon esconsced behind the heavy cream velvet draperies which covered the long windows leading to the garden. The windows behind the draperies were left open, for it was a warm summer's day and the slight breeze was welcome.

Promptly at three o'clock Ronald was announced. He entered the room with a glowing smile for Kate, obviously convinced that she had changed her mind about accepting his proposal. His blatant attentions to Miss Willoughby-Gore had no doubt influenced her he thought smugly. Once he had Katherine's promise and her father's generous settlement, he would be able to abandon his secret life and enjoy all the perequisites of a well-endowed man about town. In his own way he admired, even loved, Katherine, but he had no intention of playing the doting husband to a Cit's daughter, although of course he would do all that was proper.

"It's such a lovely day, Katherine, can we not have our chat during a ride in the Park?" he asked as she acknowledged his greeting with an effort.

This was exactly the contigency Katherine had feared and hoped to avoid, but she was too clever to object immediately.

"Perhaps later, Ronald, when we have settled our business," she agreed, all compliance. "Won't you be seated?" She indicated a divan, placed strategically beneath the windows. Courtesy demanded he accede to her request.

Before she could put her question to him he took one of her hands and looking into her face with every appearance of eager sincerity, asked, "Have you changed your mind about my proposal, Katherine? I cannot tell you how honoured I would be if that is the reason for your request to see me. I know I have been too impetuous, perhaps too demanding, but now that you have had time to consider my offer, are you willing to grant my dearest wish to make you my wife?''

Katherine, looking at his earnest face, his well-bred features and guileless blue eyes, felt a momentary pang. Could she have misinterpreted that overheard conversation? Was Ronald what he appeared, a harmless rather weak young man-about-town, hanging out for a rich wife, and not the deep-dyed villain she had thought him? She could not dissemble any longer.

"I could never wed a man whom I suspected of traitorous activities," she replied simply, hoping to surprise him into some betrayal, but his eyebrows rose a fraction and he continued to look at her fondly, ignoring her shocking imputations. Since he made no reply she was forced into bolder action.

"Last week, at Vauxhall Gardens, I inadvertently heard a conversation you were having with George Lang, who I have reason to know is a rogue of the worst sort, a dissembler and a disloyal employee, who has placed my father in the unenviable situation of being suspected by the government," Katherine explained baldly, at last getting a reaction. Ronald had not been able to hide his first startled response to her surprising tale and an ugly look darkened his face for a moment before he resumed his usual affable expression.

"Were you eavesdropping, Katherine?" he asked.

"Yes," Katherine agreed simply, then taking her courage in her hands went on, "And what I heard leads me to believe that you are involved in a plot to betray your country. I do not know the reason for such an unconscionable act, and I have misjudged you, I beg your pardon, but the conversation I overheard is not liable to any other interpretation." She spoke calmly but with determination, hiding the inward quaking which threatened to overcome her. She saw Ronald's whole demeanour alter from one of an admiring suitor to that of an enraged adversary. His face flushed, cords in his neck stood out and his eyes darkened to a frightening wildness.

"So, you were spying like some nasty little housemaid, trying to discover the secrets of her betters. And what did you intend to do with this information? Blackmail me?" he taunted, as if her efforts to bring him to account were not worth consideration.

"So you admit there is some truth to my suspicions?"

"I admit nothing but that you are a prying, encroaching bourgeois, hoping to attain a position your birth does not entitle you to, and using the common methods of a tradesman to secure your aims," he railed, his voice dripping with venom. Katherine was surprised by his complete change of manner, but convinced her that he was the man that had been sought for so long.

Ignoring his insults, she prodded, "Why did you do it, Ronald? Surely you have everything a man could want, position, a handsome face and manner, friends, fortune . . . ," she broke off sadly as he interrupted her in a passion of disgust.

"You know nothing of the life of the ton, the temptations or the expenses of keeping up appearances." His tone was bitter. "The Wexfords are under the hatches, at any moment apt to end up in the Fleet. It costs money to indulge in the delights of society, money easily obtained by grasping Cits who force the entitled rulers of this country to surrender their patrimony by their avaricious, money-grubbing methods. Your father is such a man, driving his betters to the wall, by his crude, penny-pinching demands for payment of debts." There was such venom in his voice the Katherine was chilled.

"And your way of righting this wrong was to betray your

country for money! I would respect you a great deal more if you had done it for an ideal," she replied.

"Ideals are a luxury I cannot afford. You know nothing of the pitfalls facing an aristocrat who is losing his lands, estates held in the family for centuries. When your ancestors were peasants, mine were ruling England. And we will rule again when Napoleon reinstates us with the necessary power to deal with tradesmen and usurpers," Ronald raged, not caring that he was admitting his guilt. After all, she was a poor thing, a Cit's daughter, with little standing and no influence, while he commanded the respect deserved by a Wexford. His mistake had been to offer for such a vulgar chit.

"So you have betrayed your country for personal gain and power. Have you no compunction in conspiring with another peasant, the Corsican?" Katherine jeered, now almost as angry as Ronald, completely forgetting the hidden watchers to this damning conversation.

"Like you, and all such persons, Napoleon can be used and then discarded," Ronald insisted haughtily. But, then, remembering that Kate represented a threat to his safety which would have to be removed he grasped her by the shoulders in a cruel hold.

"Unfortunately you will not be able to use whatever information you think you have learned, for I have no intention of allowing you to run to the authorities with your suspicions. And that is all they are. I can deny everything and who would believe you? But you are a danger to me," he muttered, not quite sure how to proceed. The light of madness was in his eyes, and Kate could not mistake it. He was in a grip of a great meglomania, certain that no one could thwart him.

"And what do you intend to do about it?" she challenged him bravely.

"Remove you. It should be simple to spirit you away to the country where I can deal with you at my leisure," he threatened.

"I think not, my lord," General Valentine stepped from behind the curtain and put a hand on Ronald's shoulder just as Pemberton tightened his own hands about Kate's throat. Startled, Ronald sprang up, ready to do battle, but Simon grasped him from the other side. Two captors were too much for Ronald who dissolved into a paroxym of fury.

"Take your hands off me, you scum. I am the Viscount, heir to the Wexfords. How dare you touch me," he sputtered on, fighting with maniac strength to throw off the firm grip of Valentine and Simon. Kate stood by appalled as she watched the disintegration of the young man who had once escorted her with such flattering obeisance to countless routs and balls. Ronald Pemberton, unable to face reality, had descended into madness.

Valentine and Simon needed all their strength to subdue him, and the two soldiers, summoned hastily from the garden added their efforts to the struggle before he was brought under restraint. Kate, shaking and undone by the spectacle, sought refuge in Simon's arms as Ronald was led away, raving, by his captors. General Valentine, understanding her collapse, stopped only to give her a grateful pat on the shoulder, and a heartfelt "Thank you" before he followed Pemberton and his escorts from the room.

"It was dreadful, Simon, to see him disintegrate in such a shocking way. He was mad. He must have been verging on this breakdown for ages. Why did I not recognize it? What if I had accepted his proposal, wed such a monster?" Kate cried, overwhelmed by the scene she had just experienced.

"You would never have accepted him because you were destined to be mine, you foolish girl. Come, Kate, it is not

251

like you to be so faint-hearted. You have done a splendid job. It's all over now, and you were a brave clever girl," he soothed, realizing the shock of Ronald's betrayal would remain with her for a long time.

"Yes, I am behaving like a silly dolt. It is all over, thank goodness. Was George Lang arrested, too?" she asked, restored now, mopping up the tears her ordeal had induced with Simon's handkerchief.

"Yes, we took him this morning, so there would be no opportunity for him to warn Pemberton. He is now cravenly pushing all the blame off onto his leader. Of course, the real brains of the conspiracy was not Pemberton. He only carried out orders he barely understood. Fouché, Napoleon's wily chief of his secret police, planned the whole counterfeit bullion ploy. All Pemberton had to do was coordinate the effort with Lang who was in a position to put the actual bullion into the coffers. Both Pemberton and Lang wanted the money. The ethics of the position mattered not a fig to them, the villains. But it was disgusting to see Pemberton fall apart like that, and he could have done you grave harm, Kate." Simon's face darkened as he thought of those few dreadful moments before Valentine had intervened. Some of the worst moments of his life had been endured behind those draperies as he heard Pemberton insult and threaten his love. He would have liked to throttle the devil, only Valentine's admonitory glance and his own good sense had kept him from leaping from his hiding place and milling the traitor to the floor.

Hoping to distract Kate from brooding on the recent scene, Simon gathered her more firmly into his arms and kissed her gently. This was no time for the passion which surged within him whenever he was close to her. He must show her he could be cherishing and comforting as well as a demanding lover. But her response soon evoked the warm intimacies they both desired. Katherine, relieved and excited, pressed herself closer to her lover, as if to reassure them both that they were now free to enjoy the love which overwhelmed them. It was Simon who finally pulled reluctantly back from their embrace.

"The sooner I meet with your father and we set a date for our wedding the better. It is too much to ask me to wait for long, Kate," he pleaded.

"A little forebearance is good for your soul," Kate said sternly, but her eyes were laughing.

"It is not my soul I am worrying about," Simon replied, preventing any further argument by another assault on her willing lips. Kate allowed him the last word, unable to protest and enjoying herself too much to mind.

Epilogue

Six months later the Marquis and Marchioness of Staines faced each other over the breakfast table in the wilds of Wiltshire where they had been since their September wedding. Neither one was eager to reenter the social world while they could bask in the privacy of this rural retreat. But the world intruded on them despite their best efforts to ignore its demands. Simon was reading a closely written document from his former chief, Valentine, with great attention. Kate was equally absorbed in a flowery missive, crossed several times which made its deciphering a bit difficult, from her former chaperone. Her squeal of surprise distracted Simon, who looked up enquiringly.

"What does the charming Mrs. B. have to say which occasions such a display, my love?" he asked, smiling at the delightful picture Kate made over the coffee cups. She was, indeed, in good looks, with a quaint air of matronly composure, at variance with the passionate creature who had so recently risen from bed. She was wearing a lilac cashmere morning dress, ruched with white at the neckline and sleeves, for the February mornings in the Staines mansion were chilly. She postively sparkled with health and enjoyment and now wrinkled her nose in an endearing gesture of contentment.

254

"She is not to be Mrs. B. any longer, for would you believe, she will marry Mr. Wilde within the fortnight and pleads for us to attend the ceremony," Kate was amazed at this turn of events, but remembering Mrs. Basingbroke's adroit handling of her father, could only applaud the situation. Mrs. B. was just the woman to add comfort and some relaxation of Peter Wilde's austere habits.

"Good for her. And good for your father, if we should continue to call him that," Simon said with a question in his voice.

"I think we must. No good would come of revealing my suspicions of my real father to him or the world. And it would serve no benefit to Sir Richard, who agrees," Kate said, having made that decision some time ago. Sir Richard remained close to them both, and she would have to be content with this avuncular relationship. She had made her peace with Peter Wilde, and although they would never be intimate, Simon had helped her to a more comfortable arrangement with the man she must continue to accept as her father. Peter Wilde's pride would never allow him admit otherwise, and Kate, acknowledging her debt to him, acknowledged that he could not abandon the role he had adopted years before.

"Well, I suppose we must not be selfish. We must leave this idyll to support Wilde and Mrs. B.," Simon agreed. "How will you feel about London after all that has happened?" he asked a bit apprehensively. He did not want Kate brooding about the events surrounding Ronald Pemberton's arrest. Before Pemberton could be brought to trial he had hung himself in his cell. It was not the worst climax to what would have been a shocking scandal rebounding on His Majesty's government and bringing even more unhappiness to the beset Earl of Wexford.

Wexford, informed by Valentine of his son's treachery, had taken the news stoically and realizing that his own situation was desperate, had taken the alternative he had hoped to avoid. Within weeks he wed the young widow of the Lanchashire mill owner, whose considerable dowry would enable him to pay off his debts. And he was still young enough, just fifty, that he might expect to yet produce an heir. Arrogant and foolish though he may have been, Kate had a great deal of sympathy for the unhappy Earl.

Valentine had rounded up Pemberton's few confederates, acting on information from George Lang, whose sentence had been transportation to Australia. The Marquis de Lisle, still in Paris, had the satisfaction of informing Fouché that his counterfeit bullion scheme had been thwarted. Now Simon felt they could get on with their lives, and no more secret assignments from Valentine would interrupt their domestic bliss.

"I suppose it will be permissable for me to travel. There are still some months before my condition becomes apparent," Kate informed her husband nonchalantly.

"What do you mean? Oh, God—yes—you are going to have a baby," Simon lept form his chair and rushed around the table to raise Kate into his arms all the while pelting her with questions about the expected heir, and berating her for not telling him immediately. She put an end to his frenzy by throwing her arms around his neck and kissing him with great fervor to which he responded with gratifying enthusiasm.

So impassioned was their embrace they did not hear the family retainer who entered the dining room in pursuance of his duties. Taking in the scene, he quickly backed off, and turning to one of the footmen said firmly, "That will be all, James. You need not bring additional toast yet. My lord and lady are fully occupied on family business and will not welcome any interruption," he warned, although his eyes were twinkling. He had his own ideas about the undignified goings on in the dining room and thoroughly approved.